CIRCLE OF BLOOD BOOK TWO:

LOVER'S AWAKENING

CIRCLE OF BLOOD BOOK TWO:

LOVER'S AWAKENING

R. A. STEFFAN & JAELYNN WOOLF

Circle of Blood Book Two: Lover's Awakening

For information, contact the author at
http://www.rasteffan.com/contact/

Cover art by Deranged Doctor Design

First Edition: December 2017

INTRODUCTION

This book contains graphic violence and explicit sexual content. It is intended for a mature audience. While it is part of a series with an over-arching plot, it can be read as a standalone with a "happy ever after" ending for the two main characters, and a satisfying resolution of the storyline. If you don't intend to continue the series, you may wish to avoid the epilogue.

TABLE OF CONTENTS

ONE

"My life would be so much more difficult if people actually paid attention to what was going on around them," Trynn muttered as she slipped into a vacant back office.

She was illegally and unashamedly trespassing inside the main branch of the Hellenic Bank of Cyprus, near the city center in Nicosia, though you wouldn't have known it based on the reactions of the employees she'd met so far. After pulling her laptop out of its bag, she sat in a dusty office chair and laid it on an old desk that looked like it had been stashed out of sight to hide the graffiti etched on its surface.

With a few quick taps to her keyboard, Trynn opened a program and started her attack on the bank's intranet security, feeling the familiar swoop of adrenaline in the pit of her stomach.

Footsteps sounded outside the hall and Trynn paused, waiting to see if anyone would ask her for credentials. A lone bank employee walked by the open door, giving her a curious look before turning back to the stack of papers in his hands. Trynn shook her head.

If you act like you belong somewhere, no one even bothers to find out if it's true or not.

As far as Trynn was concerned, she had the best career in the entire world. As a professional hacker for Trajan Security, it was her job to try to infiltrate high-level security systems that would be prime targets for hackers with malicious intent. After her attempt, she would report back to her employers with her findings. They, in turn, would communicate with the companies and advise them on security improvements that would prevent future problems.

So, here she was at the Hellenic Bank of Cyprus, trying to access the accounts of several wealthy bank customers. Though in reality, her assault had begun as soon as she walked in the door.

As an uncommonly tall woman, Trynn knew she stood out in a crowd—something that she often used to her advantage. Usually, the best way for her to start her mission was to ensure that she was noticed immediately upon entering a business or company's front door.

Indeed, shortly after she had stepped inside the bank, one of the tellers approached her and asked if she needed any assistance.

"Your manager called about an hour ago," she told the woman. "He said there was something going on with the internet in his office? A glitch or something?"

The bank teller had looked momentarily confused and said, "I wasn't aware of any issues going on in the building." Her Mediterranean accent was thick, forcing Trynn to concentrate on what she was saying; making sure that she didn't miss any details.

"Well, he sounded like he was in a rush, so he didn't give too many particulars." Trynn tapped her fingers on her leg, telegraphing mild impatience.

"Yes, he's often like that." The woman's words were professional enough, but Trynn could detect a slight edge to her voice.

"Look—he sounded like he was getting angry, so I should probably get started before he takes out his frustration on anyone else," Trynn said apologetically, fumbling with her bag and keys as she started moving towards the hallway.

"Yes, all right. His office is just down this hallway on the left," The teller said, sounding relieved.

Trynn gave her a wave of thanks and walked confidently down the hallway. She casually glanced back, pretending to examine the various pictures hung artfully on the walls, but in reality she was making sure that no one was watching her. She passed right by the bank manager's office and turned left as soon as she could, traveling deeper into the building, where there were fewer offices and more storage closets.

It took a bit of searching to find the room housing the bank's router, but once she did, it took only a few seconds to check the sticker on the bottom and memorize the router key and Wi-Fi password. Afterward, she found the empty office that held a few desks and the one chair she was currently occupying.

As soon as her computer was connected to the supposedly secure Wi-Fi, she located the company intranet—available to all employees, but allegedly protected against outside agents.

4

Using a Trojan horse, she was able to bypass their firewall and enter the system.

The entire hack job took her less than twelve minutes. She made a note of that on her computer, as well as comments about the entrance and how easily she was able to access the private areas of the building unhindered.

"Too easy," she said in a quiet voice, bent low over her laptop. "*Way* too easy."

"Hey, what are you doing in here?" A voice asked in Cypriot Greek, interrupting her thinking. Trynn looked up and found an older gentleman who looked like he could work for the maintenance crew standing in the doorway. She expected him to look suspicious, but found that his eyes raked up and down her legs, which were crossed in front of her.

Trynn leaned forward seductively and said, "Can I tell you a secret?"

The older man straightened up, his wrinkled face going pink as he switched to English. "Yes, of course."

"I'm new here on the executive staff, and I'm not quite used to the noise out in the lobby yet," she said, pitching her voice low. "I've been sneaking back here to do some online training. It's much quieter, you see."

"Oh!" The man said with a bright smile. "Yes. *Um*. Welcome to Hellenic. I'm surprised I haven't seen you around more."

Trynn gave an airy wave of her hand. "I'm afraid I've been stuck in meetings for the most part, or trying to do this training. I haven't really had a chance to meet everyone yet."

"Well, watch out for the other guy on my crew, yes? He's a real prankster," the old man said with a twinkle in his eye. He glanced down at Trynn's legs again before looking back into her face. "I was just checking, since no one ever uses this office. Now I know to keep an eye out for you hiding back here."

"Just as long as you don't give away my secret, or everyone else will follow me back here to talk, too," she said with a sly wink.

"Your secret is safe with me," he said genially, and placed a hand over his heart in a theatrical gesture before lifting one finger to his lips in a shushing motion. He left the room without another word, pulling the door mostly closed behind him.

Trynn let out the breath she had been holding as the man left. Of course, she had a *get-out-of-jail-free* card in her pocket, of sorts, along with her identification — but she really didn't want to have to use it. Partly because she could think of better things to do with her time than explain her job over and over again to the authorities, and partly because she had a reputation to uphold. She was the only current employee at Trajan who had never been detained by a client, and she intended to keep it that way.

Trynn told her co-workers that it was her devilish smile that disarmed people and encouraged trust, but secretly she thought she was just better than most at reading people — as she had done with the janitor, just now.

He might have had a roving eye, but at heart he was the fatherly type, wanting to keep an eye out for others' best interests.

Taking advantage of the nature of the people she came across was what made her one of the top hackers at Trajan. Many of the other employees were world-class computer experts, but could barely interact with people at a level deeper than awkward stares and delayed blinking.

"The best of both worlds, that's me," Trynn murmured to the empty office.

No one bothered her for the remainder of her attack on the bank's security system. Several other people walked by, but they were either too preoccupied with their own business to bother with her, or else the janitor had instructed them to leave her alone.

She wasn't hiding, by any means. The light in the room was on and she made no effort to keep her noises to a minimum as she worked steadily through the firewalls and protective systems around the most lucrative accounts.

Trynn embedded a marker in the deepest lines of computer code in the entire system, which would serve as a beacon to her company as proof of her penetration into the program. The beacon would self-eliminate within 30 days, so she wasn't worried about it disrupting any of their systems.

"Well, that's a wrap," she said as she logged off her computer. Standing up, Trynn adjusted her tailored pants suit and slipped her trusty computer back into her shoulder bag.

As she slipped out of the partially open door, Trynn shut the light off and walked back towards the lobby, brazen as anything. Guessing that she would run into the woman who had let her into the building, she pulled her phone out, ready to fake an urgent conversation with a non-existent supervisor.

As she rounded the corner back to the main hallway, a cacophony of sounds met her ears. There were screams and cries, but they sounded as if they were fading in the distance.

What on earth was going on?

Trynn strained her ears, trying to make sense of the disturbance—completely bewildered. She slowed her pace and looked around, apprehension rising like a cold tide. There seemed to be no one in the lobby, although the revolving door was still turning.

A crazed shriek pierced the uneasy silence of the lobby.

As if in slow motion, Trynn's eyes swiveled. She saw a man rushing towards her, covered head to toe in black, from his scuffed leather boots to his balaclava.

Thump. Thump. Thump.

Her heart rate seemed to slow as the man approached her, waving some kind of device, like an old remote control, in his hand. Trynn watched the man's mouth move, but she couldn't hear any words coming out.

He gestured angrily to one side with his free hand. Still in slow motion, Trynn looked over and saw a small group of people huddled on the floor opposite the front door, a few meters to the left of the hallway she had just come from.

"What the *fuck* are you doing? I told everyone to get down! Get your fucking ass over there with the rest of them!" the man yelled in Greek.

It seemed as if his words were sped up, pitched higher than she would have expected and twice as fast as normal speech. Yet, his motions appeared sluggish, as if she were seeing things at half speed.

"Get your ass over there *now!*" he insisted, jerking his hand with the remote control towards her.

For a moment, Trynn's rebellious nature tried to rear its head, urging her to refuse to cooperate with this asshole. Out of the corner of her eye, though, she saw a man huddled by the wall wrap his arm protectively around the woman next to him, who was quaking in fear.

I can't refuse this guy, Trynn thought, practicality returning. *What if I set him off and he kills all these innocent people?*

There was nothing for it. She would have to resist the urge to fight back and just do what the man said… for the moment, at least.

Trynn took a step forward and nearly stumbled, her feet evidently still rooted in shock. As the man turned more fully towards her, Trynn's eyes were drawn to the vest that was wrapped around his shoulders and waist.

It was a bomb. She'd seen enough photos in the news to recognize a suicide vest when she saw one.

The fear that should probably have come earlier chose that moment to body slam her. She gasped and tried to back away from the man, but he lunged forward and grabbed her arm.

"Oh, no, you don't," he growled. "You get over there right now, bitch, and get on your fucking knees just like them! I swear to God I will blow us all sky-high if you don't fucking well do what I say!"

Terror clawed its way up Trynn's back, overpowering her desire to fight as she realized that the man was clearly insane.

He jabbed her in the back with something. A weapon? His fist? The sharp pain over her kidney forced Trynn to take a few faltering steps towards the small group of people being held hostage. Fighting the paralysis of fear that was wrapping itself inexorably around her limbs, Trynn sank to the ground next to a woman with curly brown hair who was shivering where she knelt.

The madman surveyed them, looming over them. "Keep your mouths shut—I don't want to hear a word from any of you!"

Breathe, just breathe, she told herself. *You're going to have to think, Trynn. Think your way out of this.*

But it was useless. The only thing that happened when she took several fast, deep breaths was that a sharp pain crept up her throat and she felt the world spin around her. Knowing that she was in danger of hyperventilating, Trynn forced herself to take slower breaths until the spinning slowed, and eventually stopped.

The suicide bomber was shouting again, but Trynn was concentrating too much on regaining control of herself to translate his words in her mind. When her ears finally caught up with the rest of her, Trynn realized that the man was making demands.

"Don't you *get it*? There's nothing anyone can say to talk me out of this! I want a *fucking* helicopter to land on the roof in the next thirty minutes. I've got to get out of here. The government is watching our every move and I can't take it anymore! No, you *shut up!*"

By the end of his tirade, the man was screaming and clutching his head. Trynn looked around, bewildered, since everyone in the group around her had remained completely silent. She'd thought maybe he was talking to someone on a cell phone, but it appeared that he was having a conversation entirely with himself.

"*Syria, Syria, Syria, Syria,*" he muttered under his breath as he stalked back and forth, scratching his head with his left hand, still grasping the remote in his right.

Trynn wanted to ask him what exactly needed to happen for them to be let go, but her throat had gone completely dry and she didn't think she could manage to get a word out.

"I want you all to lie down! Yeah—on the ground. Now!" the bomber hissed, glancing around wildly at the large glass panes in front of the bank. Slowly, not daring to take her eyes off the bomber's hands, Trynn lowered herself onto the hard floor, turning her face to the side so that she could continue to monitor the man as he paced back and forth.

"No!" he shouted a moment later, backing away from the group with a terrified expression. "No! That's not right! Get up! All of you, get the fuck up and kneel with your fucking hands behind your heads. *Do it, now!*"

Trynn pushed herself up, just as slowly as she had dropped down, and laced her fingers behind her head.

The bomber stared at the group and, once satisfied that everyone was following his directives, he stalked away and started rifling through a desk hidden behind a half wall. Occasionally, he threw looks at them as if checking to make sure they hadn't moved, but he did not speak to them again.

"What does he want?" Trynn breathed to the woman next to her, barely moving her lips. She didn't want to draw attention to herself and have the man wearing the bomb come back towards them. "He said something about a helicopter?"

"That's right. A helicopter and a million Euros," the woman whispered back in heavily accented English. "Kept saying that the government is watching him."

Trynn felt a little ironic laugh escape her throat. "Well, if they weren't before, they certainly will be now."

"Make sure that the helicopter can out-fly Syrian border patrol!" The man yelled without warning. The brown-haired woman flinched and did not speak again.

For nearly an hour, Trynn knelt on the hard tile inside the bank, praying for an end to the situation. Although there were no police directly outside the large bay windows, she could vaguely hear the sound of a helicopter hovering in the distance somewhere. Occasionally the flash of blue light would reflect off one of the windows outside the building, giving Trynn hope that help was here and they would be rescued.

As one hour stretched into two, that hope began to die in her heart. She was in agony, having held the same awkward kneeling position for so long. Every time the bomber would turn his back, she would drop one hand to ease the strain on her back and knees for a moment.

The woman next to her shook her head frantically every time Trynn did this, even though her dark eyes were watering with pain.

Every now and then, Trynn would hear a soft sniffle from one of the hostages, none of whom were speaking. The bomber continued to pace, occasionally screaming out a string of profanity, and at other times falling into a moody silence.

Jesus. He's absolutely batshit, Trynn thought. *I'm going to end up blown to bits in fucking Nicosia by a crazy man with a bomb strapped to his chest.*

The thought sent ice through Trynn's heart, and she tried in vain to keep her emotions in check. It was beyond difficult, as she fought the tears of despair threatening to fill her eyes.

Would this nightmare never end?

TWO

Eris stared down at the elegant chess set before him. It was laid out on an antique, carved wooden table, set near the floor-to-ceiling windows in the luxurious hotel room where he and his silent, uninvited chess partner were staying. The drapes were drawn to protect the two of them from the deadly rays of the Mediterranean sun, but he glanced through the heavy fabric for a few moments as the glowing orb sank ponderously below the jagged lines of Nicosia's cityscape.

He had chosen the Merit Lefkosa Hotel partly for its extravagant amenities, and partly because a brief conversation with the hotel manager had ended with a rather hefty amount of money changing hands in exchange for the assurance that Eris wouldn't be asked too many questions. Often, anonymity was the easiest way to proceed when dealing with mortals.

Now, however, he was engaged in a furious battle of strategy. Or, as furious as a battle could be when one's opponent had not moved or spoken in over an hour, at any rate.

His companion had shown no interest whatsoever over the last few weeks as Eris planned his trip to Cyprus, only to show up randomly — not to mention, uninvited — shortly after Eris checked into the hotel. He supposed that Snag had followed him across the Atlantic out of something like affection, though the others would doubtless argue that the ancient and powerful vampire was incapable of any such emotion.

He moved his attention away from the fading light of the sun and back to the chessboard, hoping that Snag would make a decision soon about his next move. Stimulating though the contest was, by now it had dragged on long enough that Eris just wanted it to be over. Snag, however, was a deeply serious player who would plan out at least twenty moves in advance for each possible move available to him at that moment. The only reason Eris had agreed to the game — and the inevitable, humiliating defeat it would eventually entail — was that he needed to pass a few hours before meeting with his art buyer during the nighttime hours to seal their deal.

Who am I kidding? I lost the game the moment I moved the first pawn, Eris thought irritably, scratching his brow and dragging his wandering mind back to the game.

Despite Snag's cold visage, his eyes were moving around the room, as though he were growing restless as evening approached. This was not an uncommon occurrence. Eris often got the sense that his companion struggled with his private demons more as the sun was setting.

After a few moments, Snag's gaze sharpened and returned to the board. Slowly, deliberately, he reached forward with skeletal fingers and moved his remaining knight.

Eris almost let out a groan of frustration. *All of that, for a move that accomplished nothing in the broader strategy?*

"You and I need to find a different game to play," he said.

Snag's deep-set eyes rose to meet his, the pupils blown permanently wide like an owl's. He did not speak, but Eris felt a faint thread of amusement pass between them. He had the distinct impression that Snag, although clearly still uneasy about something, was enjoying his mild irritation.

Eris turned back towards the board and glanced down at all the pieces strewn across the black and white squares. With a sigh, he tipped his king over and sat back, signaling defeat.

Snag sent a flicker of annoyance towards him through their mental connection.

"Snag, why do we keep doing this?" Eris asked.

Snag looked steadily at him, but made no move to communicate.

"We sit here, day after day, playing chess at a pace slower than the Earth circling around the sun. We would have turned to stone before this game ever finished." He huffed a sigh. "Speed chess. Have you ever heard of it? *You should look it up sometime.*"

Snag still did not move or speak.

Eris shook his head, clamping down ruthlessly on the smile that tried to tug at his lips. "Well," he said philosophically, "at least you're a good listener."

A wash of hunger not his own flowed across his awareness for only an instant before it was gone. He frowned.

"You need to feed soon," Eris said. "Unfortunately, that means *I* need to feed, first."

The sudden rush of shame and buried rage was not unexpected, but it stabbed at Eris' cold heart, regardless. Snag refused to feed from humans, from animals — from any source of blood other than Eris. Even then, he fought to hold his hunger at bay until he was already weakened, like some form of twisted self-punishment.

He knew that Snag was in need of a fresh supply of blood, and soon, but he would be better able to provide for his sad, tormented friend after feeding from a human victim to replenish his own strength.

Despite the fact that Snag had eschewed verbal communication for years now, Eris made it a point to converse normally with him, attempting each day to draw him out of his self-imposed silence. Over the last few centuries, he had only heard Snag speak a small handful of times, and never in the last fifty years. Eris often wondered if Snag even remembered how, or if his vocal cords would still work after going so long without use.

Feeling more animated now that the chess game no longer loomed, Eris stood and turned toward the window. He did not open the drapes, but instead raised his hand, palm out, to touch the curtain separating them from the last rays of the setting sun. He could feel the heat under his palm, but he sensed that the sun was nearly below the horizon. It would soon be safe to leave the shelter of the hotel room.

"It's almost dusk," Eris said aloud. He felt Snag stir behind him, and he could tell that the older vampire was oddly anxious for Eris to hunt.

When the sun was safely hidden, Eris excused himself and headed out onto the darkening streets on foot. Breathing in the smell of the city around him, he allowed his mind to wander back to his mortal life.

He had been a smuggler, of sorts; although that was not the name they used millennia ago. At the time, he had considered himself a collector of fabulous treasures. The money he made from arti-facts that had come into his possession—by fair means, or foul—had eventually lifted him from humble beginnings to the halls of wealth and power. Over the centuries, much of his wealth had been retained, invested wisely in gold, platinum, stocks, and real estate.

Still, every now and then it became necessary to draw from his private collection to fund some project or another. Hence his presence here tonight, so many, many years after he had first left the beautiful island he called home. As he walked down the jarringly modern boulevard, memories assailed him from the shadows, and he felt a pang of old pain.

So many memories, so much suffering, he thought to himself. It was true. This city held a long and checkered history, and much of it still haunted him.

Not willing to allow himself to sink into list-lessness, he turned his attention to the people milling around him on the street. Hunger surged as he idly imagined luring one of them into a dark alley.

Contrary to the stories mortals often told each other, it wasn't necessary for a vampire to kill a human to feed. Vampires could lean heavily on a human's consciousness and wipe all memories of the attack, which minimized the possible fallout from panicked victims running to the authorities to babble about supernatural beings drinking their blood. Aside from feeling a bit weakened from blood loss, they suffered no further adverse effects from becoming a vampire's lunch date.

Eris' gaze wandered over the crowd, looking for a likely female target who would not put up much of a struggle. Shaking his head at himself, he realized that he was acting like Duchess, who always hunted in a crowd of men. Though she also tended to seduce her victims, sleep with them, and then feed before wiping their memories and sending them on their way — generally with vacant, ridiculous smiles on their faces.

He wondered how worried he should be that he was apparently turning into his Duchess in his old age. Though he, at least, would limit himself to a single victim at a time.

See, he told Duchess, even though she was half a world away and couldn't possibly hear him. *I still have some standards.*

As he rounded the corner, he almost ran face first into a woman who was coming from the other direction.

"Oh!" she exclaimed, dropping her cell phone on the concrete as they steadied each other. "I'm so sorry! I wasn't paying any attention at all…"

Eris smiled at her and leaned down, picking up her phone. He dusted it off, checked the screen for damage, and held it out to her. "No, no," he said. "The fault was entirely mine. Thankfully, your phone doesn't seem to be damaged, so no harm was done."

He could tell that she was taking in his appearance, subtly looking him up and down. He was playing *rich tourist* for this trip, rather than a local—a bit scruffy, a bit mussed. Khakis and white button-down shirt rolled up to the elbows, dark hair a few inches longer than what was fashionable. Judging by the pink creeping into her cheeks, she liked what she saw.

Almost too easy, Eris thought.

"You know, it's far too lovely an evening to spend it rushing around corners, engrossed in the screen of a phone," he said.

The woman touched her throat with her fingertips and laughed—a light, fluttery noise that caused new hunger to course through Eris' body in anticipation of what was to come.

"Oh, I don't know," she said, "If it results in collisions with dark, handsome strangers, maybe I should try it more often."

The exchange was so clichéd, so *predictable* after all these long centuries that Eris had to stifle a sigh of boredom, despite his need for her blood.

"And what has you so distracted that you're posing a hazard to pedestrian traffic?" he asked, playing the game even though his heart wasn't in it.

"Nothing that I couldn't whole-heartedly abandon," she replied in a sly tone.

"Well, then — why don't you tell me all about it over drinks?" Eris suggested, holding his arm out to her.

She looked flattered and shrugged agreement, but before she could reach out and take his arm, a strange feeling passed through his body like a wave. An odd, shivering vibration, deep inside his fragmented soul. It resonated within him and he looked up, alarmed, stretching outward with all his senses.

His sensitive hearing picked up the sound of police cars wailing in the distance. He knew that the woman next to him, looking at him oddly as he stood frozen in place, would never be able to hear the distant noise. Something he couldn't explain compelled him to follow the sound. He was power-less to resist the pull, like a moth drawn to flame.

"Forgive me," he said, stepping back from the woman and turning in the direction of the pull. "I've just remembered something, and I'm afraid I'm going to have to take a rain check on those drinks."

Behind him, his would-be victim was saying something about phone numbers, but he was al-ready hurrying away.

Eris could not explain, even to himself, why he felt so strongly about the situation. He jogged. Then he ran. Then, he ran *hard*, passing people on foot left and right. He could feel their stares following him, but he didn't dare slow down long enough to apologize for the jostling or to account for his actions.

Get there, get there, get there, a voice inside him chanted. He managed to control his instincts just enough to run at a speed that would not raise alarm with the humans flashing past him, but Eris could feel the strange compulsion to *be there now* eating away at him.

He rounded corners seemingly at random, drawn forward by intuition rather than by his senses. Before he had traveled five blocks, he found himself approaching a police barricade erected a few hundred paces ahead.

Not wanting to be seen running towards a large group of alarmed police officers, Eris side-stepped quickly into the dark shadows of a nearby building's recessed doorway. He could taste human fear and tension hanging in the air around him, and he wondered what had happened to cause such a response.

The attention of the officers down the street seemed to be focused on a large building with a glass paneled front. He thought that it could be a stock exchange or a bank of some kind, and tried to orient himself against his mental map of the city. The Hellenic Bank of Cyprus, maybe? That would make sense, given where he'd started from and how far he'd run.

While he was taking in his surroundings, three officers decked out in riot gear came around the corner from a nearby side street, talking swiftly to one another.

"He's got an unknown number of hostages located at the northeast corner of the lobby. As far as we can gather, there's only one perp, but the text messages being routed through JointComm are garbled," the first officer rattled off.

It sounded to Eris like he was updating his superior on the situation at hand.

"Garbled? From panic? Or maybe injury?" the second man asked.

"Unknown, sir. It's possible that the individual is sending text messages when the perp isn't looking."

"Hmm. Base command?"

"One hundred fifty meters to the north of the front door. They're working on establishing telephone contact with the lobby right now."

Their voices faded as they continued forward, approaching the barricade.

A hostage situation, then, Eris thought, wishing that he could see past the group of armed officers standing nearby with guns drawn, and into the building. *Curiouser and curiouser.*

Ducking into an alley that he guessed would span the entire block flanking the cordoned-off area, Eris passed silently around the officers monitoring the perimeter. Once he reached the back of the large building, where the police presence was minimal, he slipped quietly by an officer who was intent on the large, hand-held radio pressed to his ear.

Eris drew his power inward and shifted into mist, rising unnoticed through the evening darkness and swirling toward the building, brightly illuminated with police spotlights. He circled, following the contours of the rooftop until he saw a second-story office window cracked open to let in a breeze. His vaporous form flowed unimpeded through the screen covering the gap.

He materialized inside an office that was completely deserted. The lights were off, but his vampire senses were much more acute than a human's. He had no trouble navigating his way into the dark hallway. For a moment he stood completely still, allowing his awareness to expand outward. He could smell a faint trace of blood, the scent tainted by fear, creeping up from the floor below this one. He followed it until he found a staircase. It opened into a wide hallway, clearly a main thoroughfare through the offices. He moved forward along the passage, still listening intently and allowing the smell of human blood to fill his senses as it grew stronger.

Finally, Eris saw light ahead and knew that he was nearing the main lobby where the hostages were located. His footfalls were so quiet that even he could barely hear them. Nevertheless, he proceeded cautiously, not wanting to startle a potential gunman.

He reached the end of the hallway and glanced quickly around the corner, taking in as much of the scene in one brief look as he could.

Shifting quickly out of sight again, Eris considered what he had seen. A huddle of people crouched together at the northeast side of the lobby, clustered into a bunch as if frightened. One lone figure stood before them, pacing back and forth. Eris had not seen evidence of a gun.

So, how was he controlling them, if not with a gun?

Suddenly a shout rent the air, making Eris jerk in reaction as the unexpected noise assaulted his sensitive ears.

"I swear, if you start talking again I will blow this thing sky high! *I know you're all plotting against me!*"

Eris could practically feel the hostages trembling with fear. One female voice spoke up, as if trying to reason with the man. "No one said anything at all, we just want to get out of here."

"Shut *up*!"

Silence fell again, and Eris closed his eyes, thinking.

He's unstable, possibly hearing things. And he's got a bomb. Not a good combination. He could snap and kill these people any second.

It was clear what Eris needed to do. Blocking out the sounds of continuing shouts in the lobby, he reached down into the pit of his damaged soul and pulled forth the memory of a peace that he had not experienced in many years. Breathing deeply, he allowed the feeling to swell inside him, until it felt like it was going to overflow the bounds of his body.

These days, in his perpetual state of worry and ennui, such peace was a sham. A ruse—and one that he would pay for afterward, especially since his meal had been interrupted earlier. But it would serve.

Exhaling, Eris mentally pushed at the feeling until — with the sensation of a popping bubble — the force expanded past the boundaries of his skin. He thrust it outward until his power of suggestion was filling the lobby and the hallway all around him.

As each person was enveloped in the serenity that he was pressing outside of himself with all his will, Eris became aware of that individual's mind and swirling emotions. All of the hostages were terrified, almost to the point of collapse after being held so long at the mercy of an unpredictable madman.

The madman himself struggled wildly for a few moments against the mental sedation that Eris was forcing upon him, before relaxing into a state of blissful surrender.

Knowing that it was now safe to emerge, Eris stepped around the corner with his hands raised in the air. Although he was focusing all of his energy on maintaining pressure on the mind of the man before him, Eris knew that with enough effort, the bomber would be able to jerk himself out of the peaceful stupor and become violent again.

"Hello, my friend," he said in the most soothing voice he could muster. "I'm here to help you."

As everyone, including the captor, turned towards him, Eris' eyes fell on a device strapped to the man's chest.

Ah. A suicide vest. That made sense.

Eris walked calmly forward, keeping his gaze on the bomber, never breaking eye contact. The man blinked slowly at him, still looking unnaturally relaxed. Eris was struck, the strangest feeling overwhelming him in that moment. He knew on an instinctual level that the person before him was not a bad person, but rather someone who had become lost in the depths of an evil not of his making.

Another victim of the dark curse spreading across the world. Would he never be able to escape the dark cloud of Bael's expanding power, even here on the island of his birth?

Sudden sympathy for the damaged man in front of him coursed through him.

"What's your name?" Eris asked quietly.

The man seemed to consider the question for a moment before answering, "Ibrahim."

"Well, Ibrahim, what seems to be the problem?"

The man called Ibrahim looked around, confused. "I—I don't know. I need to go somewhere."

"Anywhere in particular?"

"I—" The man paused, swallowing hard as his eyes glittered. "I have to get away. They're coming after me! You don't understand. I need to get out of the country."

"All right. I hear you," Eris said slowly, trying to placate him. "Go on, I'm listening."

"They have eyes everywhere," the man said in a desperate whisper, leaning closer to Eris. Ibrahim's eyes were so wide that Eris could see the whites all around his irises, which were darting around as if looking for the imagined gazes on him.

"Easy, there. Let's just calm down for a minute, and we can talk about getting you out of here. Does that sound like a good plan?"

The man breathed heavily through his nose, staring at him without blinking. He nodded at Eris' words.

"Good," Eris said to the group at large, "Let's start by getting these people out of here safely, yeah?"

Ibrahim glanced down, seeming almost surprised to find the huddled group of people at his feet. Eris wondered if he had any real awareness of the night's events, or if his confused mind had erased or blocked all of those recollections.

Several of the hostages looked up hopefully, but most seemed too scared to look Ibrahim directly in the eye.

There was silence for several moments while Ibrahim considered the people at his feet. Eris continued to press heavily on the man's mind, surprised that Ibrahim was still able to resist with such force. *Shouldn't he be tiring by now?*

"Where are we?" Ibrahim finally asked a woman near the front of the group.

She swallowed hard, her dark hair cropped close to her ears. "The H-Hellenic Bank in Cyprus."

"Oh."

"Can we—I mean, do you think we could leave now?" The woman asked him, shivering as her hands closed around her own shoulders, hugging herself.

Ibrahim considered her through heavy-lidded eyes.

"I suppose so," he answered eventually. Glancing down at his chest, Ibrahim touched the hardware on the bomb. Everyone stiffened, watching him closely.

Eris, trembling now under the effort of keeping Ibrahim calm, interrupted the man's examination in a low voice. "Would you like to take that off?"

Ibrahim nodded and started to unzip the vest holding together the bomb.

"No, wait!" Eris said, reaching a hand out. The control he had over the mood in the room shifted, and Ibrahim narrowed his eyes in sudden suspicion.

"Please," Eris said more calmly, redoubling his efforts to press serenity over Ibrahim. "Let's… just… leave that alone for now. I know some people who would be willing to help get it off of you safely."

"Oh. Okay. That's a good idea," Ibrahim answered mechanically. He stood completely still, his hands dangling at his side.

"Well, then," Eris said, keeping his voice calm and quiet. "If everyone would please stand up, I think you can leave now."

A few of the people clambered uncertainly to their feet. Their eyes never left Ibrahim, who was standing obediently next to Eris.

The woman who told Ibrahim what bank they were in seemed too nervous to stand, despite the backwash from the serenity he was projecting. With an encouraging smile, Eris reached out, offering his hand to her. She glanced at it quickly, then up into his face.

Stretching a hand up, she twined her slender fingers through his.

At the touch of her skin, Eris nearly staggered under the force of an electric shock that surged through him like a lightning bolt. Dumbfounded, he abandoned his single-minded focus on calming the turmoil in Ibrahim's tortured mind.

Eris heard the woman's sharp intake of breath and knew that the impossible had happened. She'd felt the same connection between them that he had. In an instant, the peace Eris had been forcing outward into the room and around the bomber collapsed like a popped balloon. A scream erupted from the unstable bomber, who clutched at his head, scrabbling at his temple as if trying to dig something out of his skull.

Shit, I've lost him, Eris thought, a bit dazedly, all the while maintaining his electric grip on the woman's hand—afraid to let go lest she slip away into the madness and panic erupting around them.

THREE

The bomber jerked and cried out, his forearms coming up to clamp around the sides of his head. Pandemonium broke out as the hostages started running towards the door.

Ibrahim shouted a long string of garbled words in no language Eris recognized, his eyes crazed.

In slow motion, Eris watched as his thumb moved toward what appeared to be the trigger for the bomb.

Coiling his muscles to spring, Eris wrenched his hand free of the woman's and lunged toward Ibrahim. Their bodies collided with a dull thump. Eris wrapped his arms around the smaller man and brought him down hard, suppressing a cringe and a heartfelt curse as he landed on top of the bomb. Miraculously, it didn't go off.

"Yeah... I'm not going to get that lucky twice," Eris grunted. He pushed up enough to grab Ibrahim's wrists and wrench the detonator from his hand.

When he looked up, the woman with the dark hair was backing away, a look of fear on her face. The other hostages had already fled screaming from the building, leaving the three of them alone in the echoing lobby.

Ibrahim began to struggle, still pinned by Eris' tall frame.

"*Don't,*" Eris commanded through gritted teeth.

He was still staring at the woman with whom he had felt such a strong connection. Her large eyes were wet with unshed tears as she chewed nervously on her lower lip. Beneath him, Ibrahim began to screech, sounding half-strangled by the weight of the bomb vest tangled around his torso.

Eris looked down at him, trying to decide what to do next, caught between competing crises. A faint swish of noise caught his divided attention, but when he turned his head to look, it was as if the dark-haired beauty whose touch had ignited fire in his cold heart had never been.

He nearly roared in frustration, feeling his fangs lengthen and his eyes glow gold. Ibrahim's struggles grew stronger, more frantic, and Eris was already weakened from hunger and the strain of projecting mental control over a roomful of desperate people.

Saliva welled up in his mouth, and with no witnesses remaining to constrain his actions, he struck—sinking his fangs into the tender flesh of Ibrahim's neck and drawing hard at the blood exploding over his tongue.

His stunned victim twitched beneath him, a gurgle escaping his mouth. His blood tasted sickly sweet—the taste of evil and decay. Eris nearly gagged on it. The smell of Ibrahim's stale sweat rising around them mirrored the tainted taste. Eris suddenly wished that he could just leave the madman where he'd fallen and vanish from the situation.

But he couldn't... no matter how much he might want to be chasing after his mystery woman right now, rather than dealing with one of the demon Bael's sad, pathetic victims.

With the restorative power of Ibrahim's — admittedly rather disgusting — blood pouring into him, Eris found it easier to press against the man's mind, forcing him into submission. When Ibrahim lay limp in his iron hold, Eris released his neck and looked down.

Ibrahim wasn't dead, simply weakened by blood loss and sedated by the mental pressure Eris was exerting on him.

Disgusted by the whole situation, Eris swiped a smear of blood from his chin with his forearm and rolled away from his victim, staring up at the ceiling for a moment, trying to slow his thundering heart. Oddly, his anxiety had almost nothing to do with the insane man lying strapped into a bomb vest next to him, and everything to do with the woman who seemed to have disappeared like smoke.

The lobby was empty now, except for Eris and his unlucky victim.

Scrubbing a hand roughly over his face, Eris rolled onto his knees and crawled closer to the man on the ground, staring at the vest — now plainly exposed.

Fuck me, it's been a while since I've had to do this, Eris thought darkly, rubbing his brow. He'd never been a weapons or explosive expert, *per se*, but he had picked up a thing or two in the last few decades, mostly by virtue of being in the wrong place at the wrong time.

Story of my painfully long life.

He carefully examined the trigger lying on the ground next to Ibrahim, who made no effort to retrieve it. To his surprise, he found that the trigger had malfunctioned—a connection had come loose, possibly as they'd struggled. If the thing were going to trigger the vest, it would have done so when it broke. Which... wasn't to say the vest was *safe*, unfortunately.

With a sigh, he examined the zipper, which seemed to have no physical connection to the explosives strapped to the vest. That was good news, since the devices were often wired to explode if removed, once they had been put on a suicide bomber. It was clear that Ibrahim, even in his crazed state, had at some level intended on getting out of the vest without detonating himself.

"Good choice on that, mate," Eris said to the unresponsive man. With steady fingers, he unzipped the vest and carefully guided Ibrahim's unresisting arms through the holes, rolling him first one way and then the other.

"There you go," Eris finally told him. Ibrahim's bloodshot eyes darted to his face as he continued, "No harm done, eh? Now, let's get you up off this thing. I don't want any funny business, though. Are we clear?"

Ibrahim stared at him vacantly, not answering. Eris chose to interpret this as assent.

"So," he said as he helped Ibrahim to his feet and guided him away from the device. "That was fun. We'll have to do it again sometime. Only, y'know, without the terrified hostages and the deadly danger, preferably."

"What did you do to me? *They're going to get me now*," Ibrahim whispered. His eyes were no longer manic, but rather lost, as tears welled and leaked out of the corners.

"Who? Who's going to get you?" Eris asked, looking at him closely.

Ibrahim didn't respond, merely shook his head. He looked as if he had aged two decades in the last few minutes, and lived a lifetime of misery. His dirty blond hair flopped against his head as he noisily wiped his nose on the sleeve of his shirt.

Eris tugged on Ibrahim's arm, trying to get him to move towards the door, but the other man resisted. He made a pathetic groaning noise, almost a whimper of panic.

"It's all right," Eris assured him. "You're not armed, and you're going to surrender. Just make sure you explain to them about the people who are after you, and how you decided to let the hostages go because it was the right thing to do."

Eris felt no fear of exposure by this man. Ibrahim would never be able to trace the serenity that Eris was forcing into his mind back and truly understand what had happened to him. Besides, Eris had no intention of letting him leave this building with his memories intact. It wouldn't do to have him babbling about vampires and blood-drinking and hypnotism once he was in custody. He'd be packing his bags for the loony bin immediately.

Of course, as it was, he would probably be headed that direction regardless.

"Just try to stay calm for me, will you? I'm hoping this evening might end with a little less drama than it started," Eris requested.

Still trying to maintain control of the situation, he guided the stumbling man towards the front doors where he knew that the police would be waiting, guns no doubt trained on the building.

Before they emerged, however, Eris reached up and touched Ibrahim's temple. He could feel the man's consciousness wavering under his fingers as shock began to set in. With practiced effort, Eris searched through Ibrahim's mind and found all the memories pertaining to their interactions. He pushed them down deep into Ibrahim's subconscious; so deep that he would never be able to recall Eris biting him and drawing blood from the wound on his neck — a wound that had already closed under the healing power of vampire saliva.

When only one darkened door separated them from the SWAT team waiting outside, Eris turned towards Ibrahim and looked him squarely in the eye. "Go through the door with your hands raised. Walk slowly and steadily. When the police tell you to lie face down on the ground, do it."

Ibrahim stared back at him, looking like a lost and frightened child. Eris hoped that the police would find it in the kindness of their hearts to make sure that he got the help he so clearly needed.

He could *smell* Bael's hand in this, and the idea that the demon had returned to his beloved island home raised gooseflesh across his back. Especially after his encounter with *the woman*.

"Go," Eris whispered, pushing the man forward. He maintained the gentle pressure on Ibrahim's mind, keeping him at peace and holding his fear at bay.

When Ibrahim turned towards the door and started to pass through it, Eris transformed himself into mist once more, drawing all of his life force to his center until he could dissipate and flow unnoticed through the door.

He could hear the barked orders and shouts from members of the police force as he floated away into the night, his mind already intent on finding the woman who had caused him such a shock.

He was so preoccupied with the thought of her that he didn't even register the sound of a single gunshot far behind, followed by pandemonium.

-o-o-o-

Several hours later, gliding over the city in the form of an owl, Eris felt dawn approaching as he turned back towards the hotel room he was sharing with Snag.

It had been immeasurably frustrating, flying low over the area around the city center, trying to find the dark-haired female hostage who had fled from the scene after bringing Eris' world crashing to the ground like falling icicles.

He'd had no luck whatsoever. It was with bitter disappointment that he landed on the windowsill of their hotel room and scratched at the glass to be let in.

As he sensed Snag moving towards the window, Eris swiveled his head, giving the city one last sweep with his amber eyes.

The glass popped open behind him and with one swift flap of powerful wings, Eris swept inside. He pushed his energy outwards from his center, concentrating on his human form. In mid-flight, he transformed, landing gracefully on his feet and dropping his arms to his sides.

Snag remained where he was, standing by the open window. Eris turned towards his friend and studied the intent look on the ancient being's skeletal features.

Eris felt a question brush on the edges of his mind, as if Snag were raising a mental eyebrow at him.

"I've had a rough night, all right? Let's just leave it at that for now."

Nothing changed in Snag's expression, and he remained completely silent. Eris leaned heavily against the arm of the sofa set against the wall of the living area, and let his chin drop to his chest. Weariness pressed down on him as the sun prepared to breach the horizon beyond the window. Yet, tired as he was, he still felt a mounting pressure to charge from the room and find the woman as quickly as possible.

Which was both absurd and impractical, of course, given that daylight was nearly upon them.

From the corner of his eye, Eris saw Snag move noiselessly across the room. Eris turned and watched with a raised eyebrow as he pulled the chair out by the table where they had been seated before, and lowered his thin frame into it.

The older vampire laced his fingers together and rested his chin on top of his joined hands. With a quick dart of his eyes, he told Eris very clearly to take a seat across from him at the table.

Eris sighed at him darkly. "You know, for a functional mute, you can be incredibly bossy."

Snag didn't respond to the jab, but only continued to level that timeless, disconcerting stare at him.

"All right, *fine*," Eris snarled as he dropped into the chair. "What do you want to know?"

An answering burst of irritation pulsed through their mental connection. *What do you think? Don't be dim*, it said quite clearly.

Eris blinked. It was highly unusual for Snag to communicate so directly, even across mental spheres. It made Eris wonder what Snag was picking up from him that would rock the older vampire so thoroughly.

"I went to go hunt for us," Eris answered aloud. "I'd just found a likely candidate when I felt something… *strange*… happening nearby."

Snag's head cocked to one side by approximately half a millimeter.

"I think it was something across a subconscious mental channel, because I suddenly had the overwhelming sense that I was… needed somewhere else. *Desperately*."

Eris lifted his gaze from his hands, which were clasped together tightly on the table, and stared at his companion. Snag regarded him closely, but did not communicate further.

He felt another flicker of annoyance. He was having the crisis of the millennium, and here he was, talking to a vampire as old as the hills who had all the emotional range of a wilted turnip. Eris scowled at the impassive face across from him.

Snag made a nearly undetectable motion with his finger—a movement that nonetheless managed to convey the word, *continue*.

Eris sighed again. "I followed the mental pull, and found that a suicide bomber had taken a group of people hostage at a bank. He was clearly insane—he kept yelling at nothing and was obviously experiencing paranoia and hallucinations of some kind. I used mental pressure on him to calm him down, and set about getting the hostages out of the situation. Or... I started to, at least."

Eris paused, trying to gather his thoughts into something a bit less tangled.

"Everything seemed to be under control, more or less, so I reached down and gave one of the hostages a hand up—a woman who had been crouched on the floor nearby. When our skin touched, it was like being struck by lightning." He swallowed hard. "Snag, it was Phaidra. I met the reincarnation of my soulmate tonight."

Snag, who had not moved or made any sign during the speech, gave Eris a look that plainly said, "No, really?"

A perfect replay of Eris' reaction the moment his hand had touched the woman's was shoved squarely into his consciousness, every bit as shocking now as it had been the first time. The only difference was the faint hint of someone else's asperity lurking beneath the memory.

Oh, Eris realized, with a hint of sheepishness. *I guess I must have been projecting my thoughts… just a bit. Oops.*

At which point, something occurred to him, and he frowned.

"Wait. You sensed all that and *didn't come to my aid*?" he asked, nettled. Snag simply looked back at him, blinking slowly.

Eris raised his eyebrows, trying to prompt him into speech, but—shock of shocks—nothing happened.

"Stubborn bastard," he finally muttered under his breath, before continuing in a louder voice. "Anyway, she ran off in the confusion. I tried to find her afterward, but had no luck."

Snag rose and crossed to the open, west-facing window, still in the shadow of the building as night gave way to morning. He closed it with a single, precise movement and gazed out across the city, tapping the glass thoughtfully with his finger. Putting aside his earlier irritation, Eris joined him, and the two of them stood silently side-by-side as the city outside woke.

Despite his best efforts, Eris found himself grateful that the other vampire was here. For reasons that were fairly obvious, Snag was an excellent listener, for all that his skills as a purveyor of emotional support left something to be desired. And, despite his lack of action the previous evening, his immense power made him invaluable in a crisis. If he had not raced to Eris' side, it was clearly because he believed that Eris could handle the situation without help or interference.

Eris supposed he should be flattered. Or something. But still—

"I don't know what to do now, Snag," he murmured, his breath fogging up the glass. "I have to find her before Bael does. He's coming. I can feel it."

Snag twitched restlessly. His bony ribcage expanded and contracted in a sigh.

"What?" Eris demanded. "Damn it, Snag. *What?*"

Danger. The word floated across his mind's eye, borne along the mental link that connected the two of them. *For both of you.*

Eris knew that Snag was thinking about the connection between Tré and Della, which had nearly caused such catastrophic consequences for both of them. For them all.

"It won't be like that," he said, not sure which of them he was trying to convince. "This is completely different. We know what we're facing now."

Snag gave him a look. The memory of Tré with an iron dagger lodged in his heart flashed before his eyes.

Eris sighed in exasperation. *"It's different,"* he insisted mulishly. "Things will be fine. I just have to *find her.*"

But, deep in his divided soul, Eris knew better. The vortex of chaos was already surrounding his beloved, and Bael's forces would not be far behind.

"Do you think that Bael's out there, right now?" Eris asked, jerking his chin toward the window, and the city beyond.

Snag didn't answer as he closed his eyes and breathed out deeply. All at once, Eris felt the ancient vampire's power wash over him, crashing through his mind and past him like a wave, expanding in all directions.

Though he probably shouldn't have been, Eris was staggered by the force he could feel surrounding him, penetrating him, filling him up. It was as though Snag's mind had pressed outward, encompassing the entire city like a storm cloud.

Eris stayed perfectly still and silent, aware that his every thought and movement would assault Snag's senses as he scanned the area around them. He could feel the power ebbing and flowing in his mind, at times a low thrum, and at others a blazing heat. Taken unawares by a particularly powerful wave, he swallowed a gasp, trying to stay upright under the immense pressure he could feel pressing down on him.

With a sensation like a sharp wind pulling the breath from his lungs, Snag's power receded, leaving Eris feeling shaky and disoriented in its wake. A sense of foreboding, deep and wide as the ocean, brushed his mind, and he knew that Snag had sensed Bael's power nearby.

Unable to speak, Eris turned away. Turned his thoughts inward. Tried to organize the facts he knew into something coherent and actionable.

Fact. This woman is my soul mate. Phaidra, reborn. He felt that this was a solid point. Unassailable.

A vortex of Bael's evil is already forming around her. It wasn't random that she was caught up in a madman's hostage standoff. This, also, seemed a solid truth.

It will only get worse. And if Della's experience was any indication, it will do so quickly.

How could he reach her before Bael did? She'd seemed to vanish off the face of the Earth in the moment between one breath and the next. How could he protect her and explain things to her, when he understood so little himself?

These pressing questions—all without good answers—circled through Eris' mind as the sun rose, bathing Nicosia in a golden glow beyond the shelter of the shadowed hotel room. His skin prickled, and he let the heavy drapes fall back, obscuring the light.

FOUR

Holed up in her low-end hotel room, Trynn spent what was left of the night downloading information from the miniaturized recording equipment that she had worn to the bank. A small pin at her collar, which matched the color of her blouse, was specifically chosen as the means of concealing a camera. The tiny lens looked like a small stone inlaid within the design.

Trynn had not yet been able to wrap her brain around exactly what had happened to her that evening. The entire chain of events was foggy and unfocused. It seemed strange and befuddling, as if it had happened to someone else who had simply described it to her. Her reason tried valiantly to catch up with her impressions, but try as she might, she was unable to reconcile what she knew must have happened logically with what her shocked heart insisted had happened.

All she knew for sure was that the man who had rescued them—the Hot Hypnotist, as she had taken to calling him in her mind—had touched her hand, and something amazing had happened. Even though she'd been terrified and exhausted at the time, Trynn had experienced a swooping sensation in her stomach just as a soul-deep jolt electrified her. For a brief moment, then, her panic had completely faded, and she could think of nothing else but her rescuer.

It was as though her heart was screaming a message about the man, but her mind couldn't interpret it. By the astonished look on his face, she thought he might have felt something similar. Or, Trynn thought wryly, he could have simply been reacting to her hand jerking in his. It was hard to tell.

Well, what you don't understand, you research, Trynn thought. She had never yet been stumped by a mystery, and she was not about to start dabbling in failure now.

She had already pulled a picture of the Hot Hypnotist off the camera pin, and was currently running it through facial recognition software that she had hacked from a government agency in the US, as a part of a security recon mission she'd been assigned. Of course, it was strictly illegal that she had kept the program after the job was over, but she felt that it was the least the Americans could do after she discovered the huge flaw in their security system.

It's like a payment, she justified to herself. *A tip for excellent service. Besides, it's not as though I use it for evil purposes. I'm simply trying to track down the man that saved me. Us. That saved us.*

Unfortunately, the program had failed her so far. But Trynn wasn't giving up. Not by a long shot. There were hundreds of thousands, perhaps millions of faces to trawl through. Dredging up his identity was not a task her small laptop could manage in just a few minutes.

Not unless I can narrow the search parameters, anyway, she thought. *That would cut down the possibilities by thousands of people. But how? What criteria would I need to impose?*

Her fingers hovered over her keyboard for a moment while she thought to herself. It felt like her brain, which was so usually sharp and quick-thinking, was trying to dredge through an oily sludge of exhaustion that had filled her up after the attack at the bank.

No time for that. Come on, come on, think!

With a sigh, Trynn got up and went into the pathetic little bathroom. She splashed some cool water on her face, trying to dispel the anxiety that had her heart thrumming in her ribcage. She dabbed her skin dry with a towel before hiding her face in the scratchy fabric for a few moments.

The threadbare excuse for a towel was one of the handful of *amenities* this shithole had to offer, yet she was grateful for the place. The employees had accepted her reservation without even checking her ID, which, of course, was fake anyway. It was still nice to know that they were turning a blind eye.

Through her company, which had sanctioned clearance with all the top government agencies, she was issued a letter giving permission to use fake identification. So far, though, her ID had never been questioned, which was pure luck—

Trynn nearly dropped the towel in shock. Travel! *That* was the answer to her question. She could find the man's identity by searching through recent travel logs and comparing his face to security footage at the major carriers.

Hurrying back to her computer, Trynn flopped down in the rickety chair facing her desk and began to type.

I must be out of it, if I didn't think of that before. Based on the rich tourist chic *thing he had going on, he wasn't from around here. He probably flew in recently. Maybe from Greece.*

Shaking her head at her own slowness, Trynn organized the search data to scan through security footage and passport images first, then resume its scanning of the entire database. Once the computer was again rifling through thousands of gigabytes of data, Trynn sat back in her chair, swinging one foot petulantly back and forth as she considered her options.

His eyes itched and stung with exhaustion. She knew that she needed to sleep, and very soon. Her mind was racing out of control, both from the trauma of what had happened a few hours ago, and, she suspected, from lack of sleep.

After efficiently preparing for bed, Trynn crawled under the covers and settled against the flattened pillows. Through the darkness in her room, she could see a flickering glow as her computer continued to scan through documents. The clock on the bedside table read 4:45am.

Groaning, Trynn closed her eyes and tried to sleep. She struggled for what felt like an eternity, because every time she started to drift off, her body would jerk her awake to resume reliving the horrid memories or begin contemplating her mystery man.

When she finally slipped into a fitful doze, Trynn dreamt of sand and the sound of soft waves crashing on a nearby shore.

-o-o-o-

In the dream, her surroundings materialized around her from a gray haze, and she found that she was on a beach at night. Though part of her was surprised, another part of her was happy. Excited, even. She laughed joyously and stared upward towards the bright moon that bathed her in its pale light.

A hand slipped into hers and she looked to her left, where a tall figure loomed in the darkness. The man lifted his face, and she recognized his handsome features in the silver light of the moon. For a moment, she couldn't remember where she had seen him before, but her confusion didn't last long as he grinned at her and spoke.

"Victory is ours at last, my love," he said. "Flavian agreed to the shipping contract without altering a single one of the terms. We're well and truly rich now, and we won't ever have to worry again."

Trynn swung around so that her arms were draped around the man's neck and shoulders. She drew him into a deep kiss, her skin tingling and heating with excitement as he returned it with obvious enthusiasm.

As his hands smoothed over her shoulders, she realized that she was dressed oddly, her body draped artfully in an elaborate toga. Part of her accepted this without question, but again, a part of her was confused. It was uncomfortable, as though she were being pulled into two pieces, one part clearly belonging in this world, and the other that was equally out of place and bewildered by it.

The man picked her up and swung her around in glee, her feet flying out behind her. Giggling madly, the two collapsed into the sand, which felt cool underneath her. Wrapped in his arms, Trynn grinned as he rolled himself on top of her, settling between her legs. Her dress was wrapped around them, keeping their bodies pressed closely together.

She could feel the sea washing up against her feet, soaking the bottom of her skirts. Neither part of her cared, however — both of her separate halves were too enthralled by the sensation of the long, lean body pressed against hers.

-o-o-o-

His touch was intoxicating, and she wanted to bask in the sensation even as her consciousness began to slip away from the dream world and rise back toward wakefulness. She groaned in discontent as her mind pulled her out of fantasy and into reality. A reality of musty sheets, mashed, lumpy pillows, and a dark, dreary hotel room that was distinctly unwelcoming after the delightful warmth and sea breeze within the dream.

Trynn jerked upright, swearing under her breath, feeling the unpleasant tackiness of the cooling sweat that drenched her entire body like seawater.

FIVE

Clouds of Turkish cigarette smoke hung in the air. The clink of glasses crashing together or being smacked heavily down on tables seemed unnaturally loud and irritating to the man sitting at the far end of the bar, shrouded in shadows. He was wearing a long, heavy coat with the collar pulled up, the folds of thick fabric hiding the well-tailored lines of the black suit that clung to his muscular frame.

With a sigh, he swiveled a glass of top-shelf whiskey under his hand, ignoring the suspicious looks the bartender kept throwing him. A babble of voices in several languages surrounded him like the buzzing of insects, tiresome and meaningless. This shithole bar in the ass-end of Damascus was well placed to host unscrupulous meetings, situated off the beaten path as it was.

"You need another?" The bartender grunted, glancing down at Bastian Kovac's nearly empty glass.

In reply, Bastian rapped his knuckles on the top of the counter without looking up. He was wearing reflective sunglasses despite the dim lighting inside the bar. He knew that secrecy would be his greatest challenge on this mission. Maintaining a shroud of mystery around his identity would keep his contact off balance during the negotiations.

Bastian was a master of using fear and hopelessness against people, and this pathetic arms dealer from Stalingrad would be no different.

Information he had received from a faithful contact told him that this man, Matvei Timur, was highly placed in the Russian mob. Timur was renowned for his brutality, destructiveness, and, perhaps more importantly, his untouchability. Neither his fellow mobsters nor the Russian government had ever been able to lay a finger on him.

Bastian let a smirk curl one corner of his lips. There was no power on this earth that could contend with the darkness now descending on the weak and subservient humans... at least, no power *created by man*. Other than his temporary usefulness, this arms dealer was no different from any of the other pitiful beings crawling around in the mud of this world. Bastian would twist him and bend him to his will as though he were made of soft putty.

A glass slid across the counter towards him and he grabbed it. As he lifted it to his lips and swiftly tipped it back, a form moved next to him in the semi-darkness, taking the chair immediately on Bastian's left.

Bastian held back a flicker of annoyance as a man laid his elbows on the counter, taking up more space than he needed to as he requested a drink.

"Are you Kovac?" The man asked, once the bartender had taken his order. His Russian accent was thick and heavy, leaving no doubt in Bastian's mind with whom he was dealing. He nodded once, not even bothering to look up from the dregs of his whisky, wanting to make it evident to the man that he, and he alone, held the power in this transaction.

Timur seemed to be waiting for Bastian to speak for several long moments. When Bastian did not oblige, he shifted uncomfortably.

"I have heard," he finally said, "that you are in the market."

Bastian lifted an eyebrow and let it drop, neither confirming nor denying the man's inquiry. Timur watched Bastian for several more moments before saying, "I may have what you are seeking, but you will have to pay a fair price for it."

Taking his time in answering, Bastian pressed out, expanding the malevolent aura that he knew surrounded him, reveling in the involuntary shudder that Timur attempted to hide.

"Where are your men?" Bastian asked, his voice a low growl that nonetheless carried straight to Timur.

"My men?" the mobster replied. "What men?"

"You did not come alone and probably have someone planted in this bar. I will not ask you again, where are your men?"

Timur swallowed hard, but his expression was angry. "I don't see how that is—"

With lightening quick reflexes, Bastian slapped his hand down on Timur's arm. He did not press or hold, but kept the contact between them as he forced his power into Timur's arm, deep into his bones.

The man began to struggle as the taint of Bastian's evil traveled up through his elbow and into his shoulder. Bastian watched with sick enjoyment as it became ever more intense... watched Timur squirm and attempt to pull away, beads of sweat breaking out on his head. From the corner of his eye, Bastian saw a man lounging against the wall twitch, his hand wandering toward an inner pocket. Another man seated at a table nearby straightened almost imperceptibly — the answer to his question about Timur's guards.

"You will cooperate with me, or this deal is off. Have I made myself clear?" Bastian said, the words barely audible over the voices and rowdy laughter from elsewhere in the bar.

The Russian tried to pull away, but was unable to sever the connection between them. Bastian saw the moment the fight went out of him. He slumped and nodded frantically, a burst of air escaping his lungs in relief when he was released. Immediately, he grasped his arm and wrapped it close against his stomach.

"You are either very brave or very foolish," Timur snarled, looking furious now that he was free, but also afraid. "Perhaps I will change my mind about this deal and withdraw it. You sit here smelling like a cheap cologne factory and making demands of me! Threatening me! You — you have a very inflated opinion of yourself if you think you can control Matvei Timur!"

Bastian did not reply to the man's tirade, but simply returned to his drink. He knew, just as Timur knew, that the deal would proceed. It was too beneficial for the Russian mob for them to back out at the eleventh hour.

"Let's not hear of such talk so early in the conversation," he said silkily. "I harbor no ill will, Timur. Perhaps you would be interested in hearing my other proposition before you make your final decision?"

Timur remained silent and wary, but did not rise to leave.

Bastian didn't allow the smile to reach his lips as he continued, "I operate a... business, of sorts, in Belarus. It might be of interest to you."

"Interest to me?" Timur demanded in a sullen voice. "You speak in circles. It was interest in your business that landed me here in the first place."

Bastian let a slow grin develop. "This would be more along the lines of leisure time for you and your men, rather than being *strictly* about profit margins. Consider it a token of my gratitude. Something I will add to sweeten the deal, if you will."

Timur raised a heavy eyebrow, looking intrigued almost despite himself.

Bastian took another drink, raking his eyes over Timur for a long moment. "I can give you all you need to indulge your more... animalistic instincts. Everything necessary to fulfill the wildest fantasies of your most perverted men." He lingered over the words, savoring them.

Timur's face cleared with understanding. "Ah, yes. I see. Women?"

Bastian nodded coldly. "Women. Men. Boys. Girls. Whatever you need. They have long ago learned the price of disobedience; you will have no problem controlling them."

Timur's face flushed and his eyes grew hungry, the eager light in them plain, even through the darkness.

"Girls?" he asked, leaning forward and dropping his voice.

"Their beauty and innocence is incomparable. I only take the best."

The Russian sat back, stroking his graying beard and surveying Bastian thoughtfully. "You are a difficult man to understand, Mr. Kovac. You prey upon pain and pleasure in the same meeting? What am I to understand from this?"

Bastian allowed inhuman intensity to fill his voice, making it smooth as oil and dark as night. "What are you to understand? That you have *no idea* who you are dealing with."

The sentence hung heavily in the air between them as Timur continued to stare at Bastian, clearly apprehensive.

"What are you proposing? Precisely?" he finally asked Bastian. "What type of... *merchandise*... do you need? Your initial messages were oddly unspecific on that point."

"That is because I needed first to discover whether you were a trustworthy man," Bastian replied easily. "I need something very specific. Something sophisticated, uncommon, and easily transported."

"Biochemical?"

Bastian's eyes narrowed. "Am I a cut-rate terrorist looking to give his enemies a stomach ache?

Think bigger, Timur. What could I want from the Russian mob that I could not get more easily elsewhere?"

Timur cocked his head for a moment before his expression cleared in understanding. Avarice lit his eyes. "Ah. Now I understand you, I think. Yes. I have access to what you need. Six devices that can be carried in a backpack by any relatively fit man."

It was Bastian's turn to look hungry. "That," he said, "is *exactly* what I need."

"It will cost you," Timur warned.

Bastian waved a careless hand. "Money is no object. I will provide you and your men access to my... *business* in Belarus, and pay you ten million American dollars for each device."

Timur looked as if he were going to argue for a moment, but decided better of it. "Those had better be some truly exquisite girls, Kovac."

"You will not be disappointed."

They shook hands warily—Timur cringing a bit at the cold clamminess of Bastian's skin—and agreed to meet again the following day to make arrangements for the devices to be transferred. Bastian departed feeling triumphant.

As he passed out of a side door to the alley running beside the dilapidated bar, he felt a shadow loom over him. Within moments, it settled into a dense cloud that surrounded him, smothering him in cold, clinging vapor.

He fell to his knees, opening his palms skyward and waited. The power infusing itself into his surroundings pulsed and throbbed, going cold to hot, heating Bastian from his core. The cologne that he wore to disguise the putrid smell of rotting flesh steamed away as the demon Bael entered his body, coiling through his awareness to read the thoughts of his best lieutenant, his servant, his greatest creation.

You have done well, my faithful one, a voice murmured in his ear. Bastian could feel the demon's breath sliding like black oil down his neck and back. He reveled in it, wallowing blissfully in the strength and awesome power of evil.

"Yes, my master."

Death surrounded him. He could sense the reek of it rising up from earth, centuries of filth and decay filtering up through the cracked pavement of the alley, swirling around them as Bael lavished praise upon his head.

You will use those tools to usher in my kingdom, and bring back the darkness from which we have been cast.

Bastian breathed in the stench, allowing it to fill him and burn like glowing lava inside his empty frame.

"Yes." He exhaled, feeling clarity settling over him. "I will destroy the humans and bring terror and chaos where there was once love and light. You will be avenged, and I will sit at your right hand forever — your most devoted servant."

Bring about my reign, dog. Nothing else matters to you, Bael commanded harshly. *Seek not your own glory or dominion, for I am your creator, and you will always bow to me. You are but a speck of dirt on the ground, animated only by my power.*

Bastian dipped his head, feeling a horrible weight press down on him. "Yes, my master."

The weight lifted incrementally. *Before my final triumph can come to fruition, dog, I have sensed a great danger which we must face, and soon.*

"Master?"

Another of the failed six is approaching his fated mate. They must not be allowed to come together.

Bastian remained silent, sensing his master's discontent. He had learned the hard way the price of interrupting Bael. After several moments of silence, however, Bastian tentatively spoke. "How do you wish me to proceed, master? Should I find the bitch?"

Bael did not answer, but Bastian could still sense his looming presence.

"I could destroy her for you," he whispered, shivering with pleasure at the thought. His knees were pressing hard into the cracked and filthy pavement, growing damp with the sickly dew that had descended all around him. "I could break her mind and body under torture, and demolish every last memory of the vampire she so foolishly loved."

No, Bael said, so sharply that Bastian jerked in surprise. *No, we shall wait. She is near. And she will draw one of the abominations straight to us.*

"To us?"

Her mate will come, but we will be waiting. When the vampire is in our trap, we will find out what he knows, and destroy him. His cursed half-life will collapse around him like a house of cards.

Bastian nodded submissively and touched his fingers to his forehead. "It will be as you say it will be."

Yes. It shall. Go now, dog, and bring forth my kingdom.

SIX

Trynn sat up slowly in bed, wiping her brow with trembling fingers. The dream had been so vivid, it was as though she had stepped through a doorway leading back in time, to a different life that was every bit as much *hers* as this dingy hotel room.

Rather than try to make sense of something so fundamentally nonsensical, she shook herself awake and turned her attention to the single greatest comfort in her life. *Work.*

Padding across the room in her socks, Trynn sat down at the desk and rubbed her finger over her computer's track pad to wake it from power-saving mode. She looked at the screen and sucked in a breath. While she'd slept, it appeared that the facial recognition software had found a match.

"What happened to my notification alert, damn it?" Trynn murmured, since the buzzer had failed to wake her out of the seductive darkness of her dreams. She could tell that it had gone off, though, as the alert was still showing on her computer.

Sighing in frustration, Trynn reviewed the search results. It seemed that her Hot Hypnotist had indeed arrived in Cyprus via plane a few days ago. The date stamp on the security footage noted that he had arrived at approximately eleven o' clock at night, three days previously. Curiously, there was no security footage from the city of Cyprus during the day. His face was only captured after dark, under the glare of a streetlight near the exclusive Merit Lefkosa Hotel.

He could be staying there, she thought. *I wish I could find a more definite picture of him either entering or leaving, though. Seems like this guy is a bit of a recluse and a night owl, when he's not busy swooping in to save the day like some kind of mild-mannered, khaki-wearing superhero.*

Still, Trynn wasn't overly bothered by this. She, too, felt more comfortable moving around outside after nightfall. The bright sun had always hurt her eyes and made her feel overly hot in her pantsuits and sleek, tailored dresses.

She knew with complete certainty that she wasn't going to be able to let this rest without digging further. With a sigh, she picked up her cell phone. Her boss was on speed dial, and she tapped the button with a feeling of trepidation.

"Mandy?" Trynn asked in a quiet voice as soon as she heard the bark of the bossy voice on the other end. "Yeah, it's Trynn. Look, I finished up my job at the Hellenic Bank here in Nicosia, but there was, uh… an *incident*."

There was a pause on the other end of the line *"Wait. You had an incident? Tell me you didn't break your record of not having to talk your way out of a security detainment. I had a bet down that you'd last another six months!"*

"Er, not exactly…" Trynn replied, the words emerging with uncharacteristic hesitation. Despite her determination to stay collected and professional during the call to her boss, Trynn felt unwanted emotion well up as she remembered the hours of terror she had endured in the bank lobby.

Apparently her silence communicated more than her words because Mandy spoke in an anxious voice. *"Trynn. What happened? Talk to me."*

Trynn swallowed several times, trying to keep her voice steady. "I went into the bank, launched my cyber-attack, tagged the target accounts, and got out of the system clean. There was nothing triggered by my hacking. As I was trying to leave, though, I walked out into the lobby right into the middle of a… of a fucking *hostage situation*."

"A what?" Mandy's voice rose in pitch.

"Yeah, you heard me right. Some guy was standing there with a bomb strapped to his chest. He was completely out of his mind and he grabbed me before I could get out the door."

"Oh my God, Trynn! Are you okay?"

Trynn paused again. She was not sure there was a word that described the horrible sensation clawing its way up her chest or the swirl of emotions that was making it feel like she couldn't breathe.

"Yeah, um. Not great, I guess," she finally admitted. "I mean, I'm not really hurt or anything, but—"

She could tell Mandy had fallen effortlessly into Awesome Boss Crisis Mode.

"What do you need?" the older woman asked. *"How did you get away? Did the police catch the guy? Do you need me to fly out there?"*

Trynn's head was spinning under the barrage of questions. She sat down heavily on the bed, dropping her head into her hand as she pressed the phone to her ear. "No, look. I'm fine, really Mandy."

"Is that right? Because you sound like hell."

Trynn rubbed her brow, unable to hold back a weak snort of amusement. "Okay, okay. I'm not my best, but I don't need you to come flying out here or anything. I just need..."

Her voice trailed away again. What did she need? Sleep? Alcohol?

The last option sounded pretty appealing at the moment, but she wasn't about to tell her boss that she wanted to go on a major binge-drinking episode. And anyway, that really wasn't her style. She'd probably pass out from exhaustion after the third shot of tequila and get hauled off to the drunk tank.

Finally, she settled on a thought. "I think I just need some time off."

Mandy didn't even hesitate. *"Done. I'll smooth it over with the higher-ups due to the traumatic situation. Do you need to talk about it with someone? You probably should, you know. We have an employee assistance program you can access, if you need it."*

She took a deep breath and let it out, feeling her clamoring nerves start to quiet a bit. "I think I'm okay. Honestly, right now I'm trying to track down the man who saved us. I need to talk to him."

"How did you get out of there, anyway?" Mandy asked.

Trynn really didn't feel like going into detail, but she knew she owed Mandy at least a basic explanation. "A guy came in and convinced the suicide bomber to give up, which gave us all time to escape. I don't know what happened after that—I ran straight out the door and didn't look back."

She heard Mandy blow out a breath. *"Did you give your statement to the police?"*

"No, I ran through the barricade. Someone tried to stop me, I think, but I shook him off. I guess they had other things to worry about at the time."

Trynn could tell by Mandy's hesitation that she did not approve, but didn't want to push the issue, either.

"Under the circumstances, they probably understood," she assured Trynn in a quiet voice. *"Look, Trynn. Please don't hesitate to call if you need something. Take as much time as you need."*

A lump rose in Trynn's throat, but she swallowed it. "Thank you, Mandy. I think I'll be okay with just a few days."

"Good luck with the search for your rescuer," Mandy said kindly. *"If you need any help with that, I'd be glad to lend a hand."*

Trynn smiled, feeling better now than she had a few minutes ago. She was truly grateful, at times like these, to have such a wonderful boss. "All right. I'll let you know how it goes."

She ended the phone call and set her cell phone down on the bed next to her. Leaning back on her hands, she stared blankly at the ceiling, lost in thought for several moments.

I have to talk to him. I might be crazy, but I have to try to understand what happened when our hands touched.

Straightening abruptly, Trynn climbed to her feet and marched to the tiny bathroom, shedding clothes along the way. In the shower, she tried to wash away the memories of the traumatic events, scrubbing at her skin, which was tight and itchy with dried sweat. Afterward, she toweled her hair dry and applied enough make-up to hide the bags under her eyes and the pale cast of her face. Stepping back out into her room, she surveyed her supplies carefully, trying to take stock of what she had available.

She threw on a nice outfit and packed her bag with her laptop and several electrical devices that were basically props. They looked impressive to the untrained eye, but she never actually used them.

Outside, the sun beat down on her head. As it always did, her body grew uncomfortably warm within minutes. Normally, she hated the over-heated feeling, but today she felt like it was thawing out a part of her that had gone icy and cold while trapped in the lobby of the bank.

Banishing that thought, she turned her attention to the unofficial infiltration mission before her. A short cab ride later, Trynn was standing outside the grand entrance of the Merit Lefkosa hotel. She checked her reflection in the dark glass before stepping confidently into the building, nodding politely to the bellhop.

"Can I help you, miss?" a young man with wavy black hair asked from his station behind the massive front desk. His suit and tie were crisp, and his nametag read *Adrien*.

"Yes, I got a call about a server problem?" Trynn replied in a tone caught somewhere between boredom and professionalism.

Adrien's face wrinkled in confusion. "Miss?"

She let silence hang for a beat. "A server? You know, that thing that you log into on your computer," she answered with a faint note of derision, trying to put the young man on edge. To further illustrate her point, she gestured towards his computer. "I'm here to fix it."

The kid—*was he even twenty?*—looked down at the screen, then back up at Trynn. "I'm showing no errors with the computer, miss, and I can't let you past the lobby with our new security protocol."

Trynn sighed aloud. "It's only a partial outage. I need to assess the locations to figure out why your bosses are suddenly looking at kill screens and their RAM is being depleted, which, in turn, is bogging down the entire operating system."

Her voice was laced with annoyance, and she spoke slowly, as if addressing a small child. It was clear to her that this individual knew very little about computers, as his face flushed and he looked uncomfortable.

"I have clear instructions…" he said into the growing awkwardness.

"Fine," Trynn snapped, spinning on her heel. "Look, I don't get paid enough to deal with this kind of bureaucratic miscommunication and incompetence. If you're not going to let me look at the server, then why did you call me all the way out here for nothing? I'll just leave, and let you deal with the fallout. If this turns into a system-wide problem, it's likely everything will crash. Good luck dealing with your *security protocols* when all the electronic locks on the room doors suddenly pop open at once."

She made it about ten paces before the desk clerk caught up with her.

"Wait!" he said breathlessly. "Wait, I'll let you see our operations room, just let me get a copy of your ID first, please."

Trynn turned back with a put-upon sigh and passed him her fake identification. They returned to the desk, and she tapped her fingernails on the top of the marble counter in a bored rhythm as he copied the ID and scanned it into the system.

"Sorry about the confusion," the hotel clerk muttered, sliding her card back across the counter to her. "We've just been under a lot of pressure about security, what with all the crazy things going on recently."

"Yeah, sure. I understand," Trynn said, giving him a half smile. She readjusted her computer bag over her shoulder and followed him down a short hallway and into a room where the hub of the technology in the hotel was located.

"Please let me know if you need anything further," he said, looking eager to get away from her.

Trynn nodded and made a humming noise, but didn't speak, pretending to look closely at the status screen on a nearby computer.

As soon as the clerk left, Trynn sat down and pulled out her laptop, placing it on the desk in front of her. She connected her computer to the network, and immediately started hacking her way into the guest list.

Overall, she was impressed with the hotel's security system. She really had to pull out all the stops to get in, not a state of affairs that she ran into very often. When she was finally able to access the list and all the IDs that the guests had provided to the front desk, she searched through the hundreds of current hotel customers.

Trynn felt fairly certain she would recognize her rescuer as soon as she saw him, but she couldn't be totally sure. After all, she had been under a significant amount of stress at the bank, not to mention the fact that ID photos were notoriously awful and unflattering.

After roughly ten minutes, though, Trynn found him. His dark hair and five o' clock shadow gave him the look of a scruffy male model, and his eyes, which seemed to meet hers directly through the computer screen, were a startlingly deep chocolate brown.

A fluttering feeling climbed up her chest, and Trynn worked hard to quiet her rapid breathing. He was… *beautiful*. Truly gorgeous. And he had saved her life.

As unlucky as it was to be involved in that situation, she thought, *at least my rescuer was hot as hell.*

Scanning through his file, Trynn discovered that he had checked into the hotel alone a few days previously. His name was Nico Pavlaveous. For some reason, that surprised her. Trynn tried it aloud, and decided that it did not really suit him at all. At the very bottom of the page, she located his room number and committed it to memory.

Without leaving a trace of the breach, Trynn backed carefully out of the system. Logging off required her to enter a new set of credentials, which took time to override.

"God, they've really got this stuff figured out," Trynn muttered. She considered submitting the place for future consultation with her company to ensure they were continuing to maintain the highest level of security. Honestly, it would make a great model for other businesses.

When she was finally able to disconnect her computer without setting off any virtual alarm klaxons, she slipped all of her supplies back into her bag. Thanks to the beleaguered clerk, she had already passed the security checkpoint and simply needed to find room 706 in the west tower.

After searching for a few short minutes, Trynn finally followed a middle-aged woman with salt-and-pepper hair onto an elevator. She smelled like chlorine—the hotel obviously had a pool somewhere. Or possibly several, given the general level of opulence she'd seen so far. Trynn rode the elevator up to the seventh floor, pretending to be busy on her phone rather than having to make small talk with the woman standing next to her.

As soon as the doors slid open, she passed through them and turned quickly down the hall. She felt excitement growing, and the adrenaline rush drove away any vestiges of the horrors from the previous evening. It left a warm glow in her stomach, which wasn't tempered in the least by rational thoughts about the fact that she was going to bang on a complete stranger's hotel room at ten o' clock in the morning and demand that he explain to her why touching his hand had felt like touching a live wire.

Pushing all that aside, Trynn located the correct room and stood outside for a moment. Really, there was nothing stopping her from simply loitering nearby to see if he came out of the room on his own. She shook her head, too impatient to consider waiting, and stepped forward.

I've come this far. I won't back out now.

She rapped her knuckles briskly on the door a few times and stood back, waiting as the moments ticked past.

It's ten o'clock. He's probably out for the day. Damn, maybe I've missed him.

Just as she was starting to turn away, she heard the lock slide back, and the door opened.

There he stood. Her beautiful, gorgeous, brave rescuer, wearing nothing but a pair of pajama bottoms and the confused, squint-eyed expression of the unexpectedly awakened.

He had clearly been sleeping—his mop of black, wavy hair was plastered all over his head. This soft, disheveled version of her Hot Hypnotist was a dazzling sight to behold, and she stared at him, running her eyes over sleek muscles and smooth skin, words forgotten.

His eyes sharpened and raked over her. She saw them widen in shock and his mouth fell open.

It took a while for anything to come out. A few moments passed, and he cleared his throat significantly. When he spoke, there was a low, gravelly quality to his voice, clearly from having just woken up.

"What? How?" The stammered monosyllables were the polar opposite of the glib words he'd used to calm the bomber the previous night.

Without thinking or hesitating, Trynn lifted a hand up to his chest and pushed him forcefully backwards into the room. When the palm of her hand met his skin, a flash of electricity exploded across her nerves, bouncing from her hand all the way down her body. Hot pleasure coursed through her veins at the sensation. As it faded, leaving goose bumps behind, Trynn stepped closer to him. She had expected him to resist the manhandling, but he was still staring at her, open-mouthed.

"*Who are you?*" she demanded. "I'm not leaving until I get some answers."

-o-o-o-

Eris gaped at the slender, willowy woman with cropped black hair standing before him. Her brown eyes were staring at him intently, as if she could pull the truth directly from his fragmented soul.

Suddenly and acutely aware that Snag had been sitting in the chair across the room when he'd opened the door, Eris moved a step to the side to interrupt her line of sight. Foreboding rose in his chest at the thought of this woman unexpectedly seeing his companion, whose appearance was so distinctly inhuman.

He threw a quick glance over his shoulder, only to find that the room was now deserted. His relief lasted only an instant before he realized that Snag had abandoned him to have this incredibly awkward conversation without any sort of backup or moral support—*the bastard*. Eris decided then and there that he would give his so-called friend a few extremely choice words when he returned.

His unexpected visitor was still glaring at him, waiting for answers he had no idea how to give. What the hell was he supposed to say to her? How did you even *begin* that kind of conversation?

Eris wished with sudden urgency that he had taken more time to talk to Tré and find out how he broke the news to Della about the events in her past life. Because, face it—there was simply no good way to ease into something like that.

While he was standing, staring at the woman with his mouth partially open, she had stepped back, putting some distance between the two of them.

Suddenly, Eris found that he wanted nothing more than to have her hand back on his chest. He wanted to feel every fiber of his being singing under her touch. He wanted to feel the hair on the back of his neck stand up, to smell the sweet scent of her perfume on his skin.

"I—" he began before breaking off. It was useless, though. How could he possibly explain things to her?

The woman crossed her arms, glaring at him. Without consciously deciding to do so, Eris reached out with his senses and brushed the edges of her mind. He thought that he had used a light enough touch that she wouldn't notice, but she seemed to flinch involuntarily.

"Have you been having strange dreams lately?" he blurted, trying to distract her from the sensation that had stroked across her mind. *Yes, because that's a totally natural conversation starter.*

"Why?" she shot back, looking suspicious.

Eris paused, at a loss as to how to proceed. On the one hand, he didn't want her to think he was crazy. On the other hand, it seemed prudent to start with something that she could relate to. And it was clear by her demanding tone that, yes, she had been having odd dreams. The question was, how could he steer the conversation from dreams to events in real life?

"Have they been about me?" Eris asked cautiously, drawing back into the comforting shadows of the hotel room. *Brilliant. Not strange or creepy at all, Casanova. Maybe it's just as well Snag's not around to witness this masterful performance.*

It was the woman's turn to hesitate. She bit her bottom lip, her gaze sliding uneasily down to her feet. "What does that matter?" she said, obviously having to force her eyes to meet his again. "We were just involved in a major crime. It would only make sense that I dreamed about it."

Eris could tell by the tone of her voice that her dreams—like his—had nothing to do with the incident at the bank.

The woman seemed to think she owed him some kind of further explanation, because she suddenly said, "Look—I came here to thank you for saving my life. My name is Trynn."

"Trynn?" Eris repeated, the name oddly sweet as it fell from his lips. He blinked, trying to center himself. "My name is… Nico."

He held out his hand to her but she did not take it. Instead, she studied him closely, as if appraising him.

"Is that your real name?" she asked. Her voice held no hint of judgment, simply curiosity.

A smile tugged at the corner of his mouth. "No, it's not."

She gave a brief nod. "I didn't think it was. Pity, I was really impressed by the hotel's security earlier."

"You didn't think my name was Nico?" Eris asked, intrigued. "Why is that?"

Trynn considered him for a moment. "I can't put my finger on it, but it doesn't seem to fit you, somehow."

Can't argue with that, can I? He cleared his throat. "Well, you're right. My name is Eris."

"Eris what?" she asked.

"Just Eris."

Trynn resumed her intense scrutiny of his face, her eyes darting back and forth over his features.

"That seems much more like you," she said quietly.

"I'm glad you approve," he retorted, amused. "Is Trynn your real name?"

"Maybe," Trynn said.

"Trynn what?" he asked.

"Just Trynn," she replied.

He huffed a breath of amusement. "Fair enough. So, are you really here just to say thank you?"

Trynn paused. "Yes. Well... among other things."

Ah. Now they were getting somewhere. He hoped. "What other things?"

She took a deep breath as if steeling herself. "I have questions I want answered. The first and most important I already asked you. Who are you?"

Eris frowned. "I already told you, my name is—"

She waved him away impatiently.

"No," she said. "Who *are* you, really? Who are you to me and why do I feel like I've known you my entire life?"

Eris caught his breath and tried to decide how best to proceed with this conversation. Surely *not* with her still standing in the doorway to a room in a very public hotel.

"Please, come inside," he said quietly. "We do need to talk, but I would prefer not to do it with the door open."

A flicker of something like alarm passed across Trynn's face, and he silently cursed himself.

"Sorry, that made me sound like some kind of creeper, didn't it. You don't have to come inside if you're worried about it," Eris said, "but I assure you, I mean you no harm."

"Yeah, I guess you wouldn't, since you already saved my life once," Trynn replied, looking a bit sheepish.

Eris gestured her further inside and offered her the chair that Snag had recently vacated. Trynn sat primly, leaning forward to stare at Eris with an intent gaze. He became suddenly and acutely aware that his chest was bare and his hair was standing on end from having rolled out of bed so suddenly. *Brilliant. Way to make an impression.*

"Will you excuse me for a moment?" he asked, jerking his head towards the bathroom.

Trynn waved him on and curled up in the chair to wait. Eris hurried toward the bathroom, ducking into the sleeping alcove on the way to grab a shirt and trousers from his suitcase.

Once in the bathroom, he splashed some water on his face, still trying to decide how to break the news to this woman that they had been lovers in a previous life, he had become a vampire and killed her, and now her destiny was most likely tangled with his in a complicated and dangerous battle between the forces of good and ill.

Oh yeah, there was no doubt about it. This was going to go down *really well*.

After freshening up and making himself presentable, Eris walked back out into the hotel room to find that Trynn had not moved a muscle.

Patient, I like that, he found himself thinking. *Just like Phaidra.*

As his eyes met hers, he felt his heart swell with longing. At that moment, he wanted nothing more than to take her in his arms and kiss her until neither of them cared about the past or the future. He wanted her to feel his devotion, which had started as a spark when their hands touched in the bank lobby, and exploded into flame when she showed up at his door, demanding answers.

Sitting down in the chair across from her, Eris noticed that her eyes followed his every move and her pupils were blown wide. Gods above, this conversation was going to kill him, he was sure. He cleared his throat, and tried to find a place to begin.

"Do you ever feel like you don't really belong in this world?" he asked, echoing something he had heard Della say a few weeks previously.

Trynn's eyebrows drew together, and her eyes narrowed in suspicion. "What is that even supposed to mean? Doesn't everybody feel like that sometimes?"

Eris shrugged and continued, "Maybe so… but do you ever feel specifically like you don't belong here. Like you were made for… someplace else?"

Something like shock flashed across Trynn's face, but she covered it quickly. "That's preposterous, where else would I be?"

"I don't know," Eris answered. He didn't want to dump too many details on her at once, but she had definitely reacted to his words. "Perhaps… not so much another place as another time?"

Trynn was silent for a moment, digesting his words.

"Well… my grandmother always told me I have the soul of a gypsy," she offered, "but I don't know about that."

"You find it hard to stay in one place?"

She nodded. "Yes, that's why I have my current job. I can move from place to place, country to country, and no one even knows my real name."

Eris cocked his head. "Ah. So Trynn *isn't* your real name."

She simply looked at him, poker-faced. They stared at each other for several long minutes before Eris conceded defeat. Intriguing as it was, he knew the little contest of wills was a distraction from his attempt to explain the situation.

"I think I know why you feel that way about traveling," he said.

She continued to look at him, not speaking—making him do the heavy lifting in the conversation. The tactician in him admired her skill at it.

"I think it's possible that you do come from a different time."

Her eyebrows were traveling up her forehead in surprise. "What do you mean by that?"

"Do you believe in reincarnation?" Eris asked, looking at her intently.

Trynn frowned at him, clearly thrown off by the change of subject.

"I—" she stammered. "I… don't really know. It seems to make sense in some ways, I guess, but I'm not particularly religious so I've never given it much thought."

"In what ways does it make sense?"

"Just… my life, you know? Sometimes, I have these incredibly vivid dreams about times long ago. They seem so real," Trynn replied, in the smallest of voices. Something about her tough exterior seemed to have cracked, allowing a small truth—the tiniest admission—to seep out.

He latched onto it. "That's because they're not dreams, Trynn. They're memories. Those things you dream about — when you dream about me — it's *real*."

Her mouth opened and closed a couple of times before words came out. "No. That's impossible. Scientifically, inarguably impossible."

Eris didn't answer; he merely looked into her eyes. He imagined he could see something like the truth dawning there.

"It can't be true," she whispered.

"It can, and it is," he said urgently. "We were both born in the second century A.D. My name was Eris, and your name was Phaidra."

"Phaidra?"

"Yes."

Trynn's head bowed and she stared down at her hands for a moment.

"We were... *collectors*, of sorts," he continued. "We gathered fabulous treasures, sometimes by theft, sometimes by purchase, and we gained immense wealth from doing so. Until — "

Trynn lifted her head, and Eris could sense her quickening heart rate, as if memories were falling into place in her mind. His own heart beat faster in sympathy.

"Until?" she asked, barely a whisper.

"We were... torn apart," Eris said quietly. "Separated by a force of unimaginable evil. You died sacrificing yourself for me, and were reborn — who knows how many times across the millennia. We are soulmates, Trynn, destined to be together."

Eris felt like he was doing a very poor job explaining things, as his words weren't very informational. He grappled with the instinct to touch Trynn, to reaffirm their connection through physical contact, but something told him to remain where he was. Trynn was looking down at her feet again, sitting very quiet and still.

After what felt like an eternity, she looked up and Eris' heart fell at the expression on her face. It was a mixture of horror, skepticism, and open hostility.

"I can't believe I wasted my time trying to find you," she ground out in a low voice. "I thought you were some sort of—I don't know—*hypnotist*, or maybe a shrink or something, the way you were able to calm down that bomber. I thought you were a real hero. Yet here I am, alone with another complete lunatic, wasting precious hours of my life listening to you spin fairy tales about fate and destiny—"

"Trynn," Eris began.

"Shut up!" she interrupted. "*Shut up.* I don't want to hear any more of your lies."

"*I'm not lying.*" Eris could hear the desperation creeping into his voice, and hated it.

"This is completely nuts!" Trynn exploded, sounding angry now. "Reincarnation? Soulmates? The *second century*? You could've at least tried to come up with something believable!"

Frustration surged in Eris' chest and his lips curled back, his eyes glowing gold. "Believable?" he snarled. "This *emptiness* has been my life for two thousand years!"

Trynn scrambled to her feet, horror flooding her face. She backed away from him slowly, heaving unsteady breaths, and he hated himself for the fear he'd awakened in her.

"*I am not lying to you,*" Eris said in a dark, powerful voice. "In all our time together, I never once told you a falsehood. *You are Phaidra, and I am Eris.*"

The words seemed to shake Trynn to her core, and she turned, rushing for the entrance. With speed and reflexes that surprised him, she ripped open the hotel room door and fled down the hallway before Eris could even begin to stop her.

Knowing that it was full daylight outside, Eris had no choice but to let her leave. He could not follow her in any form without risking catastrophic injury under the sun's unforgiving rays.

Fury licked at his damaged soul, and he let out a snarl of frustration as he slammed the door behind her, throwing the hotel room back into semi-darkness. His sensitive eyes, however, picked out every object and color in the room.

As he turned back towards the sleeping alcove, a movement in the shadows caught his attention. Snag stood there impassively, staring at him with deep-set eyes.

"*Back so soon*? Thanks for that. You were a *huge* help," Eris snapped.

Snag did not move or speak. He simply regarded Eris with a thoughtful gaze.

"Why did you abandon me like that?" Eris exploded, feeling his temper pressing outward like a dark cloud. Snag did not flinch in the face of Eris' fury, but remained standing, solid as stone.

"Nothing to say for yourself?" Eris demanded. "Speak, silent one! Now, of all times, would be the perfect chance for you to dispense your *great wisdom*."

Eris allowed a terrible, cutting sarcasm to permeate the words, heedless of the consequences, in the heat of his anger at himself for failing to keep Trynn by his side.

Still, Snag did not reply.

"Fine," Eris snapped. "*Fine!* Don't speak. I have been here for you through thick and thin, I have stayed by your side and forced you to feed when your life was nearly spent. You would be a petrified *husk* right now if it weren't for me. And I have *never* asked anything of you in return, other than your friendship. Today, for the first time ever, I am asking for your help in understanding this mess. Yet you *refuse* to share your thoughts."

Snag merely allowed Eris to rant, pacing back and forth in the generous suite. When it was clear that no sort of response would come from that quarter anytime soon, Eris stormed back over to the bed, ripping his shirt off over his head and flopping down angrily onto the mattress. Without another word, he pulled the blankets up over his shoulder and turned so that he was facing away from Snag. He did not want to see the silent, unmoving outline of the ancient bloodsucker standing there in the dark, watching him.

Oddly, even though whirling thoughts and emotions were chasing themselves around Eris' head, he fell into a deep slumber within moments.

If he had been paying attention to anything other than his own distress, he might have noticed the way Snag was pressing serenity over his thoughts, banishing any painful dreams or recollections of the past. He might have noticed that Snag was giving Eris the peace that he needed to rest and recover from the day's events.

All the while Eris slept, Snag stayed nearby, keeping the darkness at bay and standing watch over his fellow vampire.

SEVEN

The sound of her fingers tapping against the keyboard soothed Trynn's frayed nerves better than anything else might have, as she lost herself in the lines and lines of code she was trying to sort through.

She was distracting herself with a job that had nothing to do with Trajan Security, or with a hot hypnotist who had turned out to be a freaking psycho rather than a hero. There had to be a way to break this encryption so that she could get a fix on her current target's server — there always was. And she needed a location to provide to her hacktivist organization so others could start working on the situation.

Trynn had been using her skills to assist online whistleblowers with locating and exposing dangerous individuals in the private sector for a couple of years now. Her expertise as a hacker had been vital in several projects, although no one in the group knew who she was in the real world. She used an alias and such a powerful, complicated system of encryption that it would take a technological genius to break through the multiple layers of defense with which she had shrouded herself.

Needing to clear her mind after her encounter at the Merit Lefkosa, Trynn had thrown herself into tracking down the identity of a man who was in

Damascus attempting to purchase some seriously heavy-duty weaponry. She had intercepted the communications of a suspected Russian mob figure with someone requesting munitions for purchase, but the messages had been maddeningly vague as to exactly what kind of munitions. Her gut was telling her that this was a major deal that needed to be monitored, and she hadn't gotten this far by ignoring her instincts.

Now, though, she was having doubts. Perhaps it was nothing—just one of the hundreds of back-room deals that went on in parts of the world where law and order were more of a distant dream than a reality. Perhaps this transaction would never even come to fruition, or if it did, the weapons would never see the light of day.

Or, *perhaps* it was the situation with the man who called himself Eris that had completely unnerved her and was making her question herself. She scowled, her thoughts once more drawn back to their bizarre conversation despite her best efforts. Trynn had certainly been unable to banish the preposterous notions he'd fed her, wrapped in fantastical tales that were not remotely believable.

Shit like this just doesn't happen, Trynn told herself for the dozenth time, staring straight through her computer screen without seeing it. *A gorgeous man does* not *just randomly show up in your life, save you from a suicide bomber, and then announce casually that reincarnation is real and that you were once his soulmate centuries ago before you sacrificed your life for him like some sort of lovelorn Romeo and Juliet.*

Trynn shook her head in disgust, a bitter chuckle escaping her throat. *Yeah, right.*

"Insanity," she whispered aloud, trying to keep her mind focused on the task at hand.

It was useless. Eris, with his beautifully chiseled body and sculpted features, kept breaking into her thoughts without her volition.

His mussed hair. His striking eyes. His flat, sexy abs.

Trynn swallowed, feeling heat creeping down her spine. Yet, in one part of her mind, she could not banish the image of him drawing his lips back as his eyes glowed gold.

His fangs. His fucking *fangs*.

Maybe he wasn't the crazy one after all. Maybe *she* was.

There were two possibilities here. Either she hadn't seen what she thought she saw, or... she had. Was she hallucinating? She didn't feel like she was hallucinating. Though, she supposed that was sort of the point. If you knew you were seeing things, you'd know they weren't real. Right?

She knew what the pointed fangs and glowing eyes reminded her of. But... that was nuts.

Her thoughts had carried her down such a ridiculous path that she was staring blankly into space, her warm laptop heating the tops of her thighs as the processor hummed. She scolded herself sharply for even entertaining such nonsense.

He was obviously a delusional mental case who just so happened to also be into playing dress-up. Why else would he just randomly be wearing vampire teeth at ten o'clock in the morning during the middle of summer? And his eyes? Well, maybe the light had just hit them oddly for a moment. That was probably it. If there was one thing for certain, it was that such things didn't really exist in the world.

Feeling more at peace, Trynn settled back to work. Forty minutes later, she finally had a breakthrough in her hacking project. Letting out a heartfelt exclamation of victory, Trynn practically pounced on the keyboard. With the final access key in place, she was able to pull up the account information behind the intercepted message.

The user's name was B. Kovac and his originating IP address was based in Syria. Damascus, to be exact — just as she had suspected.

"Next time, choose a better VPN service, creep," she muttered.

Still, she experienced a twinge of disappointment. This was certainly an important step forward, and one she was going to share with the other hackers in her group, but she could have guessed all but the man's name from the info they already had. Feeling let down, Trynn tried to work backwards and find more information regarding the recent communications and movements of the seller involved in the illegal deal, rather than the buyer.

After another two hours of digging, Trynn confirmed that Kovac was attempting to purchase something from a known Russian mob figure. Trynn had originally recognized the man's name from an international crime bulletin that she received occasionally from one of her former clients.

Now, she was sure it wasn't a mistake or a case of similar names. The mystery man, Kovac, was dealing with Matvei Timur, an infamous arms dealer who had access to some of the worst weapons humanity had to offer.

As she carefully translated the most recent email she'd plucked from his server, an uneasy sensation gripped her stomach. Trynn quickly hopped onto Internet Relay Chat—a hub for hackers trying to find something to do with their time. Trynn was a member of MASQUE; a group whose aims were largely to dismantle powerful trade rings within the black market, most of which were run by people that law enforcement would consider to be respectable and above reproach.

Hell, some of them *were* respectable—on the outside, at least. And some of them were power-hungry maniacs with no scruples or redeeming characteristics whatsoever.

Trynn wondered with some trepidation where B. Kovac fell on that spectrum.

Connected now, she typed out a quick message to relay what she had discovered about Kovac. She noted that she was going to continue working on intercepting messages between the two parties. Taking a deep breath, she outlined the contents of the last email and asked if it implied what she thought it implied.

Several other people chimed in, confirming her fears. After a few more exchanges, most of them encouraged Trynn to continue hunting this person in hopes of discovering what he was going to do next. One of the hackers who seemed to know what they were talking about when it came to the last email offered to take the information to the US government.

Trynn agreed and signed off. The sick feeling remained, though. These days, governments across the world were too busy trying to maintain basic order in the streets to follow up every unsubstantiated lead that came their way.

Exhaustion was pulling at her now, after the brief flush of excitement over what she'd found. It felt like her eyelids were being dragged closed and her fingers had minds of their own as they stumbled over the keyboard. After jerking herself awake twice from dozing off with her neck at an uncomfortable angle, Trynn gave up and shut down the system, wanting nothing more than the lumpy mattress on her rented bed.

She stood, stretching her back and looking at her reflection in the mirror over the beat-up dresser. Huge dark circles were smeared beneath her eyes, and she gazed at them in disgust.

Am I ever going to look and feel like myself again? Maybe it's a good thing that nothing happened with the hot, crazy guy — he'd've be frightened off as soon as he saw me without make-up. Christ.

Hoping that she just needed more sleep than she'd been getting, Trynn walked into the bathroom and washed her face. Feeling a bit more refreshed, she finished getting ready for bed and slipped out of the bathroom.

Even in a place as unfamiliar and uninspiring as this cheap hotel room, crawling into bed felt like being wrapped in a warm cocoon. Immediately,

Trynn began to drift off, sinking effortlessly into a dream that both soothed her, and heated her flesh from the inside out.

-o-o-o-

A gentle hand caressed her face, and a fingertip traced over her lips. In a flash, she darted her tongue out of her mouth, tasting salt on callused skin and drawing it inside. A moan of longing reached her ears, and she smiled around the finger.

As she languidly opened her eyes, the world again seemed to solidify around her. The light was dim, with a reddish tint. She could see drapes and hangings all around the room, covering whitewashed stone. Eris' face swam before her vision, banked fire smoldering deep in his eyes. He was leaning over her, pressing her down into the deep bedding all around her.

Placing a hand down on the bed, Trynn pushed her fingers into the cool, soft fabric.

"Phaidra, my love," Eris' soft voice whispered in her ear, trailing the finger over her chin and down the tender column of her throat. "How is it that you grow more beautiful to me every day? When we are both old and gray, I will be unable to even look upon your face, for fear that your radiance will blind me."

She turned her gaze back to him, just in time for his mouth to capture hers in a passionate kiss. Her head spun and she could taste wine on his lips. As his hands found her waist, she could feel him press deeper and settle hotly between her legs.

Trynn arched her back, trying to get him closer. His hands moved to hers, their fingers intertwining. He slid their joined hands upwards, so that her arms were pinned above her head as he continued to plunder her lips with his own.

He was like a drowning man offered air, the way he seemed to drink in her moans and sighs. Desire so intense it drove out every other thought flooded her, and beads of sweat broke out across her skin. Eris mouthed his way down her neck and then kissed each of her collarbones before dragging his tongue up to recapture her mouth.

Murmuring his name on the back of a broken sigh, Trynn tried to free her hands so she could grab his hips and pull him into her, but Eris resisted the movement. They wrestled each other for a moment – an uneven contest if ever there was one – before Trynn gave up with a breathless laugh.

"You whisper sweet words in my ear one moment, only to torture and deprive me the next," she accused, her eyes twinkling.

The slow smile that tugged at his lips made new heat flood her belly. "You love it," he shot back, with a careless shrug of one shoulder. His confidence was infectious as he stared down at her – a playful, well-fed lion, toying with its prey.

The heat of their bodies warmed the furs and blanket around them. Just as Eris shifted both of her wrists to one hand, freeing the other to slide her long, draped skirts up her legs, Trynn felt her mind drifting. She could see him, his eyebrows furrowed in concentration, but she could also feel the scratchy sheets from her hotel bed.

-o-o-o-

No, no, I want to stay, she thought desperately.

It was no good. A moment later, she opened her eyes to darkness and solitude. Her heart was pounding hard and fast, and sweat beaded her brow. The complete silence was broken only by shuffling from someone moving around in the room above hers. Snapping back to reality, Trynn groaned and threw her arm across her forehead.

Great. She had just had a major sex dream about the crazy — and crazy-hot — weirdo who had rescued her, and then tried to scare her out of her mind with a bizarre fairy story and a set of plastic fangs. Wonderful. Perfect.

Damn it.

EIGHT

The next morning, *yet again*, Trynn awoke suddenly from a sound sleep, pleasure washing through her body like a warm tide. Again, it faded abruptly as the remnants of the dream slipped from her consciousness.

She sat up and rested her elbows on her knees, cradling her head in her hands.

"Right," she told the rumpled bedclothes. "This has got to stop. I can't keep having sexy dreams about this guy. I'm going to go insane."

The sheets remained unhelpfully silent. Something about the way they were tangled around her gave the impression that they'd had more fun last night than she had, waking repeatedly from dreams just before she got to the good parts. Right now, she kind of resented them for it.

No more sleep, she decided, flipping her legs over the edge of the bed.

With her pulse still thrumming through her and heat pooling between her legs, Trynn decided that a cold shower was in order to banish the last of the fantasy that had plagued her all night long.

Once under the icy spray, she found it easier to ignore her body's demand for release as she pondered her current situation. Trynn had never struggled with a lack of libido, but what she had experienced in the last several hours was far beyond anything she would consider reasonable or average. She had been involved in a fight for her life little more than a day ago, for Christ's sake. Surely this should be a time for her mind to focus on something besides her raging sex drive.

Yet it very obviously wasn't. Sure, Trynn was deeply disturbed by what had happened at the bank, and she had thus far avoided watching the news or looking at much social media in an effort to escape frightening images and accounts of the incident. Yet, the more she thought about Eris, the more the experience seemed to fade into the background as her thoughts dwelt on him and him alone. Because, oh yeah, *that* was totally healthy.

But, *damn*. The dreams were enough to drive a person crazy.

Trynn washed her hair and body, trying to ignore the way her skin prickled under her fingers, as if longing for Eris' touch despite the chilly spray of the shower. If she'd thought it would help, Trynn would have scolded her body aloud for getting so caught up in a lunatic's twisted fairytale. *Down, girl! Have some respect for yourself!*

An hour later, Trynn was completely dressed and as ready for the day as she was likely to get, sitting at her computer and staring at a picture of Eris that she had pulled from the hotel's security system.

Why the hell did he have to be so handsome, Trynn thought, a bit sadly. *He should be married to a super-model, churning out genetically superior babies. Not holed up alone in an expensive hotel room, celebrating Halloween three months early.*

Trynn scowled at the screen and tried to resist the temptation to look him up on a social media site.

She rarely bothered with social media herself, usually finding it to be too unreliable a source from which to gain useful information. Yet, in this case, Trynn *really* wanted to see what she could find.

Unfortunately, without knowing his real last name, the search for Eris yielded no definite results. There was nothing under the fake name he'd given her at first, either.

I'll just have to go back to his hotel and talk to him again, she thought savagely. *He at least owes me that much.*

It was that certainty which drove Trynn forward through her morning. She forced down some food—even though food had seemed completely unappealing since her run-in with the bomber—and dressed in comfortable clothes for walking.

It didn't seem to matter that she was only intending to return to the Merit Lefkosa so she could confront Eris about his crazy story and weird behavior—she still couldn't help worrying about her appearance. Glancing critically in the mirror, she stared at the dark green canvas pants that she wore with a plain white V-neck t-shirt. She could pass as a tourist, she decided, with her simple tennis shoes on.

She had decided to walk back to his hotel rather than taking a cab, in hopes that the Mediterranean sunshine would do something for her ghastly pale skin. Her short, dark hair was spiked lightly and she pushed sunglasses onto her face to cover the bags under her eyes.

It sort of disgusted her that she was so worried about her looks when she going to meet a man who was plainly as crazy as a box of frogs, but on the other hand, she still felt the eerie connection—not to mention, attraction—to him.

I'm the one who's freaking crazy. What the hell am I doing stressing out about this?

It was true—Trynn was completely unaccustomed to feeling uneasy around a man. In the past, when she'd had casual relationships, she'd found it easy to be cool and aloof. She'd never been one to settle down in one place, or with one guy. For many men, it made her the perfect girlfriend—in other words, not a real girlfriend at all.

Now, though, she felt butterflies stirring in her stomach, and a sheen of sweat breaking out across her brow.

I just need to get moving, Trynn thought as she slung her handbag over one shoulder. *It will be better when I don't feel so idle.*

Walking helped manage her nervousness, and before she knew it, Trynn reached Eris' hotel. Hoping that the same young man was not working the front desk, Trynn kept her sunglasses on as she stepped into the large lobby.

To her relief, she did not recognize anyone from her last visit. Suppressing a sigh, she pushed her sunglasses up on her head and strolled confidently towards the elevators. No one stopped her, confirming her earlier suspicion that the security was not as foolproof as she had originally hoped.

When she approached the seventh-floor room for the second time, she did not hesitate to knock. This time, when Eris answered, he looked like he had been awake for a while.

"You came back," was his tense greeting. The curtains were drawn inside the room so that the light was dim, making it hard for her to parse the expression on his face as she stood under the bright glare of the hallway outside.

"I need to talk to you again," she said, girding herself as if for battle. "You owe me a better explanation than that crap you spouted last time."

Eris only nodded and moved aside, gesturing for her to come in. She stepped inside and looked around suspiciously for a moment. She'd had the oddest sensation — a cold chill, almost as though something had brushed against her arm as she moved into the room. As she glanced around the dimly lit space, however, she saw nothing.

They sat across from one another in the same chairs as last time, awkward and uncomfortable.

"So, you wanted to talk to me," Eris said after a moment, his voice heavy and resigned.

Thank you, Captain Obvious, Trynn thought, but she quashed the impulse to be a complete bitch to him. She needed to keep her wits about her so she could make sure all of her questions were answered.

"Yes," she said, trying to find words to describe her thoughts. "I need to know what happened the last time I was here."

"What do you mean?" Eris asked, looking at her steadily.

Trynn considered him. He looked genuinely unsure as to what she meant, which surprised her.

"I—" she started before falling silent. How could she tell him that she spent half the night practically humping the mattress in her sleep because of crazy dreams of fucking him silly? There was seriously *no good way* to provide that information.

"I had some intense dreams last night about you. I know that you must have some sort of...ability to influence others, because of how you handled that guy at the bank."

Trynn stopped speaking, hoping that Eris would simply confirm or deny her suspicions. He, however, seemed to be in a less than helpful mood.

"Um... okay?" he replied, obviously waiting for her to elaborate.

"Well," she said in a slow voice, "I wondered if you had done the same thing to me. You know, if you put... like... a mind-whammy on me or something?"

He blinked. "A mind *what*?"

Trynn felt her face go red. God, she sounded like a complete idiot. "I don't really have a good word for it," she snapped. "But I'm also not accustomed to having sex dreams about complete strangers that keep me up half the god-damned night."

Oh, shit. She'd said that last part aloud, hadn't she?

Eris started to chuckle, but smothered it when she glared at him. He shook his head. "No, I didn't put a *mind-whammy* on you."

She continued to glare. "How do I know that for sure?"

Eris slowly brought his eyes up to meet hers, his expression intense.

"Because if I had put a *mind-whammy* on you," he said, sketching air quotes around the ridiculous words, "it would have felt like this."

Eris' eyes glowed with that eerie inner light, and a strange, overwhelming sensation flowed through Trynn's mind. He was looking directly at her, those unearthly eyes fixed on her face without blinking or turning away. It made her feel like a mouse frozen under a cobra's cold regard.

Her heart stuttered once and pounded against the walls of her chest, all the blood in her body rushing abruptly south. She gasped and gripped the arms of the chair. Desire surged through her so powerfully that it took every last bit of her self-control not to fling herself forward across the space separating them and crawl into his lap, rutting like a bitch in heat. She could feel her restraint slipping more with every heartbeat as she twitched with longing, trying to keep her disobedient limbs under control.

She was panting, open-mouthed, so hot she was surprised clouds of steam weren't rising from her skin. Images raced through her mind of Eris plunging himself into her depths... gripping her hair... bringing his lips to her neck. They were so real that she could almost feel the ghost of his teeth against her throat, the dart of his tongue against her sweaty skin.

The ache of raw need between her legs was unbearable, and she wrapped her arms around herself, trying to stop the onslaught of sensations. Finally, Trynn could take it no longer. She scrambled out of the chair, stumbling towards him on rubbery legs. Her hot palms gripped his arms as she tried to mold her body against his, desperate for contact, for release.

Without warning, everything vanished. The heavy, drugged feeling in her mind dissipated and Trynn could breathe easily again. Although her heart rate remained high, she could feel her body calming as the glow dimmed from Eris' eyes. He maintained his steady grip on her and Trynn realized, with horror, that he was restraining her, holding her back from climbing his body like a tree.

She gaped at him, aware that he had just reached out with his mind somehow and tampered with her thoughts. Embarrassment and horror coursed through her, making her face burn with shame. It took a moment to lock her knees and get her feet back under her, but then she jerked back so quickly that the contact between them was broken.

Without the burning, ravenous desire for Eris or the electric feeling that raced through her every time their skin came into contact, Trynn found that she felt rather empty and cold.

Fortunately, anger came to her defense an instant later.

"You *jackass*!" Trynn yelled, setting herself before smashing her fist squarely against his jaw in a vicious roundhouse punch.

To her consternation, the blow barely seemed to register with him. His head snapped to the side, but he merely shook it off and looked at her in shock. Her fist, on the other hand, exploded into agony. She drew it against her stomach, cradling it and gritting her teeth.

She couldn't suppress the hiss of pain that escaped her lips.

Out of the corner of her eye, she saw movement to her left. As she whirled to see what it was, she caught Eris making a sharp gesture with his hand, though he didn't speak.

Every single rational thought fled from her mind as her eyes fell on a ghastly creature stepping out of the shadows. Although it was roughly human-shaped, its features were so distinctly inhuman that Trynn immediately knew she was in the presence of a monster.

A monster. A vampire. Jesus Christ, she hadn't been delusional before after all. Vampires were *real*. A pitiful squeak rose in her throat as she backed away in sudden terror, her eyes jerking towards the door.

"Please," Eris murmured, "*Trynn*. It's all right. You're not in danger. Don't run away again. He's a friend."

Trynn looked back and forth between the two otherworldly figures, fear and indecision writ large on her face.

Every bit of common sense she possessed demanded that she flee before she was killed. She *knew* that the creature before her was powerful. *Deadly.* Its empty, cold eyes were pitiless and frozen. A chill seemed to emanate from it, infecting her, freezing her soul.

"A *friend*?" she whispered, looking at Eris, the tone clearly saying that he had lost his *freaking mind*.

"Yes," Eris answered, glancing quickly at the monster. "A friend. This is Snag."

Trynn forced her gaze back to the... *creature*, and studied him more closely, still poised to flee if he made any sudden moves. "*Snag*? What kind of name is that?"

The creature—*Snag*—turned his head a fraction in response, but did not speak. Trynn frowned, her frantic heartbeat slowing gradually as her panic ebbed.

"Yeah, well, it's nice to meet you, too. I guess. You're... not human." Still, the creature did not reply.

Eris sighed and said, "Actually, he's every bit as human as I am."

There were two ways that statement could be taken, and Trynn could guess which one he meant. She felt her stomach clench and a cold sensation pass through her yet again. How was it possible that this was happening? She'd wanted answers, but she hadn't wanted *this* answer.

"What *are* you?" she asked, hugging herself. The knuckles of her right hand still ached and throbbed from hitting him. "How can this be *happening*?"

"Please, Trynn," Eris said, sounding tired, "sit down. I'd like the chance to try and explain things better than last time."

That was what she'd come for, wasn't it? And neither one of the pair had made any move to hurt her — not even when she'd punched Eris in the face. Trynn found her way back to her seat and crossed her arms defensively, still feeling uneasy under Snag's impassive stare. Now that her panic had faded to manageable levels, she shamelessly studied the gaunt creature on the other side of the room.

His skin was grey and papery, covered in scars. Some looked like claw marks. Some were in the shapes of complex symbols. Some appeared to be from burn marks. He was completely bald, without eyebrows, but his eyelashes were thick and dark. They framed deep-set eyes so black that she couldn't see the boundary between pupil and iris. Trynn shivered as he regarded her silently, his face completely expressionless.

Eris looked over to him and shook his head. "I know we've had this conversation many times, old friend, but you *really* need to work on your people skills."

Snag did not answer, but swiveled his gaze towards Eris, the dark depths of his eyes never flickering.

"You were going to answer my question," Trynn reminded him. She wanted answers, and she wasn't willing to wait another minute.

Eris nodded and cleared his throat. "You'll have to forgive my awkwardness. Your presence is… unnerving."

"You hang out with *this* guy, and you think *my* presence is unnerving?" Trynn asked, incredulous.

"It is, though. I never expected to find my lost soulmate," he said. "When we found Della, I thought it was a fluke. A happy accident."

Della? Trynn filed the name away to ask about later. "And you're sure I'm this lost soulmate, are you?"

Eris huffed a breath that could have been amusement or frustration. "Without a doubt. Even ignoring the spark between us whenever our skin touches... I've been having dreams, as well."

"Wait. You mean we're having the *same* dreams?" Trynn demanded, taken aback by this piece of information—though maybe she shouldn't have been.

Eris flickered an eyebrow. "Yes, Trynn. I mean that we're having the same dreams."

Silence followed his statement, and Trynn forced out a hollow laugh. "Yeah, right. Sure we are. Look! We can't be having the same dreams—that's impossible. If they're similar, it's probably just a coincidence."

"It's not. I am a vampire, and you are human, yet our souls are connected. We experience certain aspects of our lives together, especially when we revisit old memories."

"But none of this makes any *sense!*" Trynn exploded.

"I can't explain it any better than that to you," Eris said. "But, I can tell you that reincarnation is real. For example, feelings of *déjà vu* are nothing more than the mind struggling with an old memory from a past life."

"*Déjà vu* is supposed to be a trick that your mind is playing on you," Trynn said dismissively. "How do I know you're not tricking me, too?"

"You don't," Eris replied in a serious voice, "but I'm not."

Trynn studied him carefully for a moment. "Then explain more."

Eris sat back. He was silent for several moments before speaking. "It starts at the beginning of time."

"Okay, maybe not quite that much," she said. She might have wanted answers, but she had no desire for a lesson on the entire history of the universe.

"I'll try to be concise," Eris said, his tone growing mildly annoyed.

"Fine," she said with a resigned sigh. "Do please continue."

"The universe was formed around the forces of good and evil. These forces are the source of most religions. All of them believe in the struggle between good and bad, love and hate. Well, the struggle is real. There are angels and there are demons. Or, at least, there are beings that may as well be angels and demons. One demon in particular, Bael, is the force of evil incarnate on this planet."

"Like the devil?" Trynn asked, trying to remember all she could from the world religions elective she was forced to take in college. Mostly, she remembered how much she'd hated the damned class.

"In a sense," Eris said. "Not exactly. He has the power to rend souls and destroy lives. Everything bad that happens on this planet has something to do with him. He is the bringer of darkness, pain, and desolation. The harbinger of filth, disease, and rot."

Trynn shuddered at Eris' words, but she did not interrupt him.

"Bael has one great weakness, however. He has no ability to understand the unconquerable power of love. There's a saying in the Christian Bible that he seems to have forgotten."

"What's that?" Trynn asked.

"Perfect love casts out all fear."

"What does that *mean*, though?" Trynn asked, drawn in despite herself.

"For him? It means that when he decided to destroy my soul and the souls of my friends, he made one mistake that all of our soulmates exploited."

Trynn held completely still, listening. Her eyes never left Eris'.

"Their love for us protected us from utter annihilation. Instead of becoming Bael's undead puppets, we were reborn as vampires, our souls split into two pieces, the Light and the Dark — both contained in one body."

Trynn blinked once, confused.

"But in saving us, their lives were sacrificed. You were Phaidra, and you died millennia ago. Apparently, I've been waiting for your return all these endless years, and never even knew it until I found you."

"How do you know for sure it's me, though?" Trynn asked, her voice a bare whisper. "You said you knew without a doubt, but how?"

Eris stretched out his hand and touched her skin. And, yes, there was that same electric current of energy passing between the two of them, making Trynn's heart race and the hair on her neck stand up in anticipation.

"*That...* is how I know," Eris said. "We have already located the reincarnated soulmate of another of my friends. We have a bit better idea what to expect, now."

"And they had the same zap between them? Like we have?"

Eris nodded. "Exactly the same."

Trynn wasn't really sure how to argue with that. Or even, her traitorous heart pointed out helpfully, if she *wanted* to argue it.

"What does this mean, exactly?" she asked instead. "For me, for you, for this struggle between good and evil that you say is taking place around us?"

Eris scratched his head and threw a long look at Snag, who had not moved throughout the entire explanation. "I'm not certain right now. There's a lot more to the story, but that's the basic version. The important thing to know is that Bael will be trying to track you down. He doesn't want us to reunite because he fears it will fulfill a prophecy. So, he's going to try and kill you to prevent it."

Okay, then. Suddenly, her presence at the bank just when a crazy bomber showed up to take hostages took on a more sinister cast.

"What type of danger am I in right now?" she asked, her hand coming up to the base of her throat.

"The serious kind. Chaos is closing in around you, and it will only get worse. Riots, shootings, bombings, terrorism —"

"What?" Trynn yelped, her eyes going wide.

"I'm sorry," Eris answered, and he truly did look it. "I know you never asked for any of this. I am *so sorry* that your life is in danger yet again, because of your connection to me. This was never your battle, but now you'll have to fight it nonetheless."

"No, no, that's not what I meant," Trynn answered quickly, shaking her head. "You said terrorism. You said bombs!"

Her blood ran cold, her thoughts turning toward MASQUE and the intel she had intercepted about the arms dealer and his mysterious client. It seemed like way too much of a coincidence to think that Eris was warning her about chaos and terrorism while a major weapons deal that could potentially cost tens or hundreds of thousands of lives was going down at the same time.

Eris looked confused. "Yes, among other things. What —"

"Eris, I'm a member of MASQUE. I'm tracking a man right now who's trying to buy suitcase nukes from the Russian mafia. You're talking about terrorism? I... think that probably qualifies."

NINE

The ominous words settled over Eris like a pall and he realized, with a stab of dread, that he was too late. The vortex of chaos and evil was already firmly established around his mate. First the bomber at the bank, and now... *this*. He had hoped that by arming Trynn with information early on, he could spare her the same sorts of horrors that Della had experienced. It seemed, however, that he had failed—and that failure made his stomach drop sickeningly.

"When did you find out about this? Have you passed on the information to the authorities?" he asked sharply. Trynn's face blanched under his intensity.

"About the nukes? I found out last night," she answered in a small voice, looking suddenly young and scared. "I picked up his trail some weeks ago, and several of us have been monitoring the deal's progress as best we could. I informed the group of my findings right after I translated his last email. One of them is supposed to pass it on to the US government, but you can guess exactly how much good that's likely to do."

"And you don't know what sort of timeline he's operating on?"

She shook her head. "No."

"How did you find him? What do you mean about tracking him?" Eris demanded, something cold and bitter clawing its way up from the depths of his gut. It might have been fear.

Trynn ran a shaking hand through her dark, spiky hair and said, "I'm a member of a group of hackers that exposes these types of deals. We call it hactivism. Some of what we deal with is governments abusing their citizens, but sometimes it's black market crime rings and weapons deals. We monitor these kinds of exchanges and post our findings anonymously to the group. When we can, we disrupt them."

Eris stared at her. *Of course* his Phaidra couldn't be content with a quiet life somewhere. *Of course* she would be in the thick of things, chasing excitement and danger. How very like her that was.

"That... sounds like a rather hazardous hobby," he said eventually.

"Not as much as you'd think," Trynn replied with a shrug. "We never really have contact with the people we track, and they don't know our identity. Most of the time everything is going on half a world away."

Eris scowled at her. "They could find out who you are and target you."

A wan smile flickered across Trynn's face, and was gone. "I doubt that. They'd have to be a better hacker than I was."

Somehow, this wasn't comforting to Eris. Something of his thoughts must have shown on his face, because she frowned at him again.

"Oh, come on," she said, a bit of irritation creeping into her tone. "I'm fighting bad guys in the best way I know how."

"I don't want you drawn into the middle of this evil," Eris murmured, rubbing his chin in exasperation.

"Says the man who defuses hostage situations on his nights off." Her tone was still sharp.

He started to say *that's different*, but thought better of it. "Can you at least tell me more details about this deal?"

"Look—I'll tell you what I can," she said, more calmly. "Though I don't know what you could possibly do with the information that would help. A few months ago, we started seeing mentions of this mysterious guy in the European underworld. He was a new player, and was gathering all manner of black market assets. Drugs, weapons, human trafficking rings."

A prickling of foreboding played across the back of Eris' neck, and he glanced at Snag before motioning for Trynn to continue her story.

She took a deep breath. "He's become hugely wealthy in a very short span of time. Then, over the past few weeks, I've been snooping around this arms deal. I only got a name for the buyer yesterday—B. Kovac. And I only made the connection that he was our mysterious underworld figure when I realized what kind of weapons they were discussing. Very few private individuals are in a position to pay for something like that, but he's definitely one of them."

"What do we know about these weapons? Are we talking nuclear suicide bombs, here? Stroll in someplace, push the button, and take out half a city?" He wasn't sure he really wanted to know the answer.

Trynn chewed on her lower lip in thought. "Possibly. More likely something that could be smuggled into a strategic location, and then blown up by remote."

"And there's no way of knowing exactly how powerful they are?" he asked.

"No," she said. "Not unless they start blabbing about it by email, anyway."

Eris dropped his head into his hands and scrubbed at his face, trying to clear his thoughts. Right now, all he could focus on was Trynn. *Of course* his mate would be wrapped up in this mess. That was just so fucking typical—

"Eris?" Trynn asked, clearly worried.

He did not answer right away. He needed a moment to think, to consider his options and how he was going to proceed. Maybe he could convince Trynn to withdraw from the situation? *Yeah, right.* Like that was likely to happen.

Besides, as much as it was at the top of his current priority list, it didn't really help the situation. For all he knew, this *B. Kovac* could be targeting Nicosia with one of the bombs. He could convince Trynn to let the situation go, only for her to be blown to kingdom come the following week.

Straightening his spine, he looked back at Trynn. "So. What's his next move?"

"He's been making contact with a well-known figure in the Russian mob and forging business ties with him," Trynn said. "They had a big meeting in Damascus, and it's very possible he was finally able to secure what he was after."

Gods above, Damascus was a paltry three hundred kilometers away from here. Practically on their doorstep. "And where would he be likely to use these bombs, assuming he plans on detonating them?" he asked.

Trynn considered the matter. "We can't really know. I guess it depends on what his aims were."

Eris could easily guess what his aims were. "And if he wanted to cause the maximum amount of chaos and carnage?" he asked, already knowing the answer.

Trynn's voice went very quiet. "Then he'd set them off in places like Jerusalem. Ankara. Beirut. Cairo. Cities where any major attack would immediately start proxy wars."

Eris was bombarded unexpectedly by a brief but powerful flash of emotion from Snag. He flinched in surprise, his eyes seeking the other vampire. His expression betrayed no hint of what he had just broadcast accidentally, but Eris knew that Snag was originally from somewhere south of Cairo. He'd never told them where, exactly... but they were discussing the potential destruction of his ancient friend's home, too.

"What is it?" Trynn asked, glancing between them. Snag gave Eris a calculating look, but the mental channel fell silent. Eris continued to lock gazes with Snag for a long moment, before turning back to Trynn and nodding for her to continue.

"It's nothing. Please go on. If you had to guess, what sort of timeline do you think we're looking at?"

"Probably soon," she said, grim. "Once he gets the bombs, why wait?"

Why, indeed? Eris sat back, leaning against one of the arms of his seat. He rested his chin on his fingers, deep in thought.

This could all just be a huge coincidence. Perhaps this black market deal was completely unrelated to Trynn, and she was in no more danger than any other human was, these days. This transaction might be no different than any of the other dozens of cases she'd doubtless worked on as part of this group of hers. He longed to be able to believe that, certainly.

Trynn echoed his thoughts and said, "This could all just be nothing, though. We've had intelligence reports like this before and they've never amounted to anything."

Eris watched her closely before taking a deep breath and turning back to Snag.

"Do you sense Bael's hand in this?" he asked.

Snag remained silent across their mental connection, but Eris could sense his uneasiness. His companion was obviously weighing the words carefully.

After a short pause, a sense of corruption and rot permeating the sunlit paradise around them teased Eris' mind, and was gone. Snag dipped his chin the tiniest fraction, sketching a nod.

Eris nodded as well. "I feel it, too. It's as I feared. Do you think there's any chance at all that we're *not* already caught up in the vortex of Bael's evil?"

Eris sensed the answer in Snag's silence. It was an answer he'd already known in his bones; desperate though he was for Snag to refute it.

Snag's bony chest lifted and lowered as he breathed out silently. Eris felt the ancient being's power flickering around him, as if Snag's life force was surrounding him and filling him up. Eris closed his eyes, letting it in, feeling a huge increase in his own strength and awareness. As his friend's life force mingled with his own, Eris could sense evil pulsing all around them. He could feel it, like a malignant, oily cloud hanging in the air. He shuddered and shook his head, trying to free himself from the stench.

But he knew he would not be able to escape it until they'd fought the battle ahead and won. And Snag must have been aware of that the whole time.

No wonder you were so antsy, Eris communicated. *His presence is horrible, and it's covering this entire region. I felt something similar to this in New Orleans. I didn't stop to think how much worse it must have been for you.*

He shivered, feeling a flash of pity for Snag's powerful awareness.

We need to stop this, Eris thought with iron resolve. *The idea of Bael controlling someone with access to nuclear bombs is too horrible to contemplate.*

Snag did not reply, but Eris could sense his agreement. Also, his unutterable weariness.

"Something tells me you two are having a conversation without me," Trynn said, and Eris realized that she had been quiet for an unusually long stretch, watching them intently.

Eris felt Snag's power recede back into the bounds that normally encompassed it. Yet he could still sense Bael's presence, looming over them like a shadow. Snag had given him that gift, if you could really call it such a thing.

"Sorry about that," he finally said, throwing a quick glance in Snag's direction. "I didn't intend to be rude, but as you may have gathered, he's not much of a talker. I just needed a bit of help from him to see the bigger picture."

Trynn's eyebrows drew together, and Eris' attention was drawn to the small crease of discontent like iron filings drawn to a magnet. "I don't know what that's supposed to mean, in this context," she said.

Eris huffed a sigh. "It's a bit complicated to explain. Snag is very powerful. He can sense things that I can't. The demon I told you about is nearby. His evil is permeating this whole situation. Guiding it. Shaping it."

"Okay," she answered slowly. "So what are we going to do about it? How do we stop him?"

Eris stood up and started pacing, unable to stay still. He could feel both Trynn's and Snag's eyes on him.

"First and foremost," he said, "we need to ensure your safety, Trynn. I really think that you should stay here with us, where it's safer."

Something flashed across Trynn's face so quickly that Eris couldn't parse it. "Stay here?" she echoed. "With you?"

"Yes," Eris replied. "The two of us can protect you more effectively here."

She looked decidedly flummoxed, and he realized that while she wasn't actively disputing his claims anymore, she hadn't truly taken this new reality on board.

"No," she said, "I can't do that. I'm scheduled to return home soon. And I need to get back to work."

Eris shook his head. "You don't understand the amount of danger you're in. Trynn, you're being hunted by a powerful demon from the underworld. He has nearly limitless resources available to find you and follow you. Leaving this city would only end up bringing catastrophe down on your home. More importantly, Snag and I are *here*, and we're the best allies you could hope for right now."

Trynn hesitated an instant before shaking her head again. "No, this whole thing is preposterous. You don't even know for sure that this *demon* is after me—"

"We've been over this," Eris said, suddenly, viscerally aware of his growing weariness. If he could just get a few hours of sleep—and maybe some blood—Eris knew that he would be able to think and plan more effectively. Now, exhaustion pulled at him with the same relentless intensity as the sun beating down on the window outside, beyond the heavy drapes.

"Bael is after revenge," he continued. "You—
or Phaidra, if you prefer—saved my life by sacrificing your own. You *defied* him. Vampires are Bael's
greatest failures, and he will see you destroyed, if
he can. He'll do whatever is within his power to
prevent you becoming part of the Council."

"The... what?" Trynn asked, clearly over-
whelmed by the day's events.

Eris sighed and massaged his temples with his
fingers. "It's complicated, and we aren't even sure
of all the details. But I've been studying an ancient
text. It states that Bael will fall when the Council of
Thirteen unites against him. At that time, the angel
Israfael's power will be restored and balance will
come back into the world."

"God help me. That's the short version?"
Trynn asked dryly. Her eyes narrowed, and she
looked at Eris closely. "Tell me something, Eris—
and don't lie. When was the last time you got a decent stretch of sleep?"

Eris swayed where he stood and shook his
head. "It doesn't matter. What matters right now is
keeping you safe. Please, Trynn, you have to stay
with us."

Trynn's eyes moved to Snag for a moment before she looked back at Eris. "What if I just got a
room here instead? I mean... I barely know you,
after all."

Eris raised an eyebrow. "We've been in a hostage situation together, I've mind-whammied you,
and you've punched me in the jaw. Surely, all that
counts for something? Trynn, I don't want to have
to worry about getting to you in time if something

happens. I think the best option is for you to stay here in this room."

Trynn sighed in exasperation. "Look. It's not that I don't appreciate what you're offering, even if I don't fully understand what's going on. But I have a life! I have a job! Bills I need to pay! I can't just put everything on hold to play hide-and-seek with a vengeful demon."

"I would think you could contact your employer and get some kind of trauma leave, after the incident at the bank," Eris pointed out.

Trynn looked decidedly cagey for a moment, and appeared to be trying to think of another way around his suggestion. He was struck with the oddest sense of *déjà vu* for a moment, before he realized it was because he had seen that exact expression on Phaidra's face more times than he could count.

"*Trynn*," he said, coming up to her chair and crouching down so that he was at eye level with her. "I promise you, we're here to protect you. We mean you no harm. I wouldn't ask this of you if it wasn't a life or death situation for both of us. I would never ask you to walk away from something that you love on a whim, but you've *got to understand*. If you step out of those doors, there's a very real chance you could die. You might die, and there would be nothing I could do to stop it. Don't ask me to live through that again."

Eris poured as much intensity into his gaze as he could, allowing his senses to expand until they gently brushed her mind. He could sense that her resolve was crumbling; that his sincerity was winning out over her innate independence and skepticism.

He knew that he could use his power on her, to tip her over to his way of thinking. But he knew just as surely that doing so in this moment would destroy the fragile beginnings of trust they'd built.

Please, Trynn, Eris urged silently. *Please, just agree to stay here, where we can watch over you. I can't lose you again. I wouldn't survive it a second time.*

Eris tried to hold back anguished memories of cradling her lifeless frame in his arms, but the image was burned into his mind like a brand. Over the centuries, he'd become a master at the fine art of denial when it came to coping with haunting memories that would not fade, but the deep ache never really seemed to abate.

Now that he had found his Phaidra against all odds, he never wanted to let her out of his sight again. He was desperate to protect her, to spare her the horror that surely lay in wait for both of them like a crouched tiger. His hatred for Bael rose like bile in his throat and he swallowed it back down, fighting to stay calm.

"All right," Trynn said at last, a note of defeat in her voice. "Fine. I'll stay, but I need to get my stuff first. Especially my laptop."

"You can use mine," Eris offered, relief nearly overwhelming him.

Trynn gave him a horrified look. "Are you kidding? That's the equivalent of using someone else's *toothbrush*. No, no—I need my computer."

Perplexed by her vehemence, Eris made a non-committal noise. "After dark, perhaps, when we can go with you," he countered. "Deal?"

She looked unhappy, but nodded. Relieved to have things settled—for the time being, at least—Eris crossed to the desk in the corner and sat down. After a few moments' deliberation, he composed a terse email to Tré, explaining the situation as best he could in a few words.

Tré would understand if anyone would, Eris knew. After their experience with finding Della, Eris was confident that he and the others would drop whatever they were doing and come to his assistance. And in the meantime, he had Snag.

With his most immediate worries resolved, Eris let his gaze stray over the top of the bulky laptop and back to Trynn, who had moved from the chair to the couch. She wasn't looking at him. Instead, she was frowning, leaning forward in her seat to rest her chin on her hands, the way she used to all those centuries ago—clearly lost in thought. His gaze raked over her like a starving man's, taking in every svelte curve and tantalizing angle. She was tall—her body slender and coltish where Phaidra had been all softness. He longed to explore the differences.

Eris swallowed hard and looked away, trying to get a grip on himself.

He stood from the desk rather abruptly and walked past Trynn, who lifted her eyes to shoot him a challenging look. Snag, on the other hand, followed his path towards the en-suite bedroom with his customary impassive gaze.

Exhaustion still nagged at Eris, and his vision spun in ponderous circles as he flopped down onto the bed without even pulling back the covers. With a touch as light as air, Eris felt Snag brush against his thoughts a moment later, a question hanging between them.

"Please keep an eye on her for me," Eris murmured. Snag's gaze turned back towards Trynn.

Worries and plans spun endlessly through Eris' mind, making sleep impossible as thoughts of the coming darkness consumed him. In the space of a day, he'd come to appreciate what Tré must have experienced when Della emerged from the shadows and walked into his life. Eris hoped that he would have a chance to apologize for some of the impatience he'd expressed during the trying time before Della's turning. He could understand fully now why Tré had felt so protective of his mate.

A peace that came from outside him settled over Eris, and he shuddered as the tension he'd been carrying flowed out of his muscles without warning. *Damn.* He must have been projecting his thoughts more loudly than he realized. Snag had apparently had enough of listening to his internal monologue, and had decided to take action.

Eris reached out mentally. *We can't let this escalate into a nuclear war, Snag,* he said. *It will take the others time to get here, but I could go ahead to Damascus and scout around. See what's happening. We'll need some reconnaissance before we go in en masse, so we'll know what we're facing. We've got to neutralize this threat.*

In response, Eris received a surge of disagreement and disapproval. With his brow furrowed in a deep frown, Eris allowed his displeasure to radiate across the mental connection.

What the hell else am I supposed to do? he asked. *We need to move on this. We can't sit around hoping the bombs don't off before the others can get here.*

Another wave of opposition.

Wait. The single word was emphatic.

We don't have time to wait! Eris shot back, his frustration growing. *This has to be resolved before it turns into a disaster! But we also can't risk leaving Trynn unguarded. You need to stay here and protect her. I'll go ahead to Damascus and see what I can do on my own about the situation. You know how important Trynn is —*

Eris felt a flare of irritation along the connection, but ignored it.

— and we sure as hell aren't taking her along. We'd be delivering her straight into Bael's hands, he continued doggedly.

Then I will go. You will stay.

It was Eris' turn to be angry. Why was Snag making this so difficult? The logic was simple — plain as day.

Don't be ridiculous, he shot back. *You're more powerful than I am. I need you here, with Trynn, protecting her. Please, Snag, just do this for me.*

Snag did not respond but Eris felt a chill of power emanating from him. Snag's anger seemed to be growing, filling the entire suite. Eris could tell that Snag thought he was being an idiot.

It's pragmatic, and you can't stop me from going unless you plan on fighting me outright, Eris pointed out. *I'll find out exactly what we're facing in Damascus, so that we can stop whatever Bael is intending with these bombs.*

He took a deep breath and pulled out his trump card. *And I swear on my life, Snag, if you abandon Trynn or allow anything to happen to her while I'm gone, I will purposely lose every game of chess we ever play from this day forward in ten moves or less.*

There was a very pronounced silence following his words. Eris could tell Snag was musing over the threat, trying to decide if it was legitimate.

Apparently, he realized that it was. After the space of several heartbeats, Snag relented. Eris could tell by the way the tight bond of energy between the two of them relaxed. Snag was clearly still unhappy, but Eris had—somewhat to his own surprise—won the argument.

And anyway, it wasn't as though Snag was *ever* particularly happy.

Good. Now that it's decided, I'm going to sleep, Eris sent, pulling a pillow toward his chest. He settled deeper into the soft mattress, and allowed his mind to drift.

Several hours later, he awoke with a start. His dreams had been confused, a swirl of memories and worry about the current situation that left him disoriented in the wake of his slumber. Shaking his head, Eris stretched out his senses and found that the sun was setting.

That was a relief; it would be easier to embark on his mission without having to worry about the possibility of being burned by its rays if he wasn't flying fast enough across the narrow stretch of the Levantine Sea that separated Cyprus from Syria. After his unexpectedly restorative sleep, Eris felt he could wait no longer to start his self-imposed mission.

As he stretched his awareness outward, he found that Snag was gone. For a moment, this concerned him, but then he sensed the familiar presence outside, hovering in the deepening shadows. He had merely left the room when Eris started to stir, apparently to give Eris and Trynn some privacy.

Eris pushed wordless gratitude across their mental connection as he climbed from the bed and walked back into the living area of the generous suite.

He found Trynn fast asleep on the couch, one arm draped across her forehead, the other wrapped protectively around his laptop.

He stared at the computer for a beat, blinking in confusion. Hadn't he locked the screen earlier?

Fascinated by her sleeping form, Eris walked over to her and knelt down next to the couch where she was slouched. He stared at her face, drinking in the unfamiliar lines, unable to stop himself from falling back into memories of their life together, all those centuries ago. She was just as captivating now as she had been then. Even though her features were different, his heart clearly recognized its other half and rejoiced at their reunion.

I will protect you, he vowed. *I won't let anything bad happen to you. Not again. Never again.*

Trynn's breathing, which had been slow and soft, deepened as she stretched, coming awake. With her free hand, she rubbed her eyes and looked around, blinking.

Her eyes landed on Eris, kneeling next to the couch, and she pushed up on her elbows. "Where's the other guy?"

Eris hesitated, unsure how much to tell her. Trynn didn't know yet about the alternate forms that vampires could take, and he wasn't sure now was the moment to enlighten her. While part of him longed to tell her everything, all at once, the more cautious part warned that she was still struggling with the things she'd learned earlier that day.

"He stepped out for a few minutes," he said. "He's not far away, though."

Trynn relaxed back. "Oh."

"I see you made yourself right at home," Eris teased, gesturing at the laptop that had slipped down between Trynn's leg and the back of the couch when she woke.

Completely unabashed, Trynn gave him an appraising stare. "I was doing research on you while you slept."

"And?"

"You're an art thief," she accused, narrowing her eyes. "I hacked into your laptop."

Eris snorted. "I guess I should've seen that coming, huh? Though I prefer the term *collector*."

Trynn didn't respond to his attempt at humor. "That's not all I found out. I…" She swallowed. "I was an art thief, too, wasn't I?"

Eris raised his eyebrows, surprised at her reve-
lation.

"How —" he began.

"I dreamed it just now." she said faintly. "I
dreamed the past."

He caught his breath. "You dreamed it? You
dreamed… us?"

TEN

Trynn stared up at Eris' beautifully sculpted features. The remnants of her dream shrouded everything in a hazy, comforting cloud. She could still feel his hands on her, untying laces, slipping through lengths of soft fabric, dragging clothing up and off. Her heart pounded in her ears as the echo of sensation sang along her nerves.

Eris' eyes darkened, his pupils growing large as he gazed down at her.

Can he sense my arousal? Trynn wondered. She pressed her knees together, trying to restrain the urge to leap on him then and there.

If I don't get up and get some space between us, this is going to end very badly. Or possibly very well… depending on how you look at it, she thought, a bit wildly.

The dreams had been so vivid—so real that she could no longer hold onto her doubts about the validity of Eris' claims. How could her mind *possibly* formulate such vivid images and sensations based on nothing but the random synaptic firings that supposedly made up dreams? How could a dream encompass another entirely separate life?

Trynn was no idiot. She understood that there were things in the world that she didn't understand. Was the existence of angels and demons and vampires and soulmates really so far-fetched? Was it so impossible that reincarnation existed? Right now, Trynn didn't think it was.

Of course, all of these musings basically meant that her wild dreams of carefree and uninhibited sex surrounded by a room full of beautiful treasures were more than likely real.

"We were... happy once," she whispered. "Weren't we?"

His voice was hoarse. "Yes. We were."

"Maybe we could be happy again?" Trynn asked in a soft voice, watching him.

Eris swallowed hard, clearly struggling with some powerful emotion. His breathing quickened as Trynn searched his face for answers.

She laid her hand on his arm and traced her fingers up perfect skin, smooth and unblemished. She could feel the electric pulse between them... feel the goose bumps erupting beneath her touch— tiny, dark hairs standing at attention. She knew— without knowing *how* she knew—that he loved soft, ghost-like touches. She also knew that he liked the scratch of fingernails across his back, and the sensation of her legs locking around his hips, pulling him in deep.

They had spent only a few hours in each other's company, yet her familiarity with him was absolute.

She trailed her nails down his arm, pressing harder so that they dragged across his skin. He reached out with his free hand, quick as a snake, and caught her wrist in a tight grip. Trynn felt a thrill of excitement pass through her body.

He lifted her trapped wrist up to his nose, smelling her skin and rubbing its sensitive underside against his stubble.

"Your scent," he said, his eyes falling closed. "Like jasmine and musk on a summer night. How can it be *exactly the same*, after so long?"

Trynn rolled up, propping herself on her left arm so they were eye level with each other. He let her wrist slide free from his grip, his eyes flickering down to her mouth and back up. Her tongue darted out instinctively to moisten her lips.

A callused, long-fingered hand cupped her cheek, as though she were something precious. The electricity between them crackled with renewed tension.

"Phaidra..." Eris breathed, framing her face in both hands. His expression was lost. Dazed. The expression of a man staring at an oasis in the desert, expecting it to melt into a mirage and disappear as soon as he reached for it.

Something about that look pierced Trynn's heart like a blade. She couldn't bear it, and she would do anything it took to remove it. She grabbed Eris' sleep-rumpled collar in her fist, jerking him forward until their lips crashed together.

As though a dam inside him burst, Eris responded, pressing Trynn down into the soft cushions of the couch as he plundered her mouth. She kept her vice-like grip on his abused shirt as insurance he would not pull away, and moaned into the kiss as one of his hands raked over her stomach, searching for bare skin.

The first brush of his fingertips against the burning flesh of her belly was like a lightning bolt. They both gasped in reaction, and Eris pulled away from the kiss. Trynn stared deeply into his gold-flecked eyes, desire for him radiating outward from her center until she thought it must surely be pouring from her skin like a beam of light, illuminating her from within.

Slowly, his fingers slid further underneath her shirt. Trynn arched into the contact and smiled in satisfaction when his palm pressed greedily against her skin, no longer teasing. He spread his fingers, his large hand possessively spanning her flat stomach, and Trynn felt the burn of fresh desire between her legs, as the air around them seemed to heat.

Eris angled his upper body over hers as they resumed the kiss. His hand was fully underneath her shirt now, working steadily upward toward her aching breast. Trynn's legs fell open of their own accord, as if inviting Eris to cradle his body between them. The small movement did not go unnoticed, and a low growl rumbled in the back of his throat.

His tongue and teeth traced the edge of Trynn's jaw line until his lips met the soft skin of her throat. She shivered with pleasure, the sensation sending waves of hot and cold down the length of her body. She could feel the tip of his tongue teasing her skin before his lips and teeth closed over the same spot, worrying at it. He kept at it, utterly single-minded until he had driven her into a frenzied state of nearly animalistic need.

She was only vaguely aware of his rapid breathing, and the fine tremor that had taken up residence in his sleek, athletic frame. It was only when he pulled back rather abruptly and dropped down to sit on his heels next to the couch that she truly took in the wild look in his dark eyes.

That look called to her own wildness, and Trynn tried to pull him forward again to resume her exploration of his mouth. He resisted the movement.

"No," he said in a rough voice and covered her hand with his. Clearing his throat, he continued, "I'm sorry, Trynn. If we keep going, I don't think I could… stop myself."

Trynn's desire-muddled brain tried to make sense of that statement, and failed. Wasn't it the point of sex not to stop? Her confusion must have been evident on her face. Eris leaned forward to place his lips over her jugular, and kissed her there twice, very softly, the points of his teeth rasping against the thin, delicate skin.

The rush of understanding made Trynn suck in a breath, her body suspended on the knife-edge separating horror and dark, forbidden lust. The image of those sharp fangs sinking into the flesh of her neck during the throes of passion was simultaneously terrifying, and the single hottest thing she'd ever imagined.

Before she could act on the insane idea of trying to test Eris' resolve, he pulled away again and stood up, turning away from the couch and running one hand over his face as if to clear away cobwebs.

"*Gods*," he muttered—hair mussed, shirt rumpled, and still breathing heavily.

Trynn's answering groan was *not* one of pleasure. More a combination of fear, dark excitement, and a truly staggering degree of sexual frustration.

Great. He's the hottest thing I've seen on three separate continents. I've never been so fucking turned on in my life. Aaaand... now he's walking away from me. Maybe the forces of Satan really are *controlling my life.*

Before she could do anything too humiliating—like begging, or, y'know, jumping up from the couch and rutting against his leg—Trynn scrambled to her feet and awkwardly excused herself to the bathroom.

Standing before the mirror, she glared at her own reflection, roundly cursing would-be suicide bombers, ancient demons, the Russian mafia, and hot vampires with their goddamned oral fixations.

"Fuck, fuck, fuck, fuck, *fuck*!" she grated, still feeling like one giant ball of aching *need*.

She took a deep, slow breath. And another. And another.

It didn't help.

She looked around. The bathroom in this place was goddamned *epic*; she'd noticed it when she'd ducked in that afternoon to use the toilet. She'd lived in flats that were smaller, for one thing. In addition to the marble vanity with two sinks, there was a giant walk-in shower enclosed in glass, with four showerheads arrayed around the top. The entire far end of the room was devoted to a sunken, jetted tub large enough to accommodate two people who didn't even particularly like each other.

No, Trynn, stop right there. Do not *think about two people in the freaking jet powered mega-tub! Not. Helping.*

A line of bottles containing bubbles and bath oils stood along one edge like colorful soldiers. Fluffy towels hung on warming racks. A pristine white bathrobe hung on the inside of the bathroom door.

Making an abrupt executive decision, Trynn crossed to the tub and turned on the tap, adjusting it until steam billowed up from the depths. She examined the bottles and poured in the contents of a couple that appealed to her, then stripped out of her clothing and stepped in.

If I'm staying here, then I'll damned well make myself at home, she thought bitterly, as the water churned up mountains of fragrant blue bubbles, rising to cover her body. When the water was lapping over her collarbones, the bubbles tickling her chin, she turned off the tap and sank back with a sigh.

Good God. Trust me to find the only smoking hot vampire on the planet with a conscience.

Intellectually, she knew she should have been terrified by what had almost happened. She also knew that she had some pretty deep-seated issues centered around thrill-seeking and recklessness. If he hadn't stopped, could he have killed her accidentally? A dream image flashed across her mind for a bare instant, too quickly for her to grab hold of it. A shiver wracked her despite the warm water cocooning her body, but she dismissed it.

Eris would not have hurt her.

The phantom touch of fangs on skin made her tremble again, but for a different reason. He would not have hurt her in any way she wouldn't have thoroughly enjoyed, she amended.

The thought was too much for her over-wrought libido, which rose up and demanded satisfaction after the last hour of slow torture followed by sexual frustration. She closed her eyes, letting memories of Eris' touch play across her mind's eye.

He would have continued teasing her vulnerable throat until she finally growled, and rolled him off the couch to wrestle for dominance on the thick, luxurious carpet. Although she would give him a good fight, he would win, pinning her on her back with her wrists above her head, held firmly in one of his large hands.

With the other, he'd peel off her clothing, baring her to his gaze. Rather than take the time to undress himself, he would merely unfasten his fly, pulling his erection free. Would he be dripping precome for her? Her mouth watered, and she decided that, oh yes, he *definitely* would.

Her fingers slid down her belly, missing the electric tingle that his touch always spread along her nerves.

They would both be too impatient for further foreplay. He would pin her down and cover her body with his, lining himself up and thrusting into her hard enough to make them both gasp.

Her fingers slid along the folds of tender flesh between her legs and slipped inside, her passage slick with excitement despite the bathwater.

He wouldn't be gentle, and neither would she, dragging fingernails roughly across his back and urging him deeper with her heels pressed into his tight, perfect ass. He would pound into her until she screamed, and when they were both about to come, he would drag her head to the side and sink his teeth into her neck, sending them both over the edge.

Trynn pressed the heel of her hand hard against her clit and rocked, biting her lip to hold in the cry as her long-denied orgasm crashed over her. When her shudders finally quieted and she sank back against the edge of the tub, exhausted, she realized that her teeth had drawn blood.

-o-o-o-

Half an hour later, she stepped out of the steamy bathroom, feeling much better disposed toward the world even though things were probably going to be awkward as hell now. Trynn glanced around the suite, looking for Eris. Instead, she saw Snag standing looking thoughtfully out of the suite's large picture window into the darkness beyond.

Wrapping her robe more securely around herself, she cleared her throat.

With a painfully slow movement, Snag turned and stared at her with his large, dark eyes. He rarely seemed to need to blink, and considered her silently for so long that she became unnerved.

"Where's Eris?" she asked.

Snag did not answer.

Right. Either he really hates me for some reason, or he actually can't speak, Trynn decided as Snag continued to regard her solemnly. *Let's just assume option number two, until proven otherwise.*

"Okay, never mind," she amended. "I'll just go to bed now, and get out of your hair." Her eyes lifted to his bald head, and she flushed in embarrassment. "If you, erm, had any hair, which obviously you... don't. Sorry about that."

Just as she started to turn and slink away in shame toward the sleeping alcove, Snag lifted a skeletal hand and pointed at a piece of paper on the desk.

A note? Trynn kept her eyes warily on the ancient being in front of her and walked towards the desk. Still not looking away from him, she fumbled until she felt the piece of paper under her fingers. Grabbing it, she took several slow steps backwards.

He considered her for a moment longer before turning back towards the window.

Trynn felt the breath exit her lungs once those cold eyes were no longer pinning her like a captured butterfly. She took the paper into the alcove where Eris had slept that afternoon and sat down on the edge of the bed. Breathing in his smell all around her, she read the short note.

Trynn,

I am truly sorry about earlier. I know I was abrupt, but I don't believe I could have stopped myself from getting carried away. Your presence is intoxicating and I think I would have lost myself in instinctual desires. I'm in no way willing to take that chance with your safety.

I'm going out to get a bite to eat (ha!) and will return shortly. I asked Snag to watch over things while I'm away. If you happen to play chess, you could proba-

*bly convince him to start a game. He's an elite Grand-
master with a rating of 2800, so he's very good, to put it
mildly.*

*I've added you as a guest in the suite and cleared
you to order anything you would like from room service,
so please don't hesitate to get food if you're hungry or
anything else you may need. Expense is no object, so if
there is something you would like, order it.*

Sincerely yours,

Eris

Her stomach grumbled. Trynn realized with a
start that she was absolutely famished, and had not
eaten anything all day long.

Oddly, she felt more comfortable with Snag,
knowing now that he did something as ordinary as
play chess, so she walked casually back towards
the desk and picked up the room service menu.

Running her finger down the list of dishes,
Trynn thought that she was hungry enough to eat
every single one of them.

When was the last time she'd had a really good
meal? Thinking back over the last few days only
presented her with confusing memories that all
seemed to run together. She could not remember
what the hell she'd eaten, or if she'd eaten much of
anything at all.

Resisting the temptation to order a bottle of
wine, Trynn requested the most expensive dish on
the menu be delivered to the room as soon as possible.

After wolfing down the food—delicious, but
extremely spicy—Trynn found herself feeling full
and sleepy again. She didn't really want to go to

bed until Eris had returned, so she sat in the living room watching Snag out of the corner of her eye. He remained standing at the window, staring out into the night with a fixed expression on his gaunt features. She didn't think he'd moved or made a single sound since he'd pointed out the note from Eris.

"Snag?" she asked tentatively, eager to break the silence. "How long have you known Eris?"

The older vampire turned his head towards her but did not speak. He did not look angry or challenging, he simply gazed at her with a neutral expression.

She raised her eyebrows at him as if to encourage him to speak, but he remained unmoved.

She cleared her throat. "Look, I understand if you don't really like me, but I'm getting the impression that we're going to be stuck here together for a while. It would probably be easier if we could get along and interact, you know."

Snag remained completely silent and still. He didn't appear to even be breathing, which... yeah. Was a bit unnerving.

Thinking about Eris' note, she walked over to the table where a chessboard was set up, ready and waiting. She'd played chess for years online in various tournaments and considered herself to be decent. Of course, if Snag was as good as Eris said he was, she was no match for him. But it was still something to do.

Sitting down, Trynn considered the board for a moment before looking up at the silent specter and jerking her head towards the seat across from her.

"Do you want to play?" she asked, fully expecting him to remain like a statue by the window, regardless of what Eris had said.

To her surprise, however, Snag immediately walked over and lowered himself into the chair. He moved with an easy grace that she would not have expected, as if his feet were as light as air. He barely made a sound or caused the cushions in the chair to rustle as he sank down across from her.

She chose white, which always went first in a match.

They started to play at an easy pace. She did not press Snag to talk again, respecting his desire for silence even as the game became more heated.

Within ten moves, she was beaten, and tipped her king in defeat. Without a word, she put the pieces back in place, and they played again. She was able to hold out for thirteen moves in the second game. By the third, she had lasted fourteen moves.

Eris hadn't been joking. In fact, Trynn was willing to bet that he'd been going easy on her to extend the games.

The contest went some way toward thawing the ice between the two of them, and she studied Snag closely across the table. Even though he was a terrifying, spectral creature with nearly translucent skin covered in scars, no hair, and large, dark eyes that almost seemed to glow from within, Trynn could sense a kind of sadness in him. She wondered if he, too, had lost someone dear to him in the distant past.

When their eyes met briefly over the chess-board, she felt for a moment that she was seeing past the icy exterior, into the heart beneath. Though she couldn't have said why, she got the impression, before Snag's shutters fell shut again, that he was consumed with worry over Eris.

Again, she wondered how long the pair had known each other. If he was to be believed, Eris was nearly two thousand years old, and compared to him, Snag looked *ancient*. How old *was* he? What had he seen across all those countless centuries?

If Snag did have a heart buried under that impassive exterior, you wouldn't have known it by his style of play, which was highly aggressive, brutal, and unforgiving. His motions were sharp and each time he captured one of her pieces, he knocked it off the board with a tightly controlled vehemence that suggested it had done him a personal wrong. His gaze was intense, a scowl fighting to slide over his features every so often, only to be carefully suppressed before it could fully surface.

He was an enigma, and she could barely read him at all. Educational though the chess games had been, she wished that Eris would return to break the tension. They were in a lull between games, and Snag was currently sitting in the chair across from her with his eyes closed meditatively. Trynn wondered if he were thinking, or listening carefully to the sounds of life around them. Every now and then, she could detect the muffled slam of a door down the hallway, and knew that people were coming and going from their rooms, despite the lateness of the hour. It was a bit comforting, really — evidence that she hadn't truly fallen down the rabbit hole.

Beyond the door, life continued as normal.

Exhaustion was once more creeping up on her, but she knew that sleep wouldn't come until Eris returned. Indeed, she had no idea where she was even supposed to sleep. Even though she and Eris had started to act on the overwhelming desire possessing them, it still seemed foolish to assume she would be sharing his bed that night — especially after what had happened earlier.

Of course, if he *was* a vampire, maybe he wouldn't sleep at night anyway? She'd seen him sleeping — or just awoken — during the day on three separate occasions now. Perhaps they could switch off with the bed. Still, it seemed rude to assume.

Maybe she would just go grab a pillow and blanket and curl up on the couch. It had been comfortable enough when she'd fallen asleep on it earlier.

Giving up on her musings for the moment, Trynn retrieved Eris' ancient laptop and sat back down to scan the web. She needed more information to give to Eris, who clearly intended to do something about the situation with the arms dealer and their mystery man, Kovac. Though she had no idea what action he could reasonably take.

Without her own computer, she could not access the MASQUE portal, although she was able to see the public information forum and know that several of her fellow hackers were intent on following the lead she'd provided.

Wishing she could go back to her hotel and get her stuff, Trynn finally succumbed to the combination of boredom and curiosity, and broke through the light security on Eris' email account. Knowing that she was pushing her luck with a man she had barely known for twenty-four hours, Trynn scanned through his recent emails. Her eyes were drawn to the subject line—charmingly titled *'Don't be an idiot'*—of personal correspondence from someone called Tré. She opened it.

Eris,

We're headed your way, but travel from the US to Cyprus is very limited right now, so soon after the coordinated pipe bomb attacks at JFK and La Guardia. We're attempting to get something out of LAX instead, but it will delay us for an additional day or so. With luck, we'll be able to get a flight out of here sometime late tomorrow. Please don't do anything stupid before we get there.

Tré

A sense of foreboding settled over Trynn like a blanket, smothering her.

"Snag, come look at this," she said quietly.

She heard no noise of approach, but looked up to find Snag's pale face looming over her shoulder, his dark eyes staring unblinkingly at the computer screen. Something in his features seemed to harden as he skimmed over the message, confirming her fears.

"He's done something stupid, hasn't he?" she whispered.

Trynn stared up at her guard, willing him to speak. It was in vain, however, as Snag made no comment, but only straightened and returned to his place by the window.

Trynn leaned back in her chair, weariness making her limbs feel heavy.

He's out there somewhere, all by himself. How do I know he's safe?

An instant later, another thought rose up. *What does it matter? I barely know this guy. Why should I be obsessed with his safety? He can probably take care of himself, anyway.*

The internal arguments chased each other around her overtired brain. She felt dizzy, and knew that she needed sleep more than anything in that moment.

I want to stay awake and make sure he gets back all right.

Don't be stupid. He's nothing to you. Get some sleep while you can. Besides, he'll wake you when he gets back.

Pressing her fingers against her pounding temples, Trynn let out a little growl of frustration before getting up and stumbling towards the sleeping alcove. She no longer cared if it was proper or weird. She no longer cared if Eris showed up later and wanted to speak with her. Trynn's body was demanding sleep, and she could do nothing more to fight it tonight.

Trynn threw herself gracelessly onto the foot of the California King-sized bed. She crawled up towards the headboard and managed to pull down the covers so she could crawl under them. It was soft and warm, and the sheets smelled of Eris as she buried her face into his pillow. With a heavy sigh, Trynn immediately dropped off to sleep.

This time, however, instead of a room full of priceless artifacts and a man who loved her, Trynn fell into restless dreams full of impenetrable darkness and distant screaming carried on the wind.

146

ELEVEN

Bastian kicked aside a broken pallet and lowered himself onto a dusty couch with large slashes across the cushions. He brushed dust off his dark suit and tilted his head first to one side, then the other, feeling the satisfying crack of his neck.

Looking up, he found that he was being watched dutifully by a hoard of his men, their blank, dead eyes glittering in the semi-darkness.

"It is nearly time, my friends," he crooned. None of them responded to the words, or even blinked. In most cases, he had made sure to utterly annihilate their individuality, plunging them into the darkness and evil that flowed through the fabric of the world. Bastian had chosen each one carefully from humanity's dregs—the desperate and the destitute—and they had not resisted his call. Now, their souls were forever trapped, and their bodies were vessels for his master's will.

"Soon, we will take delivery of our precious cargo. Then begins a reign of destruction that will transform this world into our master's kingdom." Bastian could not keep the growing exultation from his voice. It was his dream to stand beside his master and rule at his right hand. He would be the most honored servant. Beloved. Held more dearly than a son.

Bloodlust rushed into his fevered brain as he thought of what they could do, once the world was theirs. It was a wonderful feeling, and his excitement threatened to spill over. Sensing the growing storm within him, his slaves grew restless. The mental energy he was using to ensure they did his bidding grew frenetic, and their limbs twitched under its pull.

Calm yourself, dog.

Bael's command echoed through his being, sending a shiver down his spine. He immediately clamped down on his frenzied emotions, forcing the undead in the room back under control. Keeping his mania bottled up was difficult. Bastian felt crazed, and longed to take it out on some helpless living thing. He knew, however, that his master would be displeased if he disobeyed a direct order.

To stay focused, he pulled out the itinerary that the Russian, Timur, had provided for delivery of the bombs. Bastian was expecting five individually wrapped and sealed crates containing the portable nuclear devices. He had agents standing by, ready to transport them to various cities around the region for simultaneous detonation.

The sixth device would be delivered separately to his agent in central Damascus. There was little point in bringing it out here to the war-damaged neighborhoods east of the city, just so they could turn around and take it back to the government district a day later. It would be detonated outside of the Parliament building for the Syrian People's Council. The resulting deaths would produce the maximum possible destabilizing effect in a country already torn by conflict and fighting.

Wild giddiness threatened to overpower him once more as he felt Bael's power pulse around him. It was nearly their moment. Nearly their time to rule.

The plan for six simultaneous terrorist attacks against large, soft targets in major Middle Eastern and North African cities would produce catastrophic results. It was a stroke of genius.

Thousands of lives would be lost right away. More importantly, though, every nation in the world would be thrown into disarray, pointing fingers at each other and trying to find someone to blame for the atrocity. Christians would blame Muslims. Capitalists would blame communists. The West would blame the East, and vice versa. Markets would crash, security would be increased a hundred-fold.

And all the while these petty, pathetic little countries would become more and more divided, more suspicious of one another, until someone's finger slipped and pressed a button, bringing down Armageddon. It was a masterstroke for engineering the fall of the world to Bael's power, and Bastian would be squarely at the heart of the transformation.

He and the undead had already been turned by Bael, so they had nothing to fear from the coming nuclear fallout. They could enter the hot zone and find trapped victims. It would be easy to turn them into more undead soldiers for the great army of the apocalypse. Their chances of detection would be minimal under the cloud of chaos that would descend across the planet in the wake of the attacks.

And the families of those lost would never question the lack of a body to bury.

Bastian could barely keep his energy leashed. He stood and walked over to a broken window, staring out across the ruined landscape of bombed-out buildings in the watery moonlight. A sea of bleached and crumbled concrete stretched before him, with blank windows staring into the night like empty sockets in a skull.

The bleak vista extended as far as the eye could see. Despite the torpid summer night, a chill wind gusted through the room. Dust and filth swirled around Bastian, an appropriate shroud for the power that he was about to unleash.

"What targets do you anticipate will be taken out, sir?" a voice said from behind Bastian.

He recognized the voice as belonging to one of his top men—a leader, of sorts, among the undead, who still retained a shred of personality and will. Bastian did not turn to answer him. He continued facing toward the window with his hands clasped behind his back.

Breathing in, he replied with satisfaction. "Many targets will fall, here in Damascus. Several media outlets and various government buildings will be totally destroyed in the blast. We must make sure that we surround the area before the local authorities arrive on the scene to begin rescue and recovery operations. It won't be difficult. They will hesitate to approach too near the center of the blast, due to the radiation."

Feeling euphoric, Bastian smiled, still looking out across the city towards the western horizon, where he could just make out the silhouette of the skyline denoting his future hunting ground.

I am coming for your deaths. Your utter destruction, he thought with something like glee. A shiver traveled down his spine, and his mouth began to water at the thought of all the blood that would be spilled. It would be his moment to avenge himself against humanity. Humanity had never done anything for him except toss him in the gutter and grind his face into the filth. Humanity had made him what he was, and now it would reap what it had sown.

As he stood gazing out of the window, the softest brush of something grazed against the edges of his mind. The sensation was so faint and fleeting that, for a moment, he thought he'd imagined it.

But, no. He went completely still, like a dog on the hunt. His patience was rewarded long minutes later, when he felt the presence again, closer than before.

The presence both drew and repelled; it was like him, yet not.

Turning slowly on the spot, Bastian stared around the room. Several of the undead looked up as his eyes settled on them, but again, none of them spoke. As he approached the window on the adjacent wall, he finally turned away from his suspicious examination of those with him and looked out the window again.

Could one of Bael's six abominations truly be approaching alone? Could they be so lucky on this auspicious day?

He felt certain that there was only a single vampire, but he was hesitant to stretch out with his mind and reveal himself without knowing more about the situation.

As the breeze from outside swirled through the broken widow, bringing the smells of the night with it, Bastian inhaled deeply. He caught the faintest hint of a vampire's scent on the air—sweet and metallic. A single male, approaching from the southwest. His presence was light as air, and Bastian caught the whiff of something animal. Something large, feathered, and predatory.

A wide smile split Bastian's face as he scanned the dark sky around the abandoned building. He couldn't see the abomination yet, but he knew it was close by. The strange feeling of being simultaneously drawn and repulsed grew stronger, like an approaching beacon. Bael was no longer present after his brief appearance earlier, but Bastian knew that his master must be warned of the abomination's approach.

He consciously relaxed his body and called for his master. Moments later, Bael descended like a malevolent aura around the bombed-out complex. The demon's eagerness was infectious as he, too, sensed the approach of one of his failures.

Find him, Bael commanded, triumphant. *Question him. Break him.*

"Yes, master," Bastian vowed. He could hear shuffling around him as the undead sensed Bael's excitement. The prospect of catching and torturing a vampire — one of his failed creations — seemed to fill Bael with the same frenzy that had possessed Bastian earlier as he contemplated the coming nuclear war.

Discover all that he knows about me, about the prophecy, and about the Council of Thirteen. Show him the meaning of pain.

"It will be as you say, my master," Bastian assured as he moved towards the door.

-o-o-o-

Swirling through the air over the two hundred kilometer stretch of open water near Damascus in the form of fast-moving mist, Eris allowed his thoughts to wander back to Nicosia. He knew that Snag was going to have his head once he returned, and Tré would probably tear apart whatever was left. Both had urged him, quite sensibly, to wait until the others arrived before setting off to confront whatever awaited them in Damascus.

Eris had disregarded their advice with good reason, though. He could not ignore the feeling of impending doom that had settled over his senses like a pall. His awareness of Bael's power had seemed to grow tenfold, even in the short time since he convinced Trynn to stay with them at the hotel. It was impossible for him to ignore. Soon, the demon's power would grow so strong that Eris would be unable to protect his mate.

Her kiss lingered like a phantom on his lips, and even in mist form, he could still feel the brush of her skin against his. He wanted to revel in the sensation, but needed to remain focused on his destination. He could not allow himself to become distracted now. It was important that he be on guard.

Would Bael become aware of his presence? Eris was taking care to shield his thoughts, but he knew he would have to proceed carefully in order to scope out the base where Bael's servant was holed up. If he were detected, the consequences could be catastrophic.

Though they'd have to catch me first, he thought grimly.

Eris thought back to Trynn's words about a simultaneous nuclear attack in multiple cities. This was no longer just about saving her life, even if that *had* been his primary motivator for running out on Snag. No, this was about saving all of humanity.

As vampires, fate had arrayed the six of them—seven, now—against Bael's vile power. Fighting him any way they could was, at this point, their only reason for existing. They would never surrender in their effort to prevent the complete desolation of the Light and rise of the Darkness.

In the distance, Eris thought he could make out the shore. Twinkling light from the port city of Beirut glinted off the water, and Damascus lay barely a hundred kilometers beyond. Eris sped up as his goal approached.

He would not allow Bael to destroy his mate— his *life*—again.

Stay focused, he reminded himself. He needed to remain aware of his surroundings. He could not afford the smallest lapse in concentration.

Thanks to Snag's transfer of power earlier, he now had a mental fix on the beacon blazing from Damascus like a sickly green flame in the darkness. Indeed, now that his eyes had been opened, so to speak, he could scarcely banish the nauseating awareness of it.

This is a living hell, no wonder Snag never speaks, he thought wryly.

The evil miasma smothering him like a thick cloud was both familiar... and *wrong* on every level. He could tell that the life force behind the beacon was an undead soul, twisted and mutilated by Bael, but the power emanating from it was shocking. It was much stronger than anything he had sensed before from the undead — even when he and the others had been elbow-deep in the things' entrails, fighting to protect Della and Tré.

No. This was something different. Something new.

As Eris ate up the distance separating him from his goal and passed into the city, he tried to devise a strategy to assess this new and unknown threat. The force drawing him like a moth to flame was centered to the east, away from the bustling central hub of life within the war-torn city.

He approached the source of the taint and circled, trying to get his bearings. He could tell he was very near his goal. Pulling in his life force, he transformed into a great, dark owl. Borne aloft on powerful wings, he glided gracefully through the darkness, barely flapping, approaching in total silence. One building in the bombed out area he was circling held the flickering, insubstantial light of a lit fire. He zeroed in on the structure, focusing all his senses on the interior, and the faint signs of life coming from inside.

He could see a figure standing, outlined by a blazing brazier behind him, gazing through a blown out window. Their eyes met, and dread that he could not explain gripped his mind like a vice. A moment later, the figure vanished.

Before Eris could do more than register his disappearance, a freezing cold mist surrounded him. The particles were like ice against his feathers, weighing him down, dragging him towards the earth.

The owl flapped wildly, letting out a piercing screech of anger as Eris fought to free himself from the all-encompassing icy vapor. Like quicksand, though, the more he struggled, the more he became ensnared by the trap, which closed tightly around him.

In desperation, Eris tried to push his life force out and explode into mist to escape the situation, but his power met a hard, invisible wall that surrounded him and kept him in his avian form.

Trapped as an owl, unable to fly and plummeting towards the earth, Eris let out a mental cry towards the heavens, hoping beyond hope that someone, anyone, would hear him.

If I survive, I am never, ever going to live this down, he thought as his body smashed into the windshield of an abandoned car with a deafening crash of breaking glass.

Agony shot through his left wing, which had taken the brunt of the impact. Eris felt muscles tear and heard a telltale crack as it was crushed beneath him, totally useless. His body bounced once, sliding across the hood to land on the cracked pavement.

Even on the ground, the cold mist continued to press down on him, flattening his lungs and crushing his damaged wing even more. Unable to draw breath, Eris stared up at the starry sky as the world faded into darkness.

-o-o-o-

Back in Nicosia, in the dark hotel room where Trynn slept restlessly in Eris' bed, Snag sat in a chair by the window, silent and unmoving. His head was bowed, his fingertips pressed together as if in meditation, as his consciousness expanded out into the night.

He was breathing deeply, listening to the night sounds of the hotel and world around him, gauging the growing strength of the cloud of malevolence emanating from the mainland across the Levantine Sea.

All was silent and still. But it was not the still of peace. It was the still of waiting.

From nowhere, a distant cry of pain and rage rent the stillness — terrible in its familiarity.

The ancient vampire's head snapped up; his eyes flew open.

If Trynn had been awake, she would have seen the deep-set orbs glowing white, like a cold, furious fire.

TWELVE

Trynn blinked awake to find the pale light of morning glowing from behind the curtains. *Thank god for that*, she thought as she sat up in the rumpled bed. The night had seemed to drag on forever. She had woken often, frightened and restless from half-remembered dream images.

It was a relief to finally rise and face the day.

Padding her way to the bathroom, she showered quickly and brushed her teeth with a disposable complimentary toothbrush from the hotel. As she wandered out into the suite's living area, she found Snag sitting by the window, staring at the heavy curtain as though he could see through it, miles away. His face held none of the stony neutrality it had the previous day. Instead, it was set in gaunt lines of cold rage.

She glanced around, searching for Eris, a sinking feeling growing in her stomach. After a moment, it became clear to her that he had not returned from his night's travels.

Spinning on her heel, Trynn rounded on Snag. "Where is he? Why didn't he return?"

Snag, who barely seemed to have moved since the previous evening, turned his head towards her but did not answer. His eyes glowed, deep in their sockets, and she had to cover a flinch.

"*Where. Is. He.*" She took a step towards Snag, her fists clenching. "*Tell me!*"

He remained completely silent, still staring at her with those glowing eyes. It quickly became obvious that she would get nowhere by demanding his help.

Where could Eris have gone? He couldn't still be hunting during the day, could he? Could real vampires go out in daylight? Eris had made it sound like they couldn't.

Trynn realized that she didn't really know anything about these creatures. How often did they need to hunt? How long did it normally take them?

With an uncomfortable squirming feeling in her stomach, Trynn wondered if they killed their prey. Could Eris be a murderer, too? Had she been fetishizing murder last night when she fantasized about letting him bite her?

Suddenly, agreeing to remain with them in their hotel room seemed downright reckless. What the hell had she been thinking? How did she know that she wasn't their next meal?

The memory of Eris' lips against her own and the way his mouth had grazed so lightly across her neck made her shiver, her body caught once again in that intoxicating no man's land between fear and arousal.

But… no. She didn't really think he'd been keeping her around for an easy meal.

He had been too solicitous. Too concerned for her safety. It had been as though he was terrified she would vanish in the blink of an eye.

But… if he was so worried about her, *why wasn't he here*?

Remembering the private email she'd read the previous day, Trynn recalled that the person called Tré had cautioned Eris against doing anything stupid. *Don't be an idiot*, the subject line said.

What did that mean? Was Eris likely to make a rash decision and put himself in danger?

It seemed more and more likely, the more she thought about it. Combined with Snag's taut and angry visage, Trynn felt certain that Eris must have had left against their advice and set out on his own.

"He went after the terrorist, didn't he?" Trynn asked after a moment. Her voice emerged faint and wavering.

Although Snag did not answer in words, there was a sharp edge to his expression which all but confirmed Trynn's suspicions. Eris, wherever he was, whatever he was doing, had gone after the man that Trynn had been tracking. He was alone, without any form of support or backup.

The panic that welled up inside her took her by surprise. She felt breathless, as if her muscles were tightening around her joints, trying to make her curl up in a ball.

Anger followed a bare moment later.

How could he do this to me? How could he just leave?

She had to do something. She had to *move*. She didn't know exactly what she could do, but getting back to her laptop and trying to find new information about what was going on in Damascus seemed like a logical first step.

Glancing around frantically, Trynn crossed to the table, snatched up her bag, and headed for the door. Before she could even get a hand on the doorknob, a lean figure blocked her path. Trynn looked up into Snag's set face, blinking at him in the room's dim light.

Standing so close to the spectral creature made the hair on Trynn's neck stand up. A deadly chill poured off of him in waves.

A sudden, inexplicable sleepiness drifted over her. Exhaustion seemed to settle in her bones, and she swayed, eyelids drooping. Trynn shook her head, fighting hard against the sudden feeling of sedation. *What the hell?*

She banished the fog with an effort of will, breathing deeply in an attempt to flood her body with oxygen as she stared at Snag's face. Perhaps it was her imagination, but she thought she saw a flicker of something like consternation pass across his harsh features.

The heavy weight lifted as suddenly as it came, and Trynn guessed that, somehow, Snag had tried to put her into a sleep.

Yeah, no. Not happening, Sunshine.

Deciding in a flash that she wasn't going to bow to his mind games, Trynn reached around him and grasped the doorknob. With her other arm, she tried to use her elbow to drive Snag backwards, away from the door.

Initially, Trynn thought this would be an easy move. Snag, after all, was a rail thin wisp of a creature who looked as if a stiff breeze would knock him down.

To her surprise, Trynn realized that Snag must be made of stronger stuff. He didn't flinch or move a muscle, even when she drove the point of her elbow deep into his ribs. No grunt of pain or whoosh of breath suggested to her that he even noticed her attempt at making him move, and his feet did not waver an inch from where they were planted in front of the door.

Stymied, she glared at him. "Get out of my way!" she growled. "You can't keep me here!"

Her voice rose in anger until she was nearly shouting. Snag blinked once, then pressed one bony fingertip against her forehead. This time when the woozy feeling assaulted her, she thought she'd be ready for it. But she was in no way prepared for the direct onslaught of his will as he sliced effortlessly through her mental defenses.

"No…" she moaned, her voice trailing away.

Trynn was distantly aware of the way her body listed to one side, her shoulder bumping against the wall by the door. Her head spun. Numbness spread down her body, into her fingers and toes.

Darkness was descending over her vision, no matter how hard she fought it. Within seconds, she could no longer resist the overwhelming exhaustion pressing down on her mind. She slumped forward, caught by wiry arms that supported her weight without effort as she fell into a deep sleep.

-o-o-o-

Eris came back into awareness slowly, feeling like his thoughts were trudging through the much-

reviled swamp mud that surrounded the old plantation house he and the others had stayed in
outside New Orleans. Oh, how he'd hated that
damned swamp.

The first sound he became aware of was that of
quick, excited breathing.

*Right. Yes. Damascus. Suitcase nukes. Bael. Focus,
Eris.*

He realized in a rush that he was flat on his
back, bound to whatever hard surface he was lying
on by thick ropes and straps of leather. He tested
the restraints, jerking against the bindings, only to
feel blinding pain erupt in his shoulder. That was
also roughly the same point at which he realized he
was naked.

A soft chuckle echoed through the room.

"I wouldn't do that, if I were you," a voice
said.

Eris tried to open his eyes but found that they
were gummed together against his lids with something that felt like glue.

"Thanks for the advice," he croaked. His throat
was parched and raw, as if he had been screaming.
He swallowed, trying to moisten it before he continued. "Bit much for a first date, though. Don't
you think?"

He made a vague waggling motion with the
hand of his uninjured arm, indicating the bondage,
and the being naked, and… well… *all of it*, actually.
He had a feeling that Snag was going to be really,
really cross with him at some point in the very near
future.

There was no answer from his captor, but Eris heard the unmistakable sound of metal being dragged across metal. The noise made the hair on the back of his neck stand up; it sounded like two sword blades being pulled slowly across one another.

With a sinking sensation in the pit of his stomach, Eris thought, *Damn, if Snag doesn't kill me, Tré will. This is really not shaping up to be my finest hour.*

For some reason, mental focus seemed much harder to achieve than it normally was. He had a vague recollection of crashing through a car windshield and then being suffocated... which, yes, okay, probably had something to do with it. Feeling dizzy, he tried to breathe deeply, but found that this only made the spinning worse. Also, his ribs hurt rather a lot whenever he inhaled.

"You are probably feeling quite weak right now, but don't be alarmed. I did that on purpose."

"Wait... did what?" Eris slurred, trying again to concentrate. "What did you do to me?"

"When you flew so unwittingly into my clutches, I decided to drain your blood to weaken your life force."

"Drained... me?" Eris ground out, trying to get his brain to sync up with his mouth.

"Yes, that's right," the man said with a low chuckle. "I prefer more...compliant victims, shall we say?"

Lovely.

Eris struggled again, but his efforts only seemed to sap him of more energy.

His captor clicked his tongue disapprovingly. "Now, now, lie still and be a good boy."

Slumping back against the hard surface of the table, Eris blew a derisive breath through his lips. "Sod off. I was never *good* even when I *was* a boy. And you need to work on your people skills. I've got a friend—the two of you could start a self-help group."

"Perhaps it's past time someone taught you a lesson."

The relish in the man's voice was obvious, but Eris allowed no trace of alarm pass across his face.

"Oh, good," he said, mock cheerful even though his voice was still gravelly. "A sadist. This is going to be fun, I can tell already."

His nonchalance seemed to aggravate the man, who began pacing in circles around the table to which he was bound. Eris sort of wished he could pry his eyelids open… but, then again, there was something to be said for not getting an eyeful of the torture instruments before they were put to use, he supposed.

"You will learn some manners before this day is done," his captor snarled.

"Many have tried—" Eris began, only to be cut off when the man swooped down on him silently and gripped his hair in an unforgiving fist.

Jerking Eris' head back painfully, he brought his face close to Eris' exposed throat. He was mere inches away, and Eris could smell the man's putrid breath on his face. It was all he could do not to gag.

So, he thought as the sadist ran a ragged fingernail down the thin skin over his jugular, *I guess this is how the other half lives. At least I have the good manners to hypnotize them first.*

Suddenly, the earth underneath them shook, and the grip on Eris' hair disappeared.

"Yes, my master," the man breathed. "What is your bidding?"

Eris strained to open his eyes, even just a sliver. Finally, he managed to rip one of them apart a slit, feeling as if several of his eyelashes had parted company with his skin during the process. He was able to see a small portion of the room through the tiny gap, though it was blurrier than he thought it probably should have been.

"What was that about?" he asked mildly. "Got new marching orders, have you?"

The sadist didn't answer, but Eris could sense him moving away.

"What's the matter? Cat got your tongue?" Eris called after him. "And I thought we were getting along so well!"

Something about goading his captor seemed to be pouring life back into him. Perhaps it was merely the small act of resistance that fueled his surge of energy. He knew it would not sustain him forever, though. After that, the mental image of Trynn would be his talisman against the tempting darkness swirling at the edges of his mind, whispering of sweet oblivion.

Out of the crack in his eyelids, Eris saw movement and tried to flinch away, but his reactions were far too slow. A streak of stinging pain opened along the length of his cheek. He hissed, feeling hot blood trickle down his face. Blood that he probably couldn't afford to lose.

"My master grows weary of your impertinence. If you do not hold your tongue, I will slice you to shreds with this knife," the man threatened.

Well, that certainly escalated quickly.

Eris breathed heavily through his nose, forcing his reaction to the fresh pain under control.

Stay focused. Think. Concentrate.

Reaching out with his consciousness, Eris discovered that he and his captor were alone in the large bunker-like room in which he had awoken. There were other presences nearby, but not so close that he could shout out for help and expect to get it. And even if they had been, the presences felt... *off.* More than likely, he was surrounded by Bael's mindless puppets, which certainly didn't make things look any brighter.

"Now that I have your attention," his captor said in a softer voice, "I want you to know how this is going to work."

Even without decent eyesight, Eris could tell that the man was pacing around him again. They'd barely gotten started, and he was already finding the habit intensely irritating.

"I'm going to ask you a question—"

The man's voice was interrupted again by the sound of metal sliding across metal.

"—and you are going to answer the question, completely and truthfully. Do you understand me?"

"Not really."

"What do I need to clarify?" his captor replied in a dangerous voice.

"Oh, nothing. I just don't really get why you think that's going to happen. It seems pretty unlikely."

The sadist laughed. "Ha! I hardly think so. I will break you under my ministrations. Slowly. Deliberately."

The evil that poured out of the man while he spoke made Eris feel as if black oil were coursing over his body and face.

"People skills," he reiterated. "Just saying."

Without warning, a fist slammed into his face, breaking his nose and making blood spray everywhere. Despite his attempts to remain stoic, Eris let out a grunt when he was struck and felt his eyes immediately begin to swell.

Well, fuck. So much for being able to see.

"Do you know who Bael is?" the sadist asked, looming over him.

Eris spit blood out of his mouth, only to have it dribble down his chin. "A loser."

"Want to rethink your answer?"

"Not so you'd notice." The words made it sound like his sinuses were clogged, which felt somewhat less than dignified.

This time the unexpected blow was to his diaphragm, knocking the air out of him. He couldn't seem to drag it back in, his mouth gaping open like a fish. Being a vampire, he could almost certainly go without for a bit if he had to, but that didn't make it any more pleasant.

"I will ask you again, do you know who Bael is?" the sadist demanded, this time pacing back and forth on his left.

"A demon," Eris choked out, when he was finally able to breathe again.

"Very good. That wasn't so hard, now, was it?"

The man leaned over the table, his clammy hand pressed against Eris' exposed leg. Eris shuddered and tried to pull away, but the ropes around his ankles were too tight.

"I don't think you give my master enough credit," the man said conversationally.

As he spoke, Eris felt the tip of a knife press into his leg. He held his breath as the man slowly pressed harder and harder, until the blade pierced his skin.

Eris gritted his teeth together, struggling not to cry out as the knife was forced downward, towards the table, slicing through his skin.

"And you are a vampire, correct?"

"Correct," Eris gasped, squeezing his swollen eyelids together as pain streaked through him in sharp bursts. "As you're well aware."

"One of the thirteen?"

Eris hesitated. Even if he had been in his right mind rather than strapped to a table being tortured, it was too complicated a question to answer.

There was so much that they still needed to learn regarding the prophecy. So much they didn't understand.

"I've no idea," he said truthfully.

The man withdrew and could be heard rummaging some distance away.

"You will find," he said, his voice echoing around the chamber, "that I was fully prepared for you to refuse to cooperate. Tell me, which part of your body do you value most?"

"My brain, I suppose," he said.

"We'll need that for a bit longer yet, I'm afraid," the sadist said, coming closer as he spoke. "Such as it is."

Without warning, Eris' skin erupted into fiery agony. It was unbearable, unendurable, and Eris arched his back, struggling wildly against his bonds despite his shattered arm.

He let out a deafening scream as the sun's rays blistered his exposed skin. Behind his swollen eyes, glowing red seemed to grow out of the darkness, as though he were being consumed by the undying inferno at the heart of a star.

Eris lost track of himself, of his surroundings, of what was being done to his body under the pain and agony of direct sunlight. He could no longer hear himself screaming at the top of his lungs or feel the cool metal table underneath him. He was trapped in the scorching flames, unable to escape.

Quite as suddenly as the torture had begun, the flames were extinguished. The sun's rays were blocked, plunging him back into blessed, cool shadow. He lay limp in his bonds, his strength spent after mere moments under the unforgiving glare.

I will not. I will not. I will not.

He was still in pain from his blistered skin, yet it was so much better than being in direct sunlight that he thought he could withstand it eternally, if it meant never undergoing that unbearable agony again.

He started to shiver, his body slipping into shock after the abuse it had sustained over the last few hours.

"Are you one of the thirteen?" The man repeated.

Eris' teeth were chattering so much that his answer was barely understandable. "I d-don't kn-know. W-we s-s-still have m-much to learn about-t the p-prophecy."

"Hmm... yes," his captor said thoughtfully. "It is a bit of an enigma, is it not?"

Eris did not reply. It was taking all of his strength and determination to remain conscious; he was not going to give the man what he was seeking.

"How many are there in your coven?"

And so the true test began. Eris tried to turn his face away in refusal. He would not betray his friends. He would not make them a target for this madman. He would die before giving away their secrets.

"So be it," his captor said in a resigned voice. He stood again and moved off towards Eris' feet.

Eris could hear a drawer sliding in and out and then the man returned to his side.

"It didn't have to be this way, you know," he said in a condescending tone.

Eris felt a metal rod being pressed against the worst of his burns. For a moment he was confused. Then, the cold hit him.

Iron. Second only to living wood when it came to damaging vampire flesh.

Against his blistered skin, the iron rod felt like a block of ice. Rather than the cold penetrating only the top few layers of his skin, though, it seemed to seep through his muscles and right into his bones, further draining his life force.

With a groan of pain, he tried for what seemed like the hundredth time to yank his flesh away, to protect himself. Yet to no avail. He was trapped in the clutches of this minion of Bael with a taste for cruelty and torture. His skin started to crystallize under the rod, only to have Bael's servant move it to more and more sensitive areas on his body.

Eris abandoned all pretense and screamed as loudly as he could, desperate to draw attention to himself, for someone, anyone, to come to his aid.

"You can scream all you want. The ones outside obey only *my* command," the man said maliciously.

Removing the rod, he left Eris lying on the table, panting and soaked in icy sweat. He was completely spent, his body desperately weakened. He convulsed; his muscles jerked and spasmed, completely outside of his control.

"I want you to tell me all you know about the Council of Thirteen," the undead man demanded, coming close to Eris' face again.

Eris, who was bordering on delirium, giggled feebly. Breathing in heavy gasps, he tilted his face blindly toward his captor and mumbled, "Can you guys smell each other? 'Cause, I'm sorry, but… you really smell bad. Even with… that cheap cologne thing… you've got going on."

Despite his numbed brain, Eris could hear how slurred the words sounded. Despite all the pain he'd experienced, he was still resolutely set against giving this man any information about Trynn, the council, or his friends, though. He would protect them at all costs.

He began to understand that this struggle, this battle, could and probably would claim his existence. He had no idea how long he could hold out without being pitched into insanity. His best bet would quite likely be to goad his captor into destroying him before he accidentally revealed anything important.

But how long would this man tolerate his defiance? Would Bael himself come down to finish the job he'd started millennia ago?

I will never get to see Trynn again, he realized, his chest aching from more than the screams. Grief welled up, and he struggled for a moment with the impulse to drop into the darkness pressing all around him. He was so very tired—his reserves spent from who knew how many hours of torment.

"Tell me who you are," Eris demanded.

He wondered idly if the sadist would answer, or just start torturing him again.

"My name is Bastian Kovac," the man growled, "and I am my master's greatest creation. His *success*. I am the embodiment of his victory."

"Sounds very gratifying for you," Eris rasped.

Bastian gripped Eris' face with alarmingly strong fingers. Sharp fingernails pressed into Eris' skin.

"You are the failure! Vampires are the perversion of my master's power, useless and weak! Your frailty makes me sick. You, who cannot tolerate a weak ray of sun on your skin — "

He paused for a moment and Eris imagined he was shaking his head. "You can be destroyed by a stake through your heart."

To emphasize his words, it seemed, Bastian pressed the rod against Eris' bare chest, directly above his heart.

Eris arched and bucked as Bastian laughed, the sound cruel.

After several moments, Eris was released from the icy agony. With no warning, his mental connection with Snag exploded into life within his mind, and he groaned. Apparently, the threat of iron so close to his vulnerable heart had broken through the mental shields he'd erected to keep Bael from sensing his thoughts.

The connection surged, strong and vibrant. Eris could feel Snag's fury at him for landing himself in danger, just as he felt Bastian's consciousness probe at his vulnerable mind.

In response to the oily touch of Bael's servant, Eris felt Snag wrap a mental shield around him, forcing Bastian out and away. A low growl sounded in Eris' mind, and he knew that Snag's rage was about to spill out of control. The usually silent, sedate, and impassive vampire's power was building. He was drawing, it seemed, from the very earth itself.

Bastian let out a snarl of anger at being forced away. His self-control appeared to snap, and blows rained down on Eris' body, seemingly at random. Eris felt a couple of ribs shatter, and sank back into his mind, allowing Snag's strength to cradle his fading consciousness. The pain grew duller and he lay completely lifeless, unable to fight any more.

Meanwhile, Snag's anger mounted, and the air around Eris seemed to crackle like an immense weapon charging, ready to rain down destruction.

As he began to slip into unconsciousness, Eris heard Snag's voice, low in his ear.

You deceived me. You forced me to remain behind and protect her, and all the while you intended to sacrifice yourself.

Eris could not reply. Could not defend his actions by stating the truth, that he'd been a fool and underestimated Kovac's power, probably at the cost of his own life. He couldn't muster the energy necessary to do anything more than send a single plea.

Keep... her... safe...

There was a long pause.

I made you a vow. I will not break it.

Comforted by the promise, Eris slipped gratefully into darkness. He did not hear Snag's final words.

I will keep you both safe.

-o-o-o-

Trynn groaned as consciousness returned. Every inch of her body felt heavy and painful, as if she'd endured some tortuous full-body workout that pressed her muscles far beyond their endurance.

Her eyes cracked open—even her damned *eyelids* hurt—and the world around her spun momentarily before coming into focus. She was lying on her right side on the comfortable couch, facing the partially open window. Hazy, sodium-yellow light filtered through, adding to the indistinct glow illuminating the room.

Pushing herself into a sitting position, Trynn squinted and peered around, trying to remember what the hell had happened. She stared blankly through the window for several moments, and saw that the yellow glow was from the roof light on the building across from the hotel.

It was pitch black outside.

Shit. *Shit.*

"Snag!" she yelled, furious, scrambling upright on shaky legs. She staggered forward a few steps towards the door and nearly collided with the pale vampire, who seemed to have appeared from nowhere.

"*You!*" she accused, pointing her finger into his chest. "You knocked me out!"

Snag did not respond to her accusation—*surprise, surprise.* Instead, he simply stood there, staring down at her. Perhaps it was the low light, but his features seemed even more sunken and spectral than usual.

"How dare you?" she railed, too angry to even try to calm down. "You had no right to do that to me! I am *not your hostage*. I can leave whenever I damn well please—*you are not in charge of me!"*

Again, Snag remained infuriatingly silent in the face of her tirade. He blinked at her once, the moment stretching between them.

Desperation sang through Trynn's veins, her desire to storm from the hotel growing stronger every moment. *She had to find Eris. She had to make sure that he was safe.*

She let out a wordless yell of rage and spun on her heel, pacing back and forth along the length of the couch she had just vacated. Running her hands through her hair, Trynn considered her options. How could she find Eris when the only clue she had was a vague suspicion that he'd gone after Kovac?

On her next pass, her eyes fell again on Snag. Something about the look on his face made her think he was well aware of what was going on, and where she could find Eris. She knew he wouldn't answer if she asked him directly where Eris was, but maybe she could provoke him into speaking some other way?

Trynn knew she could be a manipulative bitch when she put her mind to it. And she was *damn* well going to put her mind to it right now.

"You're a terrible friend," she snarled, staying just out of reach in case he got any ideas about putting her to sleep again. "How can you stand there blinking at me like a simpleton when Eris is out there, somewhere, in god-knows-what kind of danger? *How can you just sit by and let it happen?"*

Snag didn't move an inch, nor did his expression change. His lack of response didn't surprise Trynn in the slightest. She hadn't expected him to give over the information that easily. But that was fine. Trynn was not, in the end, a particularly nice person. And she had plenty more ammunition where that had come from.

"Do you even care about him at all?" she demanded, narrowing her eyes. "Maybe you were relieved when he headed off into danger, so you could stay here, safe and sound. Maybe all you care about is your own sorry, pathetic hide."

Snag did not react outwardly, yet something made the hair on the back of Trynn's neck stand on end. The atmosphere of the room filled with electricity—like the instant of eerie stillness in a storm just before lightning struck.

But if there was one thing Trynn had never learned how to do, it was *stop*.

"*What did he ever do to you*?" she hissed. "He's been nothing but a friend to you, and for how long? How many centuries? Yet you betray him like it's *nothing*."

A muscle at the corner of Snag's jaw contracted. As Trynn watched with a sudden surge of trepidation, he raised his right hand to his temple and closed his eyes.

Without warning, images exploded into life in front of her mind's eye. They were vivid. All-encompassing. She was still in the hotel room, but it was daylight, and the viewpoint had changed. Instead of standing by the couch, she was seated in Snag's preferred chair by the window. She could sense that Eris was lying in the bed within the walled-off area of the sleeping alcove, though she couldn't see him from her spot by the window.

We don't have time to wait!

That was Eris, speaking without speaking. Trynn could hear his rich tones as clear as day, though he was still in the other room.

This has to be resolved before it turns into a disaster! But we also can't risk leaving Trynn unguarded. You need to stay here and protect her. I'll go ahead to Damascus and see what I can do own my own about the situation. You know how important Trynn is —

Trynn felt Snag's flare of irritation at his friend's words.

— and we sure as hell aren't taking her along. We'd be delivering her straight into Bael's hands, Eris continued doggedly.

Then I will go. You will stay.

Snag's mental voice was deep and commanding. But now Trynn could feel Eris' anger, as well.

Don't be ridiculous. You're more powerful than I am. I need you here, with Trynn, protecting her. Please, Snag, just do this for me.

Snag did not respond, but Trynn felt a chill of power emanating from him. His anger was growing, filling the entire suite just as it had moments ago in the real world, when she had goaded him.

It's pragmatic, Eris pointed out, *and you can't stop me from going unless you plan on fighting me outright. I'll find out exactly what we're facing, so that we can stop whatever Bael is intending with these bombs.*

The image before her shifted and changed between one breath and the next. They were someplace unfamiliar. She could see a dark chamber with a light above a table where a lone figure lay.

Immediately, she recognized the man as Eris, yet he looked completely different from when she'd last seen him. His face was bloody, bruised, and swollen—his eyes crusted over with some sort of black sludge.

"Eris! *Eris!*" Trynn cried, but her voice was lost before it ever reached her lips. No matter how hard she tried, no sound escaped.

She could see burn marks upon his marble white skin, and large swatches of purple flesh where he had clearly been badly beaten. She tried to reach out and touch him, but her hand was as insubstantial as smoke.

He was barely breathing, and his skin was covered in a sheen of sweat.

Trynn felt a presence beside her, and looked up to find Snag standing next to her, staring down at Eris' broken form. He looked up slowly and met her eyes. As their gazes locked, she felt what he felt—Eris' agonizing pain and terrible weakness, the strain on the fragile thread binding his soul to his ruined body.

An instant later, Trynn was back in the real world, crouched on her hands and knees in the hotel room, trying in vain to throw up her fucking *toenails* onto the soft rug beneath her. After retching for what felt like hours and bringing up only stomach acid, she clumsily tried to push herself upright—only to fall to the side, leaning against the front of the couch.

"Oh, God," she croaked, shaking in reaction like a leaf in the wind.

She looked up at Snag through tear-blurred eyes. He was still standing in front of the doorway. As she watched, he lowered his hand from his temple and let it hang limply at his side.

Trynn swallowed several times, choking on bile, and tried to speak again. "W-we have to stop this. We have to help him! Snag, *please!*"

She was begging by the end, staring up into Snag's dark, pain-filled eyes.

He didn't answer, and hope began to die in her heart. Just as the first sob of wretched grief tried to rise and jerk free of her chest, a strange rushing sound filled the room.

Trynn looked around wildly, trying to find the source. A cool mist was swirling through the open window — something that was clearly impossible on such a sultry Mediterranean night. The cloud of vapor filled the whole room, wrapping around the two of them like a soothing caress.

Snag closed his eyes, his chin dipping, and breathed out in a slow sigh.

THIRTEEN

The swirling mist seemed to suck the air directly out of Trynn's lungs. She jerked back, her shoulders banging against the couch.

"What the hell?" she rasped, looking up at Snag. The ancient vampire still had not moved.

Trynn blinked, trying to clear the tears from her eyes. When she opened them again, the cloud of mist had disappeared, and five people stood in the center of the room—three women, and two men. She remained frozen, kneeling next to an acrid puddle of bile as she stared at the mysterious intruders.

What? How—?

"We caught most of that, Snag," a tall man with dark hair said. His tone was that of someone who was used to being obeyed. His unnaturally light grey eyes flashed toward Trynn, who remained in the unflattering position she had been in before their arrival. "Do you know where Eris is? Can you track him?"

Snag did not speak, but the newcomer nodded as if he had.

Trynn looked over the remaining members of the group with wide eyes. Next to the leader stood a short, curvy woman with long, honey-colored hair and a mole on her face, like some old Hollywood movie actress. She returned Trynn's gaze with a look of sympathy and reassurance.

"We should go after him right away," the second man said. He had brown hair and striking green eyes that seemed to see right through her. There was an air of easy charisma about him that permeated the room as he spoke. Trynn had the distinct feeling that whatever he wanted, he generally got.

The two women standing closest to the window were also watching Trynn with poorly veiled interest. One was a haughty vision of beauty, with porcelain skin and pale blond hair flowing around her shoulders. Intelligence blazed from her bright blue eyes, but so did cynicism.

The other had mocha skin and large, soft brown eyes. She was also a picture of loveliness, her perfection marred only by a state-of-the-art prosthesis where her left ankle and foot should have been. She looked friendly, where her companion was aloof, and Trynn was instantly drawn to her. She bestowed a quick, tense smile on Trynn before she turned back towards their leader, who was speaking.

"I don't like it much, but we'll have to split up." His silver eyes turned back towards Trynn, regarding her thoughtfully. "Snag, you've fulfilled your vow. Go. Della and I will remain behind and guard Phaidra."

Trynn felt a flash of annoyance at the mistake, though she knew it was petty.

Before she could even draw breath, Snag dissipated into a vaporous cloud right before her eyes, and hurtled out through the window. The blond woman and the dark woman were right on his tail, followed an instant later by the brown-haired man. The eerie sound of rushing wind echoed behind them for a moment, and then all was still once more.

Trynn abruptly realized that she was still crouched on the floor by a puddle of her own sick, and scrambled to her feet.

"My name's not Phaidra, it's Trynn," she said, happy when her voice barely quivered.

The Hollywood pinup girl stepped forward and steadied Trynn with a hand on her shoulder when her balance threatened to desert her.

"Of course it is," she said. "You'll have to excuse the lapse. It used to make me crazy whenever one of them slipped up and called me Irina, so believe me, I understand. My name's Della, short for Delaney, and this is Tré."

"Uh... hi," Trynn said automatically, still completely bewildered.

"Now," Della said in a no-nonsense tone. "You look like you've been through the wringer. Come on, you need to freshen up. I expect we'll be stuck here waiting for a while."

Before Trynn could protest, Della was herding her towards the bathroom with surprising effectiveness given her petite frame.

They were halfway across the suite before Trynn recovered her wits enough to put the brakes on. "I don't need to freshen up, I need answers!" she snapped.

Della looked at her sympathetically. "You'll get answers, don't worry, but first you really do need to get cleaned up. No offense, Trynn, but vampire noses are sensitive, and not to put too fine a point on it, you smell."

She wanted to be affronted by the gently delivered insult, but when she drew in breath to say something sharp, an unpleasant smell assaulted her. With a sinking feeling, she pulled her shirt up to her nose and sniffed.

Dear God. Okay — a shower was definitely necessary.

"Trynn, look. We aren't going to hear anything for a while," Della said. "You might as well take care of yourself first."

There was a certain logic to that, even if Trynn didn't much like it. She took a damned shower.

Fifteen minutes later, she stepped out of the bathroom wrapped in a fluffy robe, her wet hair plastered to her forehead. She found Della and Tré seated at the table, speaking quietly. When she came around the corner, they both looked up and Della smiled, though it was strained.

"Feeling better?" she asked.

"Yes and no," Trynn answered cautiously. "No longer stinky. Still need answers."

"Please, join us," Tré said.

Della pushed the third chair out and gestured for Trynn to take it.

Sitting down, Trynn wrapped her hands around the steaming mug that had been placed on the table in anticipation of her return. It was tea.

She sipped it and looked at the two vampires expectantly.

"Xander always says that Americans drink too much coffee and not enough tea," Della said. "So we try to humor him—even though tea-drinking isn't our natural instinct, so to speak."

"Natural instinct?" Trynn echoed, confused. Then it dawned on her that these two were vampires, and probably preferred blood to bergamot. "Oh! Right… vampires. Uh, sorry. This has all been a bit much, to put it mildly."

Della waved her off. "Don't apologize. It takes a lot of getting used to."

"So, what can you tell me?" Trynn asked, looking back and forth between the pair.

Della and Tré exchanged a look.

"We were actually about to ask you that question," Della said.

"*Me*? Why?"

"We know what we overheard from Snag's mind as we were arriving. But we don't know everything," Tré said. "We need you to tell us more about what's been going on."

Trynn swallowed and scrubbed a hand through her damp hair, gathering her scattered thoughts. "Um, yeah. Well—I'm a member of an online hacktivist group. We uncover and disseminate secret information when we feel it will have beneficial humanitarian effects."

Della and Tré listened intently, letting her explain at her own pace.

"I don't know as much as I'd like to about what's going on, honestly," Trynn said after a moment of awkward silence. "Just what I've been able to gather from emails I've been intercepting."

"What kind of emails?" Tré asked, leaning forward and folding his hands on the table.

Trynn swallowed. "There's an Eastern European underworld figure who has been amassing power and wealth at an astonishing rate. We have a few guesses about where he came from and how he's doing it, but no one can really confirm any of it. We think he gained the vast majority of his wealth from illegal trafficking of weapons, drugs, and humans, all of which can be extremely lucrative."

"Go on," Tré prompted.

"Recently, it appears he's been amassing his own private stockpile of weaponry and not reselling it." She took a deep breath. "Our latest information suggests he's planning a simultaneous attack with suitcase nukes in several cities around the region. The closest I've gotten to details was finding out about a scheduled meeting between this guy and a powerful Russian mafia kingpin in Damascus a few days ago."

"Okay, *that* is legitimately terrifying," Della said, her brown eyes growing wide.

Tré's already pale skin went a bit paler, though his eyes grew sharp. "And your information is good? How certain are you about the details of this plan?"

Trynn hesitated. "We usually have excellent intel, since we hack it all ourselves. Most of these criminals assume that their information is safe behind firewalls and security devices. I can't say that we're right a hundred percent of the time, but I am absolutely confident that this guy, B. Kovac by name, met with someone who has access to nukes and bartered a deal. I saw an email with my own eyes — one arranging transport of the weapons."

Tré swore under his breath in a language Trynn didn't recognize, and ran his hands through his dark hair.

"This reeks of Bael," Della observed quietly.

"Bael? The demon thing?" Trynn asked. "Yeah, that's what Eris thought. He seemed pretty convinced of it."

Della shivered visibly. "So, we think Bael has got this Kovac guy trying to destroy the world?"

"It seems quite likely," Tré answered. "I'm not at all certain we have enough muscle to manage this."

"Muscle? What do you mean?" Trynn asked.

Tré looked grim and angry. He pushed away from the table, rising to pace a few steps across the room. "I mean that four vampires may not be enough to avert this disaster — even when one of those vampires is Snag. I can't guarantee they'll be able to stop this attack and rescue Eris at the same time."

Trynn's stomach clenched. What was he saying? That they wouldn't even try to save Eris? Selfish anger rose. Yes, the thousands of possible victims in this act of violence mattered. Yes, it would be a devastating blow to the world if the radioactive fallout killed or injured thousands of others. The course of humanity would be irrevocably changed.

Yet, panic welled up at the thought of losing Eris. Didn't his life matter, too? These people were his friends! Shouldn't they be doing everything in their power to rescue him?

Trynn thought back to the malicious words she'd hurled at Snag. The accusations she'd made. At the time, she'd only been interested in goading him into speech. Now, she felt sickened by the exchange.

She'd goaded him, all right, and he'd ended up communicating far more than she had expected or intended. It was obvious that he cared for Eris deeply. After what she had seen in his mind, she would have known that even if he hadn't hurtled off without a moment's hesitation to rescue his friend, the instant he was released from his vow to protect Trynn.

Surely he, at least, would not abandon Eris to his fate.

Christ. She needed to apologize to Snag when he got back—probably on hands and knees.

Even that thought was chilling, though. With powerful demons and evil men wielding nuclear weapons arrayed all around them, how could she be sure that Snag *or* Eris would return? She didn't know if she would ever see either one of them again.

The growing sense of helplessness ballooned inside her chest, constricting her heart, nearly overwhelming her.

Della was looking at her as if she could see right into Trynn's thoughts. Hell, maybe she could.

Now was not the time to be selfish. She had to focus on all of the lives that could be lost to these attacks. She needed to be thinking up a plan to help, not blubbering in the corner like some kind of damsel in distress. She needed to figure out a way to *stop this*.

Trynn took a deep breath and searched desperately for some way to resolve the bomb crisis and save Eris at the same time. She dropped her head into her hands, staring at the darkness behind her closed eyelids. She squeezed them shut so hard that lights flared like red starbursts. Before the whirling patterns had fully faded, an idea came to her, springing from her subconscious fully formed.

Trynn jerked upright. "*Shit*! I know what we can do!"

Della had jumped in surprise at Trynn's outburst, and Tré spun around, his intense silver stare pinning her in place.

"Okay—you're not going to like this part," Trynn said quickly, "but I have to get back to my hotel room across town and pick up my computer."

"If Bael is after you, that's ridiculously dangerous—" Della said, but Trynn interrupted her.

"You don't understand! I *have* to, Della—untold human lives depend on this information! *Eris'* life depends on this information!"

The two vampires stared at her intently, then at each other. With a flash of irritation, Trynn realized that they were conversing silently—discussing her as though she weren't sitting right in front of them.

"I'm serious," she said through gritted teeth, shoving her chair back from the table and jumping to her feet. "I'm not crazy. *I have an idea*."

"All right," Della said unhappily, standing up as well. "We'll take you, but we have to go now, while it's still nighttime."

"I'll get dressed." Trynn nearly sprinted the length of the suite. Her shirt was ruined, but her sensible trousers were wearable. After a bare moment of hesitation, she rummaged through Eris' luggage for one of his casual button-down shirts and rushed into the bathroom to change. She emerged moments later with his sleeves rolled up to her elbows, the hem of the shirt hanging to the top of her thighs. She snatched her handbag and threw it over her shoulder as she headed towards the door, where Della and Tré were standing, ready to depart.

They passed out of the palatial hotel peacefully enough — most of the inhabitants were fast asleep at this hour. Trynn felt an unnatural stillness press against her as soon as they stepped outside. No breath of wind was stirring, and the air felt heavy with a coming storm. Sirens wailed in the distance.

"It's already starting," Della said. "I can feel it. We'll need to hurry."

The normally sleepy city seemed to be holding its breath, waiting for something. Trynn's hair stood on end, gooseflesh erupting across her arms even though the street in which they were standing was calm and no sign of disturbance reached them from the nearby buildings. Trynn glanced towards the west, and saw a flickering, insubstantial glow of orange reflecting off the distant buildings.

Fire.

"It's normally not like this," Trynn whispered, hesitant to even lift her voice enough to penetrate the darkness. She swallowed hard, feeling as though a shadowy presence was closely watching her every move.

"It's part of the vortex forming around you," Tré said grimly, his eyes scanning the shadows. "You are the eye of the storm."

Trynn shifted uncomfortably for a moment before taking a steadying breath and heading in the direction of her hotel. An agonized scream rent the air a few blocks away, and she flinched hard, nearly stumbling over her own feet.

"All of this can't really… be because of me, can it?" she whispered.

Della steadied Trynn with a hand on her back. "In a manner of speaking, yes," she said. "The same thing happened to me, you see."

Trynn stared down at the shorter woman, dumbstruck. "What do you mean, it happened to you?"

"I used to be just like you, Trynn," Della said. "I was living in New Orleans and working in an *insurance office*, for god's sake. One day, everything was fine, and then… all these terrible things started happening in the city."

Della's voice trailed off. They walked silently for several moments, as Trynn waited for Della to continue.

"So many lives were lost," she finally said, her voice brittle with bitterness and old pain. "I didn't realize that it was all my fault until I met Tré and the others."

"It wasn't your fault, *draga mea*. There is only one being at fault for the pain and death… and his name is Bael," Tré interjected. Della shook her head, frowning. Trynn could tell they'd had this argument before, perhaps many times.

"But it was like it is here?" Trynn asked, suddenly breathless. "There were fires, and shootings, and suicide bombers, and other horrible things?" Her eyes lingered on the orange glow, shining more brightly now as they made their way further into the city. Heavy, acrid smoke hung in the air. Sirens screamed in the distance, but everything around them was completely quiet as they moved along the deserted street. It was eerie, in a way that chilled Trynn to the bone.

"Yes," Della confirmed. "Just like here."

"But *why*?" Trynn asked. "I haven't *done* anything!"

Della and Tré met each other's eyes, communicating silently again. Trynn felt an unexpected stab of jealousy at the obvious bond between the two, even amidst all the chaos and uncertainty. Trynn felt like her whole world was a breath away from falling apart, and the two of them were busy making doe eyes at each other.

"Sorry," Della said a moment later, tearing herself away from her lover's gaze. "Inside joke. I said pretty much exactly the same thing—on more than one occasion, as I recall."

"To answer your question, we have some theories on that," Tré said quietly. "We think Bael becomes aware of the reincarnated souls of our mates when we wander close enough to them for the bond between us to reconnect. Once he finds them, he pursues them to wherever they are staying. For you, it was here. You got too close to Eris and Bael discovered your presence in Nicosia. His greatest power is in turmoil and violence, so he unleashes the full weight of it and uses it to revenge himself on his enemies."

Trynn scratched her neck, thinking. "Why am I his enemy, though? Why should he care whether Eris and I are reunited or not?"

Della huffed in sympathy. "That's what I wondered, too. What you don't understand is that your existence is a threat to him. You are the one the few people who has ever defeated him."

Her footsteps stuttered to a halt as she turned to looked at Della. "I… *what*?"

"You don't remember?" Della asked, frowning. "You haven't dreamed about it?"

Trynn tried to force down the flush that tried to stain her cheeks at the mention of dreams. But—

"No," she said. "I… uh… I know we were together. In someplace that looked like… Ancient Greece, I guess? We seemed really happy."

"It was ancient Cyprus," Tré said, his voice low. "You're walking the streets of your ancestral home as we speak."

A dull spike of shock pierced her, but something about his words also seemed *right*, like a puzzle piece slotting into place.

"Oh," she said.

Della's words were gentle. "Trynn, for whatever reason, Bael singled out Eris and attempted to turn him. Bael tried to make Eris into his servant, a shell completely immersed in darkness, who would do his bidding without hesitation or conscience."

"Turn him?" Trynn asked, as the three resumed their progress towards her hotel. "How?"

Tré shivered and looked away, making Trynn wonder.

It was Della who answered. "He attempted to tear Eris' soul into two halves, the Light and the Dark. If he had been able to complete the turning, Bael would have drawn the Light out of Eris and cast it forever into the pit of Hell, leaving only Darkness behind."

Trynn gripped her hand to her chest, picturing it. "And I stopped that? How?"

"Only you and Eris know for sure," Della said, "but certain ancient texts tell us that only the willing sacrifice of true love can protect someone from Bael's destructive power."

"Sacrifice?" Trynn echoed, her mind whirling. *Jesus*. She'd wanted answers, but…

Gathering herself, she spoke again. "So he survived and I—what? Died?"

Tré and Della's silence was all the answer that she needed. It was an odd feeling, knowing that she had been so in love with Eris at one point that she had willingly sacrificed her life for him. Now, she was tortured by the idea of something bad happening to him, but she hadn't really worked out how she felt about Eris, or what their next steps would be.

Assuming he survived. Assuming *she* did.

The uncertainty was unpleasant for Trynn, who was used to being able to confidently take control of a situation; who always knew what she wanted from life.

The past few days had thrown her into a tailspin, unable to grasp what was happening around her. Trynn's life had burst out of its seams, unraveling before her eyes. Demons? Vampires? Reincarnation? A great war of good versus evil?

What could possibly be next?

Yet, it was all real. She'd been thrown into a nightmare from which there was no waking up, no blessed relief that it had all been in her head. She was walking down a darkened, silent street next to two vampires, being smothered by stifling smoke that hung in the air as the city of Nicosia burned around them. They were standing in the terrifying eye of a vicious storm, praying that they could pass through and come out the other side alive.

It felt like the entire city was teetering on the edge of a chasm, about to slide into chaos and utter destruction. Tension crackled in the air, waiting to explode into violence.

"We need to hurry," Trynn said, quickening her steps as they rounded the corner and her hotel came into view. Next to the grandeur of the Merit Lefkosa, the place appeared dilapidated and worn down. Shabby bushes flanked the front door, through which the three companions entered warily.

The sleepy attendant cracked open a wary eye before tipping further back in his chair, his feet propped up on the desk as they passed by.

Down the hall, Trynn unlocked her hotel room door and walked inside, flipping on lights.

To her relief, nothing had been disturbed. Seeing her laptop still sitting on the desk where she left it, Trynn pounced on the device like a cat on an unlucky mouse.

With frenzied clicks, she logged into her computer and began working as fast as she could, praying that her plan would work.

Della sat on the edge of Trynn's bed, watching her without speaking.

"What are you doing?" Tré asked, wandering around behind her and looking over her shoulder. "What does this plan of yours entail?"

"I'm sending an email," Trynn answered, the words clipped and terse as she worked, focusing on her screen as though Eris' life depended on it.

Because, *oh, yeah…*

It did.

FOURTEEN

Silence met Trynn's simple words, and even though her eyes never left her computer screen, she could tell that Della and Tré were communicating telepathically again.

They probably thought she'd lost her damned mind.

"Trynn," Della said hesitantly, "how will that help?"

A vicious smile spread across Trynn's face as her fingers flew over the keyboard. "I'm about to turn the tide against our friend, Mr. Kovac. He's going to fucking well learn what happens when he tries to attack the world on *my* watch."

Despite the tension in the cramped room, Tré let out a snort of laughter at her assertion. "Yes, you're Eris' mate, all right. Now, take a breath and *explain*."

"Hold on just a second," Trynn murmured, clicking between several screens as she tried to ensure she had all the relevant information available to her, while composing a message in Russian in her head.

After several moments, she spoke. "Okay, so we intercepted this information in the form of emails, right?"

"Right," Della said, and Tré shrugged agreement.

"But we don't know the true identity of the guy purchasing the suitcase nukes. Nothing beyond the name B. Kovac, which could be any one of hundreds of people—maybe thousands," Trynn continued. "He always sent these encrypted emails through a series of different servers to hide any identifying information."

Trynn could feel herself falling into teaching mode as she explained her theory. "Now, we've been trying for months to discover who this guy is and where he came from, but maybe we were going about things all the wrong way? We didn't know until recently if this information was even legitimate, so we've been trying all the while to establish whether this guy is truly a threat. Well, we're past that point now. He's obviously a huge threat."

"Obviously," Tré agreed, frowning at her—clearly not getting it.

"We haven't paid much attention to the suppliers because we know who they are. That part wasn't a mystery, since there are databases used by the US government and Interpol that track all the active members of each criminal organization. We already knew their part in the plan, so we never really dug deeper than that."

"And that's what you intend to do now?" Tré asked.

"No. I'm not acting as a spy in this war anymore," Trynn corrected. "Fuck that. I'm picking up a gun and changing the course of the battle."

"But *how*?" Della asked, looking just as confused as Tré.

"I told you, we already know all about Kovac's supplier," Trynn said in measured tones. "So… what do you think would happen if the Russian mafia suddenly received correspondence from Mr. B. Kovac, stating that he wasn't going to uphold his part of the deal? For example, something stating that he wouldn't be making the full payment?"

Neither Della nor Tré answered, but slow smiles spread across their faces. For the first time, Trynn could believe that they were predators—she'd seen just such a smug expression once on the face of a cat, contemplating a bird with a wounded wing.

"I don't think they'd be very pleased, do you?" Trynn finished blandly.

"They probably wouldn't, at that," Tré replied.

"I imagine they'd be a bit cross, yes," Della put in.

"Plus," Trynn added, "they're not really known for their patient and forgiving natures. If a major deal like this went south at the last second…"

Her voice faded away as she threw them a wide-eyed, innocent look. "Who *knows* how they might respond?"

Turning her attention back to the email, Trynn scanned through what she had written one last time and sent the message.

Once it was away, she pulled up Twitter and focused on finding the users she was looking for. She'd noted several of the more outspoken players in the Russian mafia over the years, and searched now for their handles on the social media website.

Where are they? C'mon, c'mon, don't leave me hanging, here, she thought, scrolling through the fast-moving feed. Trynn knew that many members of the Russian mafia communicated through Twitter. She was hoping to see evidence of a sudden shock within their criminal organization as word spread of Kovac's betrayal. Trynn turned back towards the two vampires.

"Is there a way for you to communicate with the others?" she asked grimly.

"The other vampires who are going after Eris?" Tré asked.

Trynn nodded.

"There's a growing distance between us, but Snag is incredibly powerful. I think I can reach him from here."

Tré fell silent and cocked his head, as if trying to listen to an elusive sound. After a few moments of quiet, he nodded. "Yes, he can hear me. What should I tell him?"

Trynn ran through the details of her plan in her mind again, wanting to keep her message short.

"Tell him that we are trying to disrupt the arms shipment and that the Russians are likely to retaliate against Kovac."

Tré nodded. "Della — *draga mea*, lend me some of your power for a moment." He closed his eyes, and Della did, too. Trynn watched in fascination as Tré took several deep breaths, as if to center his thoughts.

Finally, they both opened their eyes and Tré nodded, which Trynn took to mean that the message had been successfully delivered. A combination of excitement and apprehension flooded her stomach as she stared back at the screen, contemplating the events she'd just set into motion.

A memory of her childhood in Canada popped inexplicably into her mind.

"Snow angels, Mummy!"

"Yes, darling. Yours are beautiful, just like you!" Her mother replied, her pink cheeks visible over the scarf wrapped around her chin. Bright eyes followed Trynn's progress as she knelt carefully in the snow next to the head of the snow angel she had just created.

Trynn reached out a gloved hand and carefully drew a smiling face into the snow.

"My snow angel is really a superhero in disguise, Mummy. She's going to save the world," Trynn called in a high voice. Her dark hair fell over her shoulders, tied back by the headband covering her small ears.

"You think so, darling?"

"Yes, of course. That's what good angels do. They save the world!"

She'd been young then, in that bright and happy time before everything had gone bad—her father's death. Her mother's second marriage. Breaking glass and quiet crying, the snap of a leather belt, the dull thump of fists hitting flesh.

Trynn had run away at fourteen, leaving the smiling angels behind. At twenty-seven, perhaps she'd finally found them again.

She blinked several times, jerking herself back to the present.

"Trynn?" Della asked, concern in her voice.

"Sorry," Trynn murmured. "It's nothing. Just thinking about snow angels."

Della looked bewildered, but Trynn just waved her off. She turned her attention back to the Twitter feed as the first confused messages started to fly back and forth.

"*Oh, yeah*," she said, voice fierce. "*That's* what I'm talking about. Shit, meet fan."

Trynn snapped her laptop shut and scooped it and the power cord into her bag. Taking only a moment to stuff a handful of clean clothes in her bag, she returned to the two vampires, and all three of them hurried for the door.

-o-o-o-

"You are my life and soul, beloved… I give mine willingly for you. I will be in the very air you breathe, now and forever. Every time your heart beats, I will be there, my love," Phaidra's soft, breathy voice whispered in his ear.

Shrouded in darkness, Eris twisted his head back and forth restlessly, trying to find the source of the voice, and the delicious warmth emanating from it. Confused and disoriented, he could not understand what was happening. The evil that had possessed his spirit was receding. He felt more like himself, yet something was different. His senses were sharper, and he felt a terrible chill stealing through his soul. There was empty space within him, where before there had been light and happiness.

He moaned, feeling himself being pulled awake against his will. The nightmare of his turning gave way to the nightmare of the present. He knew he was too weak to withstand any more torture, yet his body betrayed him by dragging him back into wakefulness.

The world spun, and Eris felt certain that the table on which he was still bound was tilting, a hairsbreadth away from crashing to the floor. Even though his equilibrium was screaming in alarm, Eris made no effort to fight his bonds.

He turned inward, trying to slip away into sleep again, in hopes of finding a kinder dream this time, and felt his consciousness start to drift. At the edge of his awareness, Eris thought he could sense Snag's presence. Yet, it was so elusive that it, too, might have been a dream.

Losing himself felt like sinking into swirling water, being buffeted by deep currents. His breathing grew more and more labored, as though a great weight were pressing on his chest. His heart rate sped up, fast and thready as his body tried to compensate.

Without warning, Eris felt his senses sharpen and his awareness expand beyond his shattered physical form.

He could sense Snag again. It wasn't a dream. This time, his presence was as plain as day. To his horror, he realized the presence was nearby, drawing ever closer. *Snag had abandoned Trynn to come after him.*

He let out a weak groan of denial, hoping against hope that the sound had not attracted the attention of his captors. He had not been able to restrain the small noise of anger and betrayal.

No! Snag… goddamn you! You promised me… you would… keep her safe…

Even his thoughts sounded breathless. The strain of communicating telepathically with Snag drained him of the paltry amount of energy and life force he had left.

For a moment, sickly flashes of light wavered across the blackness before his eyes and he could do nothing but lie there, feeling giddy and sick.

Well, that's gratitude for you, another familiar voice said in his mind.

Xander?

Who else?

But— Eris tried to blink his eyes open. One cracked open partway, only to be dazzled by a powerful spotlight above him, drowning out the darkness beyond, making it impossible to see anything beyond the ring of light. *But—how?*

We're flying to you, genius. What did you think? Shit, they really have done a number on you, haven't they? Even you aren't usually this dense.

Eris could sense others pressing close to the mental link, but he didn't have the strength left to tune them in. It was like staring into the bright light above him and trying to discern the shadows beyond its edges. The more he strained, the less he could make out, and the more it made his skull ache.

His confused thoughts turned back to Trynn, who must even now be in grave danger without Snag's protection. What the hell did Snag and Xander think they were doing, trying to rescue him? *She* was the one who needed their help!

He had clearly been left alone here, the gritty dryness in his mouth proclaiming that he had been unconscious for several hours, at the least. It was likely that in the absence of any useful information from him, his captor had abandoned his broken body to petrify, slowly but surely hardening into stone as his life force leached away.

Their experience led them to believe that vampires could not die natural deaths from illness, starvation, or age. If the old texts were to be believed, there were only a few ways to truly kill a vampire. But in the absence of the animating force they drew from human or vampire blood, they would eventually enter a petrified, husk-like state that was not truly life, either. He'd seen that firsthand; Snag had been nearly in that state when Eris had stumbled upon his tomb, millennia ago.

A snort of disgust echoed across the mental bond. Clearly Eris had been unable to shield his thoughts from the others in a weakened state.

Sounds deeply unpleasant, Xander observed. *You had to know we weren't just going to leave you to that fate.*

It would have taken a very long time, Eris retorted, feeling distinctly waspish and wishing more than ever that he could just go to sleep. *Trynn needs protecting right now.*

Merde, another familiar voice scolded. *She's well protected, you idiot. Tré and Della are guarding her. For once, could you worry about yourself right now?*

Oh, good, Eris thought. *Duchess is here, too. My day is now complete.*

I heard that.

Well done, mate, Xander congratulated. *Way to insult the rescue party.*

Leave him alone, both of you! We're coming, Eris, all right? Just hang on a little longer.

That was definitely Oksana, whose mental voice sounded decidedly strained. She and Snag seemed more aware than the others of the extent of Eris' highly weakened state. Or perhaps the other two were simply dealing with it in the way they knew best, namely through sarcasm and bitchiness.

Pain was sweeping through his body in horrible, sharp waves; growing worse the longer he remained conscious. He tried to shift himself to the right to ease the pull on his shattered arm… but no luck there. He was tied fast, and, if he were being honest, so weak he probably couldn't have moved anyway.

How the hell did the four idiots think they were going to get him out of here, anyway?

Snag growled at him across the link.

As plans went, *blind rage* left something to be desired, in Eris' opinion.

He squeezed his eyes shut against the light. He'd always hated winging it.

You didn't exactly leave us much choice, Xander observed. *Since you went off half-cocked without any sort of a back-up plan. Or any sort of original plan, from the looks of it.*

I had a plan, you ass, he managed. *It just happened to be one that failed. It happens, all right?*

He was honestly too worn down to feel much in the way of shame or embarrassment, which was probably just as well. The fact of the matter was, he'd been stupid. He'd underestimated the enemy, when the enemy was a demon who could rend souls and rain down chaos.

He'd acted rashly, and now he was reaping the consequences. It had been desperation to protect Trynn that had driven him straight into the arms of Kovac. The truly fucked-up part was, he'd probably do it again under the same circumstances.

Fog settled over his thoughts. He was vaguely aware of the mental voices jabbering at him, but he couldn't make out what any of them were saying over the fast beating of his heart and the sound of his labored breathing.

Maybe he'd finally be able to pass out again now.

Eris, no! Stay with us! Oksana commanded. The urgency in her voice jerked him out of his twilight state, and he moaned in displeasure.

We need you to show us where you are, Xander said. *What do you remember about your arrival?*

East of the city center, I think.

Not the most specific directions you could have offered, Duchess retorted, her irritation bleeding through the link.

Call to me. Snag's wordless command brooked no argument.

Eris sighed heavily, exhaustion pulling at him. *I'll try.*

Yet he found it hard to remain conscious with the tantalizing promise of painless sleep hovering over him like a cloud. He struggled against it, but his surroundings dimmed as warm darkness wrapped around his thoughts.

A savage mental blow buffeted his mind—an image of Bael wrapping sharp, bloody claws around Trynn forced itself in front of his mind's eye. He exploded into motion, struggling against the chains as a roar of rage tore free from his throat.

Fuck's sake, Snag, Xander cursed. *Are you trying to kill him? Eris? Best stay awake, mate, or I'm not sure we can keep him from doing that again.*

Adrenaline coursed through Eris, like fire burning through his sluggish veins. He yelled again in rage, but still could not free himself.

As his awareness sharpened and all thoughts of sleep were forcefully driven from his mind, Snag surged forward and melded their minds more fully than he had done in years. His awareness of the older vampire was so strong that he could actually see the world through Snag's eyes.

The group was circling over the ruins, drawn by his life force towards what looked to be an abandoned warehouse. Parts of the roof had caved in and almost every single window had been blown out. Streaks of sooty blackness caked along the roofline and above the windows told Eris that there had been a vicious fire in the building.

Snag's powerful nose was able to pick up the faint whiff of smoke and burned flesh. Eris recoiled at the smell, but Snag did not let him break the connection.

He swallowed against his rising gorge and focused his waning strength on a message of warning. *Undead nearby. Don't know how many.*

He felt Snag's acknowledgement as he and the others swirled downward.

As one, the four vampires streaked as mist through the closest of the blasted out windows and took human form in the corner of the warehouse. Standing back to back, they scanned the area with eyesight much more acute than a human's. Large containers and crates of supplies loomed in the darkness, creating a confusing labyrinth in the enormous building.

"Which way?" Oksana whispered, her voice so low that no human would be able to hear it.

Snag shut his eyes, cutting off Eris' telepathic view of his surroundings.

Instead, he felt Snag's mind expand with a cold, white light. The ancient vampire pressed outward, filling the entire space with his life force. Through it, Eris could sense the other vampires more fully.

He could tell that Oksana needed to feed on human blood. Her last meal had been Bon Bons, which she was now regretting in light of the coming battle.

Xander was fighting a vicious hangover—so in other words, he was perfectly normal.

Duchess was the picture of health and vitality.

An oily sensation with the stench of decay slid across Snag's awareness—a large group of undead soldiers about one hundred meters to their west. It seemed to both Snag and Eris that they were standing guard over something, possibly an entrance to the basement beneath the factory building.

Snag projected the impression to the others and gestured in the direction they needed to go.

Brilliant, Xander projected with false cheer. *This is going to be shed loads of fun, I can just tell.*

Eris gritted his teeth, frantically yanking his good arm against the ropes, hoping to free himself and help with the fight. It was useless, of course.

A cold sweat broke out over his body and bile rose in his throat as Eris sensed the group of vampires creep forward towards the unsuspecting undead. Snag's power pulsed through the building.

Bael's minions must have been completely mindless to not realize something powerful was approaching. But where was Kovac? Eris wriggled his less-injured wrist, which was now soaked with sweat. To his delight, he was finally able to drag his hand out of the loop of coarse rope wrapped around it.

He closed his eyes and sank fully into Snag's consciousness.

Snag was peering around a large metal container, looking at a light source he could make out through the damaged door.

"It looks like a lantern or small fire," Xander murmured under his breath.

"How many creeps are there?" Duchess asked, cool and unruffled as a spring morning.

Snag reached out and slid his consciousness over the undead in the other room. A few of them looked around in confusion at the sensation, but there was no sense of alarm. Clearly, the unfortunate creatures had been so thoroughly immersed in evil that they could no longer even recognize the presence of the Light.

Oksana was concentrating on the mental link. "Nine behind the door, which leads to a passage down to the basement—probably where they're holding Eris. There are more underground."

"Then let's get this party started," Xander answered, his eyes lit with green flame. His lips curled back, baring his fangs.

The four of them fanned out, approaching the door. Snag gave Xander a significant look, and the younger vampire moved forward, ready to burst through the door and lead the charge into the midst of the oblivious group of undead.

Just as his fingers were about to grip the handle, the door was pulled open from within. One of the undead stepped out, staring at the ground before bumping stupidly into Xander's chest.

"Well, hello there," Xander greeted as the thing's head snapped upward and its mouth fell open in shock.

Through Snag's eyes, Eris could see that its teeth were rotted and green. He smelled the pungent, suffocating stench filtering through the doorway.

Before he could even draw breath to yell for help, Xander slammed his knuckles into the zombie's face, its head flying backwards under the force of the punch.

The incapacitated foot soldier stumbled backwards and fell into the room, knocking over the lantern that was sitting in the middle of the floor.

Its fellows leapt to their feet with snarls of surprise and fury.

A vicious fight ensued. Although these undead were no more capable of independent thought than those the vampires had fought in New Orleans, they were clearly trained to fight, and battled relentlessly.

Several more poured out of the door before the vampires had a chance to respond. The new arrivals waded in, battling ferociously.

Duchess was locked in hand-to-hand combat with a man nearly twice her size, and although her centuries of experience at fighting kept her one step ahead of the monster, she was unable to finish him. Instead, she danced lightly in a circle, evading blow after blow aimed at her head.

Eris felt Snag draw his mental power into a hot ball in the center of his chest. Every time one of the undead approached him, he simply forced the creature back with a blast of his life force. The Light penetrated the Darkness inside the undead, making them stumble, recoil, and fall to the floor. Yet, with each burst of power, Snag weakened his own reserves.

Unfortunately, the others were faring about the same. Xander was wrestling with a man roughly the same size and strength he was, and, following Duchess' example, Oksana was using her light frame to evade, rather than deal a deathblow.

Snag snarled in impatience and sent another undead soldier flying backward.

"Doing the best we can here, mate," Xander gasped. His opponent had managed to get him in a headlock, and he wrestled to free himself.

Snag sprung forward and struck the zombie in the temple with his elbow, causing the creature to lurch away, stunned by the blow.

Xander gasped and clutched his throat, dragging air back into his lungs.

Snag pressed his hand against the zombie's head and forced sleep into its mind. The creature struggled for a moment, and then went completely limp as his animating force drained away into nothingness.

Oksana let out a cry of victory as she finally knocked her opponent backwards onto the floor with a burst of strength. The thing's chest was impaled on the sharp end of a broken metal pipe cemented into the ground. It shuddered once, and went limp.

Her victory was short-lived, however, as more of the undead leapt through the door, ready to take their fallen comrades' place in the battle.

"This is meant to delay us!" Xander called, and Eris felt Snag's agreement, echoed a moment later by Oksana and Duchess.

As one, they pulled their life force inward and dissolved into a swirl of mist that circled the group of bewildered undead and plunged through the open door. Experiencing the flight through Snag's senses made Eris feel sick and dizzy.

He pulled his mind back and opened his eyes, back in his own body. He could sense that Snag was close now. He'd managed to pull his right wrist free earlier, but the effort had cost him. He was too weak to do more than lie there and drag in one shallow, rasping breath after another as the bright light pointed at his face stabbed into his slitted eyelids.

Groaning, Eris fought the sudden urge to give up completely as he saw Bastian Kovac stride into the room, hatred etched in every feature.

"Oh, yes, I am aware that your little ragtag band of rescuers is close, but make no mistake, nightcrawler. You will not leave this place alive. I will not allow them to take my prize from me."

Hopelessness washed over Eris, and he had no strength to fight it. He could sense a huge, billowing darkness building within Kovac. Bael was coming to aid his servant, and Eris' poor judgment had drawn his friends into a trap.

Even if the others got to him, it seemed unlikely they would ever be able to fight their way back out.

There was only one small glimmer of hope. None of them had ever seen Snag's power fully unleashed. Eris knew him to be one of the strongest creatures in existence. Idly, he wondered if that power would stand against this bastion of the Dark.

Heh. Bastion… *Bastian*. The ridiculous thought suddenly seemed inappropriately amusing…

Eris jerked, realizing that his consciousness had started to slip away at the worst possible time. He could sense that Snag and the others were right outside the door. They were held up by another battalion of the undead, and struggling to repel the Dark force emanating from Kovac.

Finally, with a massive effort, the four vampires burst through the door at the far side of the cavernous room in which Eris was being held. Oksana slammed it behind her and turned the lock with a loud *click*.

The four vampires stood in the shadows facing Kovac, who stood in front of the metal table, blocking their access to Eris.

"You have made a grave mistake, coming here tonight," Kovac said darkly.

None of the vampires answered, but Snag took one step forward. As his foot touched the ground, the concrete under it buckled and cracked.

A shudder ran through the building. Dust fell onto Eris' face and he knew that the ceiling had been compromised somewhere above them.

Kovac had not moved a muscle as the concrete around them cracked and shifted. Completely impassive, he regarded the vampires who were slowly spreading out to surround him with a sneer. His attention caught and held on Snag.

Oksana took the opportunity to slip behind a pile of boxes, making her way closer to Eris on the table.

Tension filled the air as Snag and Kovac stared each other down. They were completely silent, but he could tell that Snag was straining against Eris' captor, grappling with him mentally, seeking to wound or to control.

While Kovac's attention was fully occupied, Oksana continued to skirt around the room in the darkness, making her way towards Eris' head.

Kovac whirled in place with no warning, a black cloud swirling out from around him and spreading in all directions. Everything that the cloud touched exploded or was hurled aside. Xander and Duchess flung themselves on the ground as the disk of darkness passed over their heads.

Oksana crouched behind the table on which Eris was being held and the dark force passed inches over their heads.

Snag had not moved, but as the darkness rushed towards him, he threw a hand up, palm out, and exhaled in a rush.

Light exploded from every part of his body, even brighter than the spotlight above Eris' head — blinding him with its intensity. The mushroom of light expanded toward Kovac, and the swirling darkness still pouring from him blasted apart as the two forces met.

Extreme heat filled the room and Eris felt Oksana's cool hands on his face.

"Let's get you out of here, *ti frere*," she whispered.

Eris blinked. Both Xander and Duchess had appeared at his side as well.

He twisted his head to better see the battle raging between Snag and Kovac.

Just when he thought that Kovac must surely fall under the intensity of the Light, Bael's servant raised his arms and a great wind picked up in the underground chamber.

Papers flew everywhere. Old crates skidded across the floor and crashed into one another. The wind became so intense that the vampires struggling to free Eris were forced to cling to the table to stop themselves from being hurled against the wall.

Eris could see Xander's mouth moving, but his words were lost in the deafening howl of sound that had filled the entire room. Snag's aura was receding, being pressed back into his body.

The ancient vampire was sliding backwards, his feet dragging across the crumbling floor as he struggled to remain upright. Finally, he swung his arm around, almost as if he were going to throw a right hook at Kovac. Fire exploded in a ring around Eris' tormenter. It raged higher and higher, consuming everything around him.

Despite his weakness and complete exhaustion, despite the fact that almost every ounce of his lifeblood had been drained from his body in the hours he had been held in this desolate bunker and tortured, Eris was overcome by a sense of awe at the sight.

Snag's power, his absolute fury, the waves of destruction that were pouring off of him should have annihilated anyone foolish enough to cross his path. Yet the battle between the two beings seemed even. Neither was able to deal a fatal blow; they were merely holding their own against each other.

The spectacle was so incredible that Eris momentarily forgot he should be trying to help free himself from the table.

Oksana's impatient voice brought him back to reality. "Eris, come on—help us out here. We've got to get you out of here."

"Wait," Xander said, going abruptly still. "Do you hear something?"

Over the crackling of power from Snag and Kovac, not to mention the sound of parts of the building collapsing under the force of the battle, the four vampires could make out the sounds of a dull, growing rumble.

"Earthquake?" Duchess suggested through gritted teeth. "Because, you know, that would be the *perfect* denouement to this day." She was tugging on the restraints at Eris' left wrist, finally freeing his fractured arm.

"No, I don't think so. I think…" Xander's voice trailed away. With a gasp of understanding, he began working more frantically, finding weak points in the leather and metal to pull against, exerting all of his considerable strength.

"We seriously need to get out of here," he said urgently.

"Why? What's happening?" Eris asked, his words slurring as his injured body protested the manhandling.

"It's about to get very crowded," Xander said unhelpfully.

Finally, with a snap of parting rope, Eris was free. Oksana and Xander tried to pull him to his feet, but he was too weak to stand. He crumpled backwards onto the table with a harsh cry.

This seemed to attract Snag's attention. He looked at the ceiling, taking in the growing rumble of approaching vehicles. Understanding flashed across his face.

Go! The mental command echoed across their mental connection with such force that Oksana, Duchess, and Xander knew better than to question him or argue.

They stepped backwards quickly and transformed into mist. Before Eris could draw breath, all three had vanished into the darkness.

"Your friends have abandoned you," Kovac taunted Snag. "Soon, my master will descend and crush you. But, before you die, Ancient One, I will make you watch as I consume this one's flesh, one slow strip at a time."

With a roar of fury, Snag threw himself forward. Eris watched in horror as he and Kovac were entangled in an ever-shifting web of Light and Dark. The power locking the two great beings together made the hair on Eris' head stand on end. The electricity in the air was so strong that sparks zapped Eris' skin where it made contact with the metal of the table. A buzzing whine grew louder and louder until it completely drowned out the roar of engines outside and the shouts of men coming their way.

For Eris, time slowed to a standstill. Everything was frozen except his eyes, which rolled weakly as he tried to focus on the battle. The web locking the two beings together pulsed with power, an angry, actinic glow. Eris' heart beat sluggishly, loud in his ears as he waited for something, *anything*, to happen.

A colossal noise ripped through the static-filled air, a combination of an explosion and the crack of a lightning strike. Indeed, a bolt of electricity flashed down between Snag and Kovac, throwing both of them in opposite directions as the web shattered. Kovac's body smashed backwards through the door, which was blown off its hinges under the impact. He crumpled in the hallway, insensible, glass and concrete raining down around him.

Snag staggered backwards toward the table, but he remained on his feet, victorious at last.

Men in black combat gear poured into the passage outside, shouting to each other in Russian. One pointed a Kalashnikov at Kovac's crumpled form and fired at least two-dozen rounds into him. Eris blinked rapidly, trying to clear the sweat and blood from his eyes. When he opened them again, he was staring down the barrels of several automatic weapons pointed at him.

In an instant, Snag was there, throwing his wiry body over Eris' as gunfire erupted around them in a deafening *rat-a-tat-tat*. The retorts and the echoes from the concrete walls mixed together, a tangled din that made Eris' head pound in agony.

At the same time, he felt his life force being pressed inward by a strength not his own, and both he and Snag dissolved into mist as the high-caliber bullets riddled the place where they had been.

Eris did not have enough power left to move or even hold this form, but Snag enveloped him, supporting him and pulling his insubstantial cloud of vapor through the building—now swarming with mafia foot soldiers. The pair burst into the open air, and Eris huddled further into Snag's protection as he became aware of the deadly sun slipping above the eastern horizon.

His body, even as mist, screamed in agony, protesting both the movement, and the terrible heat and light. Snag gathered him close and raced through the fickle morning shadows, fleeing for safety with no thought given to anything but speed.

Eris wanted, with every fiber of his being, to black out so he could finally escape the pain and slip into blissful nothingness, but it seemed that Snag's power was strong enough to not only transport him, but to also keep him tethered to life and consciousness.

The elder vampire seemed to be following some internal beacon as he wound expertly through bombed out, half-collapsed buildings.

Deep in the heart of the war-torn neighborhood, Eris could see a large structure that appeared to be mostly intact. At one time, it must have been some sort of government building or courthouse. The stone was cracked and burned, but still held strong. Most of the windows on the front were blown out, but Snag whisked Eris inside one of them and raced down a dark hallway towards the interior of the building, blessedly sheltered from the early morning light outside.

The smell of sweet wood smoke wafted through the air, coming from deeper inside the building. Eris felt Snag pressing his life force outward, materializing both of them into their human

forms. Eris landed on his feet but immediately collapsed, unable to stand. With inhuman reflexes,
Snag caught him before his body could hit the cold
floor.

Although Snag's physique was frail and seemingly fragile, he lowered Eris carefully to lie
propped against him, seemingly without effort.

His mental call echoed through the bond, making Eris' ears ring. He winced, but continued to lie
still in Snag's embrace, limp and spent. A door
nearby was thrown open and Oksana appeared,
looking chalky pale despite her dark complexion.

"How is he?" she asked, fear evident in her
melodic voice. "And you? Snag, you're burned."

Snag did not answer, but rose with Eris still in
his arms, carrying him as if he weighed nothing.
Eris' let his eyes slip closed, trying to resist the nausea clawing up his throat from the sudden change
in elevation.

He was lowered gently onto a pallet of dusty
couch cushions that had clearly been scavenged
from elsewhere in the building. It was covered with
old blankets scrounged from the rubble and one
small, faded pillow.

Eris gasped in distress as his broken bones
ground against each other. Once separated from
Snag's life force, he immediately started to drift
away into the darkness beckoning at the edges of
his mind.

Hazy voices passed back and forth above him,
discussing their next move. Eris could take no part
in the conversation. He was beyond the point of

caring. All he wanted was to slip into the quiet warmth of oblivion.

"He's far too weak to be moved," Duchess said, laying a hand on Eris' forehead. "I can barely feel his life force."

"He'll need to heal for days before we can return to Cyprus," Xander said from close by. "What do we think? Are we safe enough staying here?"

"We're a couple of kilometers away from the site of the battle," Duchess observed. "They could still find us fairly easily if they came looking… but will they bother?"

Snag shared the images from their last moments in the basement of the warehouse.

"Sustained automatic weapons fire will probably have destroyed most of the undead, or at least made it hard for them to travel any sort of distance. And the Russians have no reason to come looking for us. Why would they?" Oksana said. "Come on. We should build a bigger fire in the grate. We need to keep him warm while his body recuperates."

The others moved away and Eris continued to float, confused, just below the surface of consciousness. On some level, he understood their words, but it seemed to take a long time for his mind to catch up with what was being said.

Something brushed across his lips, leaving a salty, metallic smear behind.

Eris knew that he needed the offering of healing blood desperately, yet he could not make his jaw move or his throat swallow. He was too tired — *far* too tired — to think of feeding at the moment. All he wanted was to see Trynn one more time, and then…

You will feed.

The words were a command, implacable and unassailable. Skeletal fingers pried his jaw open with surprising gentleness. A moment later, blood dripped into his mouth and slid down his throat, even as his consciousness finally slipped away.

FIFTEEN

Trynn sat curled up on the couch in Eris' hotel suite, her laptop perched on the arm of the sofa. After a brief discussion back in Trynn's hotel room, Tré had decreed that the more defensible location on the seventh floor of the Merit Lefkosa hotel was worth the added risk of going back outside. Trynn agreed, and so did Della. It wouldn't take much for rioters to burst into her ground floor room at the no-name hotel in the bad part of town.

The trip back had been far more fraught than the trip out, but apparently the presence of two vampires was sufficient to intimidate the gangs of young men with bandanas pulled over their faces who were roaming the streets, breaking shop windows and setting fire to cars. She wasn't sure whether it was the eerie, glowing eyes, or whether the mind-whammy was in play. Either way, she wasn't complaining.

Trynn was sporting a fresh bruise on her temple where one of them had clipped her with a thrown bottle, but she'd also gained a new appreciation of the benefits of being a vampire when, an instant later, her assailant was being pinned against the nearest wall by five-foot-nothing of curvy Hollywood starlet. Della hissed up at him with bared fangs and gold eyes. The kid staggered off a few moments later looking docile and confused.

Back in Eris' hotel room, Trynn was burning holes through her laptop screen, following the constantly updating Twitter feed, hoping for some news from the Russians regarding the raid they planned against Kovac. She felt a huge sense of accomplishment, knowing that she had instigated the attack, but also a mounting sense of trepidation.

The worst part was, there was *nothing* online. Not one single word, since the initial flurry of Tweets when the news spread. Not a solitary mention of the events that had happened over the course of the past few hours.

The higher-ups must have ordered radio silence, Trynn thought.

With a huff, she set her chin in the palm of her hand, her eyes drifting out of focus. Dawn had risen and the morning passed without any word from the other vampires.

Tré had told her that his connection with Snag had been severed as the group approached Damascus.

"Why? What happened?" Trynn had demanded.

"It takes concentration to maintain that kind of connection over a great distance. My guess is Snag had other things to worry about besides keeping us in the loop on what's going on."

She'd known he was right, of course, but the hours of hearing nothing were wearing at her.

"I'm going to go mad at this rate!" Trynn exclaimed, straightening and shifting restlessly. "I have to know what's going on!"

"No news is good news," Tré said with that same infuriating calm. "If there'd been a detonation, we'd have heard about it by now."

He was right about that, too, damn him. There was no mention on the news, nor any intelligence coming in from MASQUE, that indicated an attack had occurred. They were stuck waiting, relying on some kind of contact from the others to tell them what was happening.

If they were still alive.

Feeling an overwhelming surge of exhaustion, Trynn tipped her head back against the couch and closed her eyes. What she wouldn't give for even one night of uninterrupted sleep. Looking back, she couldn't remember the last time she'd slept undisturbed. At least, not without having first been hypnotized by a skeletal creep who she was totally going to *strangle* if he didn't hurry up and *let them know what was going on.*

Della sat on the other end of the sofa, scanning through news channels on the huge, flat screen TV, trying to find any information that might give them a clue about what was occurring in Damascus. She clicked the remote so quickly that Trynn wondered if there was any way she could even see what was flashing across the screen before the channel was changed.

Tré, who sat at the desk staring unblinkingly at Eris' computer, had not moved or spoken in over an hour. Occasionally his finger would scroll down on the mouse he was holding, but otherwise he might as well have been made of stone.

Suddenly he inhaled sharply. Even though the sound was barely audible, Trynn jumped to her feet, nearly sending her computer crashing to the floor.

"What? What is it? What's happening?" she snapped.

Tré held up a hand for silence, and she thought she'd have a breakdown right there and then.

"It's over," Tré murmured eventually, his hand dropping back to the desk.

"The battle?" Trynn clarified.

"Yes."

"What about Eris? Are the others okay? What's going on? When are they coming back?" Trynn knew she was firing off questions without giving him a chance to answer, but she couldn't seem to stop herself.

Della stood and moved behind Tré, her hands closing on his shoulders. The picture made Trynn's heart—which already felt like it was lodged somewhere in her throat—ache with longing.

"Eris is badly injured," Tré answered in a faraway voice. His eyes were glowing with that eerie silver light.

"How badly?" Della whispered.

"Badly. Snag is trying to help him, but he was severely weakened in the battle, as well. Apparently it was pretty much a cluster—" His voice trailed away as his eyes flickered toward Trynn and away again. "Well, let's just say it wasn't the smoothest rescue mission ever conducted."

In her mind, Trynn recalled the agony that Snag had shared with her, the result of hours of torture that Eris had been subjected to. She swallowed hard, and made a decision.

Taking a deep breath, she squared her shoulders and lifted her chin. "I *have* to get to him now. I don't care how dangerous it is."

Tré opened his mouth—to argue, she was sure—but Trynn saw Della squeeze his shoulders.

He craned around to look up at her, his brow furrowed, and they communicated silently for a moment before Tré relented.

"I understand, Trynn," he said. "Just as *you* need to understand that Della and I have vowed to keep you safe. But... let me see what I can do."

Trynn nodded tightly and hugged herself, trying to stay calm while she waited for Tré to do whatever it was he was doing.

After a quick consultation with Della, he pulled out his phone and started placing calls. He seemed to be arguing with whoever was on the other end, trading sharp words in a Baltic language Trynn couldn't quite place.

"Don't worry," Della said, sitting next to her and curling a leg under herself like a contented cat. "I've been exactly where you are right now. We'll get you to him. I've never seen Tré fail yet."

Tré was apparently multi-tasking, because he paused in the sharp exchange long enough to cover the phone's speaker with his hand and quip, "Your lack of faith wounds me, *draga*. Failed *yet*, she says..."

In the end, his cockiness was not completely misplaced. All in all, it took Tré about an hour and a half to secure transportation to Damascus for them.

"We'll have to wait for nightfall," Tré told her when everything was settled. "I'm sorry, but there's no way around it if you want to arrive with living bodyguards at the end of the journey, rather than matching piles of ashes."

Trynn shivered. Almost two days had passed, and Eris had been the prisoner of a vicious sadist for much of that time. Had he suffered the effects of the sun's rays? She let out a growl of frustration at the idea of waiting, and pressed her fingers against her temples.

"You should try to get some rest," Della suggested. "No offense, sweetheart, but you look like hell."

"Fine," she replied in clipped tones, and more or less stormed off to the bathroom.

Trynn couldn't really argue with Della's blunt assessment as she gazed at her reflection in the bathroom mirror. Dark circles were smeared beneath her eyes like smudged mascara. She looked raw and edgy, as if she were on the verge of crawling out of her own skin.

After cleaning up, Trynn collapsed face down onto the bed. Maybe she'd overestimated her own endurance, because she immediately fell into a deep, blessedly dreamless sleep.

What seemed like seconds later, Della was shaking her insistently awake.

"Come on, Trynn, you need to get up. We've got a flight to catch. *Trynn*."

Della obviously wasn't taking no for an answer, and Trynn tried to reboot her groggy brain. "Huh?" she asked, sitting up suddenly and pulling her arm away.

"We need to leave," Della said, slowly and clearly. "We have a flight to catch."

That brought everything back in a rush.

"Shit!" Trynn immediately sprang from the bed, straightening her rumpled, borrowed shirt and rummaging around for her things. "I'm up. How long have I been asleep?"

"Hours," Della answered with a shrug. "You were really out of it; I could barely wake you. I don't doubt you needed it, but now we have to move."

Trynn tossed all of her scattered possessions into the duffle bag she had brought from her own hotel room. When she had everything—and there wasn't much, really—she threw the bag over her shoulder. "I'm ready. Let's go."

Tré and Della had clearly not been idle while she slept. All of Eris' and Snag's belongings had been packed and were now waiting by the door.

To her relief, she realized that they would not be returning. That suited her fine. She didn't know how much more of being solicitously guarded and confined to this room she could stand. It might have been gilded, but it still felt like a cage.

Della hailed a cab, and the three of them rode through the restless streets of Nicosia. Trynn was more than a little shocked to see the extent of the damage in parts of the city. The fires had damaged or destroyed whole blocks, and many of the roads were impassable.

Eventually, they made it out and into the sub-urbs beyond. Their destination, it turned out, was a small, private airstrip just north of the city.

"How did you manage this, anyway?" Trynn wondered aloud as they pulled up to the small fa-cility.

"Persuasion," Tré retorted in a dark voice.

"And by *persuasion*, he means *money*," Della added wryly.

Trynn peered at them in the dim light of the cab's dashboard. "So you're rich, then?"

"Long-term investments become simpler given our… unusual circumstances," Tré said, still grim. "But no one said I used my own money. Actually, I used Eris'. It only seems fair under the circum-stances, and I daresay he can spare it."

She'd known, intellectually, that Eris was well off. That much was obvious from the hotel room and his own thoughtless, casual elegance. Plus… *art thief*. So maybe it shouldn't have come as a sur-prise. She just hadn't quite made the connection between *staying at the Merit Lefkosa* kind of money, and *chartered flights from a private airfield on short notice* kind of money.

Movement caught her attention through the back window, and she tensed as a private security team approached the car on foot, guns drawn. Their cabbie began making frightened spluttering noises and put his hands in the air.

"Our apologies, my friend. Please relax—you're in no danger," Tré assured the man. Trynn wondered if there was a bit of vampiric suggestion behind the words, because the cabbie seemed to grow very relaxed, very quickly under the circumstances.

Handy, she thought, *as long as it's not being aimed at me.*

Tré stepped out of the vehicle with his hands raised at shoulder height in a token of non-aggression.

"Peace, my friends," he said in the same arresting tone of voice.

To Trynn's astonishment, the men, who had been walking towards them quickly and with purpose, slowed. Their steps faltered and they stumbled to a stop, standing under the glow of a streetlight and looking vacantly at Tré.

"Who are they? And what did he do to them?" Trynn whispered to Della as they pulled their bags from the trunk of the car.

"I imagine they're airfield security, and were coming over to check our documentation," Della said, keeping an eye on the men but not seeming overly concerned. "He just temporarily stunned them. They'll be perfectly fine in a little bit."

Trynn nodded knowingly. "Ah. The mind-whammy. Right."

Della let out a bark of surprised laughter, and quickly covered her mouth with one hand. "Oh my god," she said from behind her muffling fingers. "You call it that, too? You should have seen the look Tré gave me the first time I said it…"

Luggage in hand, they walked around a low building to where Trynn could hear the sounds of a helicopter's engines starting up. The unmistakable *thwack thwack thwack* carried across the small airfield.

Within moments, they were approaching the nervous-looking man standing just outside of the zone of turbulence created by the chopper's blades.

"You have the cash?" he demanded in a low voice, throwing a look over his shoulder as though he expected someone to be spying on them.

Tré pulled out a thick wad of Euros folded into a money clip, and held it up for the man to see. Immediately, the pilot's hand snaked out and grabbed it, flicking through it to make sure that he was not being shorted.

"It's all there. Let's get moving—we have a long journey ahead of us." Tré seemed mildly irritated by the delay as the man rubbed one of the bills between his fingers as if to ensure it wasn't counterfeit... though he hadn't batted an eye at the outrageous cost of the flight.

"Yes, yes, let's go," the man said in a heavy Greek accent as he turned towards the chopper.

Trynn followed the others to the sleek aircraft, keeping her head ducked to minimize the turbulence from the spinning blades. Having never been on a helicopter, she didn't know exactly what to expect. She found a headset with earphones and a mic sitting on a seat across from Della and Tré, so she picked it up and slid into the seat, adjusting it over her ears.

"Buckle up," the pilot's voice barked over the radio, and she hastened to obey.

All in all, the flight itself wasn't too bad. The takeoff off made her stomach drop uncomfortably, but the rest of the time they simply hurtled through the dark night towards their goal across the narrow stretch of sea.

It was a testament to how exhausted she was that she dozed off halfway through the flight, only to jerk awake when a hand fell on her arm.

"The pilot says that the place where we need to go is too badly bombed out for him to land and take off," Tré told her. "He's going to land in a vacant area close to the airport, so we can avoid having to answer awkward questions. We should be able to find someone willing to rent us a car from there, though we may also have to travel some distance on foot. Snag indicated that the roads around the building where they're staying are blocked by rubble."

Trynn nodded, but did not speak.

She wondered how much Tré had told the pilot about their journey, and guessed that the man actually knew very little, other than their destination.

Behold, the power of large wads of cash.

By the time they touched down in Damascus, Trynn was beginning to feel a jittery sense of anticipation. She needed to see Eris with her own two eyes before she would believe that he was still alive. She *needed* to, like she needed air and water and food.

"Della," she whispered as they stood waiting for Tré to finish haggling with a man about the price to rent his battered four-door Skoda. The pilot had taken off practically the instant they'd disembarked and moved out of the landing zone, which made Trynn wonder what threats or coercion Tré had used to get him to take the job in the first place.

"Yes?" Della replied.

Trynn swallowed. "Did you ever question whether or not you really were one of these...*fated mates* of a vampire?"

"There were times that I did, at first," Della recalled. "The whole story was so crazy and out-there that it seemed insane."

"I hear you on that," Trynn muttered.

Della snorted, then grew thoughtful. "And yet... I had these dreams. It's like my heart was saying *yes*, but my mind just couldn't accept the reality. It's a tough place to be, especially since I didn't really believe in the paranormal beforehand. But... the more I was involved with Tré, the more distant those doubts became."

"Really?" Trynn's voice was wistful as she thought about how little time she'd truly had with Eris, to try and figure things out.

"Yes, really. It will be the same for you, I'm sure of it. You and Eris have barely begun getting to know each other again. Soon, you'll be sharing memories, and when you're together you'll realize that you've just been half a person without him."

Trynn raised her eyebrows at the flowery proclamation, unable to help herself. She'd just never been a hearts-and-flowers kind of girl.

"Don't look at me like that," Della chided. "I'm serious! You'll see. You'll be amazed what you find once you have a chance to truly be alone together and talk."

"Maybe," Trynn replied evasively. "Honestly, I think I'm still in shock."

The driver stopped arguing with Tré and reluctantly handed over the keys just as Della leaned closer, bumping shoulders with her.

"Yeah, that's pretty normal," she said. "If there even is a *normal* for this situation. It's a lot to take in all at once."

"I don't think I'll ever get used to it," Trynn admitted as Tré took the keys and handed over another, smaller wad of cash.

"Of course you will," Della retorted. "I feel now like I was always meant for this life. Kind of like I spent all those years as a mortal hurtling forward towards the moment when I met Tré and then was made a vampire a few short days later."

Trynn had been trying really hard not to think about the *being turned into a vampire* part, but—

"Did it... hurt?"

Della didn't answer for a moment, but dropped their small bags into the trunk of the car before sliding into the front seat next to Tré. Trynn got in behind her and sat in the back, staring out of the window at the lights of Damascus.

It seemed like a very long time before Della answered.

"It did," she admitted. "It was physically and psychically painful, it's true... but I don't really remember it."

"You don't?"

"No, not really. It faded in the face of what came after. Trust me… the joy and all the amazing feelings of being with the one you were meant for more than make up for it. *That's* what I remember."

They fell into silence, each consumed by their own thoughts. Trynn was assailed by a sudden image of Eris screaming in the moonlight, flailing in the sand, his fingers curled toward her like claws.

She caught her breath, her heart beating faster. The memory was startling, especially since Trynn didn't know where it came from or how it got into her head.

"Do you know exactly how Eris was turned?" Trynn asked, breathless.

"No, we weren't there," Tré answered. "Except for Snag, Eris is the oldest of any of us, by quite a stretch."

"*You* were the only one that was there," Della reminded Trynn. "In a manner of speaking, anyway."

Even though neither of the vampires in the front seat could see her, Trynn nodded, trying to follow the memory further.

There was a confusing rush of sounds and darkness. Even in these odd dream-memories, Trynn could feel a pounding sensation in the back of her head that made her think she'd either been struck by something, or had fallen to the ground and hit her head.

Trynn could remember stumbling blindly into the swirling darkness, choking on the horrible stench that filled her nostrils. She'd fought her way towards Eris, feeling as if she were battling a cloud of stinging insects that scrabbled against her exposed skin.

Screaming filled Trynn's ears and with a rush of surprise, she realized that it was her own voice raised high, shrieking to the heavens. The dark cloud solidified around Eris, making an impenetrable barrier that kept them apart. Trynn flung her body forward over and over again, unable to get through and reach her beloved.

Refusing to give up, she lunged forward the final fraction, and was able to touch him.

"Trynn?" Della's voice broke through the memories in which she had become lost. "You still with us, there?"

She blinked. "What? Uh... yeah. Sorry. I... think I'm starting to remember more details about the night Phaidra died, is all."

Saying it matter-of-factly like that helped Trynn feel more in control, despite her fluttering heart and the clammy sweat breaking out on her skin. It felt like she could bring it into reach and understand it better if she owned it, rather than hiding from her past.

Della only nodded, a sad smile pulling at one corner of her full lips before the expression collapsed into sympathy

"How much further?" Trynn asked, trying to focus on the present.

"I don't really know," Tré answered. "Though we're definitely going to have to walk to our final destination."

"Then we'll walk," Trynn replied, brooking no argument. She was not going to let a little rough terrain stop her from reaching Eris tonight.

About an hour later, Trynn, Tré, and Della reached the end of the road. Quite literally, in fact. There was a makeshift roadblock in front of them, illuminated by the headlights. Behind the roadblock the pavement appeared to be gone, leaving only a pile of twisted rubble.

"I think this is our best bet," Tré murmured, getting out of the car. "They're directly ahead of us, and I doubt we'll get any closer via a different road."

Della and Trynn got out without a word and grabbed their bags from the trunk of the car. Tré hefted the bag containing Eris and Snag's belongings and peered into the darkness before them.

"This could be a rough journey," he warned. "Especially with human levels of night vision."

"It's fine," Trynn said. "Let's go." She couldn't understand why they were standing around talking when they could be making their way towards Eris. When the two vampires started their trek, she hurried ahead, clambering over large embankments of concrete that had been ripped up.

After reaching the top of a portion of the street that had buckled around a bomb crater, Trynn looked down into the pitch black hole beneath her. The lights from the occupied part of the city no longer reached this far, and the rest of their path was cast into shadow.

"I should've brought a headlamp or something," Trynn muttered as Della and Tré joined her at the top.

They peered towards the bottom and Trynn wondered if their superior eyesight could see through the darkness.

"That would've made things easier," Tré agreed. "But on the positive side, I don't believe there are any of the undead around."

"*Undead*?" Trynn echoed. "Jesus Christ. Do I even want to know?"

Della sounded distinctly uncomfortable when she replied, "Yeah, you probably don't. Think zombies with attitude and you're not far off."

Okay, then. Frankly, Trynn's brain was operating just about at capacity at the moment, so she decided maybe she'd just pretend she hadn't heard that particular nugget of horror.

"Can you see the bottom?" she asked instead.

Tré squinted downward. "Mostly. It's very dark back here, but I think that the drop will be onto concrete, just like how we climbed up here."

She nodded. "Okay, I guess I'll try to slide down on my feet."

Tré made a noise of protest. "Or you could let me go first, so there's someone to catch you if you fall."

"This is really no time to get into a feminist debate with you, but you can go first if you want," Trynn said between clenched teeth. "As long as *someone* goes."

Tré stepped over the edge and slid down into the darkness with a controlled grace that did nothing for Trynn's irritation.

A moment later the scraping noise stopped and Tré called up to them, "It's not too bad. You should be able to make it down if you're careful."

"Arrogant son of a..." Trynn muttered, hopefully too low to be overheard. She and Della followed him down one at a time. Trynn got a small spot of road-rash on the palm of her hand, but was otherwise unhurt.

They walked onward, Trynn stumbling repeatedly in the dark despite the weak light of her cell phone's flashlight app. She really hoped that Tré or Della had some sense of where the hell they were going, because she was hopelessly lost in the twists and turns they took to avoid significant damage and debris in the road.

Finally, Tré pointed to a dark silhouette in the distance. There was no light visible from within, only a denser darkness that told Trynn they were approaching a large structure. It took them another good half hour to get to it, but finally they reached a relatively undamaged stretch of pavement in front of the place.

"Looks like it used to be a government building of some kind," Della murmured, staring through the gloom. Evidently, vampire eyesight was, in fact, strong enough to pierce the darkness.

"Xander says we're going to have to reach a second story window to get inside." Tré said.

"Great, climbing up a building in the pitch dark," Trynn grumbled. "What could *possibly* go wrong? Why can't we just go in the front door? Or the back door? Or the *side* door?"

"Everything is boarded shut," called a voice from high above them.

"Duchess!" Della called back. "It's good to see you!"

"Snag thought you might need a little help getting into the building, so he had me hunt down some rope," said the other vampire, the hint of a French accent coloring her words.

"Brilliant!" Della exclaimed. "I wasn't sure if we were going to have to make Trynn scale the side of a building or not."

"Will you be able to climb up to the second story with a rope?" Tré asked her.

From the window above, something was tossed and landed on the ground with a dull *flump*.

"I guess we're about to find out," Trynn said skeptically.

"We'll carry your luggage," Della offered.

"Any chance you could carry me?" she countered.

"Unfortunately, Snag is the only one of us strong enough to fly with a human," Tré said. "And I'm afraid he's otherwise engaged at the moment, tending to Eris."

Trynn felt her way forward and tested the strength of the rope. She could tell that it was tied fast to something solid. Examining the wall of the building, she found that the stone was not smooth, but had uneven edges and recesses where she could place her hands and feet.

In the end, the task was done—though she hoped never to have to repeat it. Trynn used the rope to pull herself up over parts of the wall that she could not scale without assistance. Della stood below her calling up encouragement, while Tré hovered nearby in case she fell.

After pulling herself clumsily through the window and toppling onto the floor, Trynn heard a rush of sound and found that Della, Tré, and their luggage were standing next to her as she pulled herself to her feet.

"That's a handy parlor trick," she grumbled, trying to dust herself off.

"Come on, this way," Duchess insisted, sounding impatient with her griping. She led them swiftly down a dim passage. The moon emerged from behind the clouds, a faint glow reflecting through the smashed windows on the west-facing side of the building. According to her phone, it was nearly dawn, and Trynn knew they needed to remain under shelter for the vampires' sakes.

Duchess stopped before a closed door. Flickering light crept out from the gap underneath. Glancing back towards Trynn curiously, she pushed it open and led the way inside, closely followed by the other three.

Trynn pushed her way forward, and her eyes fell on a horrible scene. On a pallet of soft blankets and cushions, Trynn could see Eris. His face was bruised, swollen, and bloody. He seemed to barely be conscious, stirring fretfully under the threadbare blanket covering him. He moaned unhappily as Snag pressed a bony wrist to his mouth, and tried to turn his head away.

The dark-skinned woman was crouched on his other side, running a soothing hand through his hair. "Come on, Eris, you need to feed again. Please."

"Oh, Eris..." Della said, her voice fading away.

Trynn walked forward on numb legs, anger and shock welling up inside her.

Why would anyone do this to him? Surely, not because of me?

She couldn't voice the thoughts aloud, but Snag, who seemed to have been listening, turned towards her with rheumy, sunken eyes. He looked exhausted and even paler than usual. Blisters and angry red marks peppered his exposed skin.

"*Snag*," Tré said. "When was the last time you fed?"

The ancient vampire didn't answer. He merely turned his gaze back towards Eris.

"You can't feed him alone," Tré insisted. "Not when you're this weak. Let one of us take over for a while."

His voice seemed to startle Eris, who jerked and turned his head towards the door. Through the slit in his swollen eyes, Trynn could see the glitter of his dark gaze, staring straight at her.

"Trynn," he whispered, his voice cracking.

Her name was all it took. Restraint breaking, Trynn ran forward and threw herself at Eris, who didn't even raise his arms. She collapsed against his chest, crying silently, her fingers hovering over his injured face, afraid to even stroke him. His breath rasped beneath her cheek after the strain of speaking. After a few moments, he took a deep breath and exhaled slowly.

After a long moment, Trynn sat up and looked around, though she still leaned over Eris protectively. "What's going on? What did you mean, Tré? Shouldn't we try to get him to a hospital?"

"A hospital can't help him. That's the last place an injured vampire should go," Tré said. "Eris needs to feed from another vampire. By sharing their blood and life force, he'll be able to heal himself. There's only one problem."

"Which is what?" Trynn demanded, looking around the room at the others. If that was what he needed, why were they all standing around? Why had it looked like Eris was trying to refuse Snag's blood when they first entered?

"Snag is insisting that he has the strongest life force and therefore he should be the one to feed Eris—" Tré explained.

"Okay," Trynn interrupted.

"—but Snag is severely weakened. He's just battled one of the most powerful beings we've ever come across, and hasn't given himself time to feed and recuperate."

"Not only that," the pretty black vampire added, "but he won't even feed from one of us to replenish his strength."

"It's fine," Eris choked out, his voice slurring. "I'm fine."

Some of the anger that Trynn had been holding inside for days snapped and started pouring out of her. "No, you're not *fine*! Have you looked in a mirror recently, Eris? Because it's not a pretty sight! Goddamnit, how could you possibly think of running off like that? Tré told you to wait. *Snag* told you to wait, but you just had to go and take matters into your own hands!"

"I had…to keep you…safe," Eris whispered. It sounded as if every word cost him a great effort.

"How did this keep me safe? Besides, I didn't *need* to be safe," Trynn shot back, tears springing to her eyes again. "I needed *you*, to help me figure out this craziness! Just you!"

Before she could stop them, sobs choked their way from her throat, despite her efforts to hold them back. "How c-could you even th-think of l-leaving me?"

Eris' eyes slipped closed—as if he could not bear to see Trynn's tears.

"I'm sorry," he whispered. "I realize now that I played right into Kovac's hands."

"*You think*?" Trynn fired back angrily, trying in vain to wipe her streaming eyes and nose.

"Can you forgive me for being so pig-headed?"

Trynn looked at him and found that his swollen eyes were staring unblinkingly at her. It was unnerving, seeing him like this—his face was so damaged that he was not immediately recognizable as the devilishly handsome man who left the hotel a few days previously.

She wanted to stay angry with him. She wanted that rather desperately, in fact. But, try as she might, she couldn't do it. She knew he'd just been doing what he thought would help stop something terrible from happening. He'd been playing the hero, yes—but only to keep her safe. Her, and the untold thousands of other people who might have become Kovac's victims.

"I forgive you, you bastard," she whispered. "Just don't ever fucking do it again, all right?"

Eris seemed to slump in relief. "Good," he breathed.

She could feel him weakening under her hands. His body sank into the makeshift bed of cushions, and his breathing grew sluggish. There was no time. He needed help, and the one trying to give it was in no condition to help anyone right now.

Trynn wasn't quite sure what game the old vampire was playing by refusing to feed from any of the others, but she had an inkling—there was an obvious solution that no one had broached yet. The consequences for her were life changing… but Trynn had already spent half a lifetime leaping before she looked. Why should now be any different?

"Snag?" Trynn asked, seriousness etched in every word. "Could you feed from me?"

He didn't respond, she had not expected him to. Instead, she turned towards Della and Tré, the look on her face stubborn and set. She stood up and folded her arms, ready to take on any challenge.

"He could," Tré finally answered. "But, to my knowledge, Snag hasn't fed from anyone but Eris in centuries. He doesn't hunt humans."

Surprise threaded through her haze of worry. She looked at the old vampire and saw him in a new light. Good god, no wonder he and Eris were so close. She took a deep breath.

"You wouldn't be hunting me. I'm offering. Eris and I are bound together somehow. Whatever bond you have with him that makes you willing to drink his blood extends to me, too. You can feed from me to restore your strength, so you can help Eris. I'm asking you to turn me, Snag," Trynn told him.

Blank shock followed her words and no one in the room spoke for a moment.

"Don't you want to think about that for a minute before—" the man called Xander began.

Trynn didn't let him finish his question. "No."

"Trynn, this is a really big—" Della started.

Trynn turned and gazed at her new friend, her expression hard and determined. "No. This is right. I can feel it in my bones. This is what I need to do. I am where I've always been meant to be."

She looked down at Eris. "By his side."

No one spoke or dared argue with her.

The tense atmosphere in the room had roused Eris back to consciousness, it seemed.

"Ph-Phaidra? Are you sure?" he asked, his voice wavering. "Are you completely sure?"

Trynn slid her fingers through his tangled hair. "My name is Trynn. And I'm more sure than I've been about anything in my life. Eris…"

Her voice trailed away, and her eyes moved to the vampires scattered around the dark room. They were all regarding her solemnly as she spoke.

"The seven of you are fighting the most evil being on this planet. This war… this *horrible* war will continue to tear people apart and destroy all the good that we've been trying to build in the world. Humanity will be consumed unless we do something to stop it."

She turned back to Eris. "I may not truly understand it, but I'm connected to you. That makes me part of this battle, whether we like it or not. I didn't ask for this, but I'm in it now, and I'm not going to hide in the shadows and wait for this *evil* to snap me up."

Eris looked up at her, anguished. It was clear that he was undergoing some painful internal struggle.

"Eris," she said, forestalling his words, "I know. I get it. You don't want to see me turned. It's all right, though. I love you. I am in love with you and I want to be together for all eternity. I think... maybe... this is fate."

He searched her eyes. They stared at one another for a long moment, but Trynn did not break the silence.

Finally, he said, "I could never refuse you anything. Never."

His voice was feeble, as though the decision had taken every last ounce of his strength.

Despite Trynn's assurance that she had no second thoughts, sudden nervousness crept over her as she turned her eyes towards Snag.

How did vampires feed from humans? Della had warned her it would hurt…

The only point of reference she had to go on were old movies she'd watched as a kid. In each of those films, a tall, dark figure had trapped a helpless, screaming woman in an alley or abandoned house and sunk his fangs deep into her throat.

Still kneeling on the ground, Trynn turned to face Snag. He was looking at her with keen interest, as if he had never seen anything like her in his long life.

With careful movements, Trynn dragged her shirt away from her neck. She turned her head so that soft skin was exposed and she shut her eyes. She might have made her decision, but she didn't really want to watch it happen.

Somebody in the room made a faint, strangled noise, but she didn't open her eyes to investigate the source. A soft swish of movement told her that Snag had lowered himself to his knees in front of her. A rush of adrenaline flooded her body, trying to throw her into fight-or-flight mode. She breathed through it, her heart pounding like a drum.

It was going to happen any second now. She was going to become a vampire.

An icy hand touched her arm, making her jump. Her eyes flew open and she looked around, despite herself. Snag was indeed kneeling, but well back from her, having to lean forward to touch her arm.

She watched as he cradled her wrist in his hands and raised her arm towards his mouth. Their eyes remained locked on one another the entire time, as if Snag was testing her resolve. She stared back without blinking. Could he see her fear? Sense the way she was frozen under his gaze like an un-lucky mouse before a cobra? He paused, his head tilting to one side.

Trynn let out a shaky breath and inhaled again, hoping that the pain would be minimal but having nothing with which to compare it. *Do it*, she urged, knowing that he'd be able to hear her if he was listening.

She felt Eris' hand slip into her free one. She could only imagine the effort it cost him as he tangled their fingers together and squeezed.

Snag's lips touched the inside of her wrist, and a shiver ran up her spine. In some ways, it was a shockingly intimate sensation, and a red flush of embarrassment crept up her neck. Suddenly, she was very glad he'd ignored her neck when she offered it. His lips drew back, and Trynn saw his brilliantly white fangs press against the smooth part of her skin.

She only had an instant to notice that one of them was crooked—*snaggle-toothed, oh, I get it now*—before a flash of movement and a spurt of red, red blood made her gasp. Snag's fangs sunk deep into her arm. It was surprisingly painless. He shuddered, his eyes slipping closed, and began to drink.

Oh. This isn't so bad, I guess, Trynn thought, as the world around her grew increasingly hazy and distant. She could feel him drawing blood out of the vein in her wrist. She could see the stain of red coloring his lips.

Warmth crept through her, and sleep played at the edges of her mind, making everything drift. Trynn fought to keep herself from sinking into slumber. *Why was it getting so hot in here?*

The prickly sensation of heat increased, and sweat broke out across Trynn's forehead. She frowned, her eyes wandering aimlessly around the room. The other vampires stood, resolute, watching Snag drain her blood. Trynn's eyes moved back towards Snag, and she opened her mouth to say something. Was it supposed to feel like this? Had he taken enough blood yet?

Before she could, the smoldering heat flared, igniting her flesh from the inside out. She was on fire, burning up, consumed by invisible flames. A searing pain wrenched her chest as her soul started to pull apart at the seams.

"What's happening?" Trynn cried, consumed by agony. The vampires looked on with expressions of empathy, but no one spoke.

Her balance deserted her, and she collapsed sideways onto the floor near Eris' bed, rolling onto her back and shaking like a seizure victim. Dimly, Trynn was aware that Eris rolled onto his side to face her, groaning with the effort of doing so. He reached out and stroked her hair off her sweaty forehead, shaking nearly as badly as she was. He murmured words of comfort that Trynn could not understand.

The tearing sensation grew exponentially, and blackness flooded her mind. The void expanded, bringing ice and Darkness where there was once life and Light. Yet, the Light had not vanished. Not completely. Trynn could sense it, pulsing angrily near her heart, where it had been ripped free and tossed aside.

She screamed at the sensation, terrible shrieks that scraped her throat raw and stabbed like tiny knives at her lungs. As she thrashed, Trynn felt a cold, bony hand clutching at her shoulder, restraining her flailing body. Someone was trying to calm her, pressing peace into her mind from an outside source—the sensation causing a harsh dissonance when it touched the horror of her rent soul.

Tears streaming down her face, Trynn's grip on the world started to slip away.

"Hold on, Trynn. I will if you will," Eris whispered in her ear. "I'll see you on the other side."

With one last whimper, Trynn surrendered herself to the darkness.

-o-o-o-

It was odd, hearing the sound of waves. Damascus was a dry place, wasn't it?

But, no. She could hear the ocean. She could smell it—a salty tang in the air. Where was she?

She opened her eyes and found herself standing in darkness, the pale light of the moon splashed across her face like wan silver mist. She brushed sand away from her hands and arms. Had she been lying on the beach? The grains clung to her legs as well.

Salt water teased her feet and ankles, white foam clinging to her skin as the tide ebbed and flowed around her. The sea breeze lifted her hair off her neck and filled her nose with the smell of salt.

"Come dance with me," a voice whispered in her ear.

She looked to her right and saw Eris standing beside her in the darkness, the light of the moon reflecting in his merry eyes.

Giddiness stole over her and she laughed, smiling up at him. "Of course, my love."

Eris pulled her into his arms and led her in a rollicking dance, twirling her around and around until she shrieked with glee, dizzy and flushed. When he put her down, she stretched up to kiss him, grinning against his lips.

With a mischievous smile, she grabbed his hand and dragged him back into the surf with her, the two of them laughing as they crashed through the waves. Her long dress floated up around her legs, as soft as silk against her skin.

"This is our victory!" Eris proclaimed to the heavens. He threw his arms wide, sweeping them towards the small town situated at the ocean's edge. The hearth fires burning inside the huts and cottages were visible through the darkness, promising warmth and light. "Now that the shipping deal with Flavian is sealed, this island will be our kingdom! We'll never want for anything. We'll never have to steal and scrounge and hide in the shadows again!"

She framed his face with her hands. "You will be my King, and I, your Queen."

"Nothing can stop us from having the life we always wanted, Phaidra," Eris declared, covering her hands with his as he laughed, clear and happy. "Not now."

His simple, toga-like chiton was soaked from their dip in the ocean, and his hair dripped from the spray.

Phaidra smiled, happier than she'd ever been in her life, and pressed her lips against his... just as the wind around them changed.

Pulling away, she shivered and looked around in confusion as a cold breeze wafted over her damp skin. Shaking off a brief flutter of unease, she smiled again. "Come out of the water, my love — the evening is growing chill. Help me find some seashells! I'll make us two necklaces so we might remember this night always."

Eris beamed at her and lifted her slight frame into his arms, spinning her around in a circle as he had done earlier. "Anything for you, my sweet."

He bent and kissed her neck before setting her on her feet and leading the way back up the beach. They gathered all the shells they could find. Phaidra tucked them in the folds of her toga, where they clinked together when she walked.

As they searched, they spoke of their newly acquired wealth in reverent tones. Thieves they might have been once, but now their quest to become honest traders had finally reached fruition. With the Roman shipping contract in place, they would soon have enough money to purchase all the land around them. Eventually, they would control this entire part of the coastline.

The chilly breeze grew positively frigid. Phaidra straightened and looked around in alarm.

"Is a storm coming?" she asked, turning towards Eris.

Eris checked the sky, his eyes drifting out over the darkened ocean. "No... there are no clouds on the horizon, only millions of brilliant stars."

A gust of wind nearly knocked Phaidra off her feet. She staggered into Eris' arms. They turned towards the town of Lapethos, only to find that the flicker of fires they had been able to see earlier had disappeared. A dense, clammy fog was descending on them as they crowded together.

"I don't like this," Phaidra whispered, feeling fear climb up her throat. "This is no natural wind. It's the work of the gods; it must be."

An explosion of sound echoed around them. The two lovers clutched their ears and fell onto their knees. Phaidra screamed—she could no longer see the sky, the moon, or even the vast expanse of the ocean. She was lost in the black fog, and her grip on Eris' strong arm was the only thing holding her to reality.

"No!" Eris shouted, pressing her behind his solid form. *"No!* Begone, demon!"

"What?" Phaidra asked, confused. She could see nothing but impenetrable blackness.

Suddenly, a deep, cruel laugh reverberated around them. It was so powerful that it seemed to shake the foundations of the earth itself, making the sand swirl and shift beneath her. She sank as if into mud, until her hands and legs became trapped in the quaking surface beneath her.

"You have grown powerful, little mortal." The disembodied voice rolled around them like thunder. *"For that, you will now pay the price. You have become…* useful *to me, and now I will turn you into my creature."*

Phaidra stared at Eris, who gazed upward with a look of horror on his face.

"Your soul is mine," the voice continued. *"I will rend and devour it, until your flesh is nothing but an empty shell, ready to be filled up with my will. You will be consummated by my evil."*

Even as he gasped for air in the smothering cloud of darkness, Eris straightened his spine in defiance, though his hand on her arm was trembling. "My soul is not yours to take! It belongs to another. It is for her and her alone that I sought power and wealth. I will not serve you, filth!"

The evil laughter echoed around them once more. Sudden agony burned Phaidra's skin, as if the black mist had turned to vitriol. She screamed, jerking violently in an attempt to get away.

The mist receded, the pain disappearing as quickly as it had come. With shaking arms, Phaidra managed to pull herself free of the sucking sand, which had grown still now that the demon appeared to have focused its attention on Eris.

Eris! She looked to her left and saw the dense darkness swirling around him. She could just make out the outline of his body, lying face up in the sand. His back arched in torment, yet he made no sound. The beach had gone completely silent, as if the heavens themselves paused to listen.

"*Eris, no,*" Phaidra whispered, petrified with fear. Her lover did not respond. Unnatural green lightning, the likes of which she had never seen before, crackled across the beach.

The central mass of fog coalesced into a monstrous, twisted figure. It was huge—larger than life. The creature bent menacingly and gripped Eris with slimy, bloody claws. The reek surrounding it made Phaidra's stomach churn.

The thing's attention turned towards Phaidra, and she recoiled in disgust. It had the body of a man, but the head of a toad. The head gulped wetly, its long tongue shooting out to lick one eyeball. The wide, slack mouth looked as if it could swallow Eris whole.

"*No!*" Phaidra shrieked, struggling forward to try and reach Eris through the cloud surrounding man and beast. The urge to flee was nearly overwhelming, but she would *not* leave Eris at the demon's mercy. She threw herself forward, over and over, but the mist surrounding the two figures had grown thick as treacle. Finally, she lunged forward a final fraction, and was able to reach him. Her fingers found the edge of his toga, soaked now with sweat and blood as well as seawater.

Even pulling with all her might, Phaidra was barely able to move his writhing body a finger's width. The creature was clearly amused by her attempts. It cackled with glee, and the hair on the back of Phaidra's neck stood on end at the horrible sound.

It was evil. Pure evil.

"*You cannot save him, insect. You are nothing more than a worthless whore. A warm place for him to stick his cock. He is mine now,*" the toad said.

Phaidra swallowed a sob and shook her head, trying to draw on the defiance that Eris had shown earlier, even though she was still too petrified to speak or look directly into those horrible eyes.

"*His inner Light will be cast into the underworld and tortured for all eternity,*" the beast continued. "*I will make him my slave until this world crumbles to nothing. He will serve me loyally, feasting on blood and skin and sinew.*"

Phaidra recoiled in revulsion at its words, and tried again to pull her lover's body out from under the suffocating cloud surrounding him. Still, her meager strength was insufficient to free Eris from the demon's clutches.

"M-my life for his." Phaidra forced the words through chattering teeth.

The black miasma swirled around her, flooding her nose and mouth, making her sputter and cough for air.

"*You would give your pathetic life to save his?*"

The terrible voice crooned the words in her ear like a lover. She shuddered in disgust as the toad's tongue traced up her neck.

"*My life for his.*" She repeated the words with more force this time.

Her love for Eris burned brightly in her chest, filling Phaidra with a strength she had not known she possessed. Will overcame fear as she looked up at the demon and stubbornly set her chin. "You will take my life, offered freely, and spare his in turn."

Phaidra glanced down to find a faint golden glow emanating from her skin, luminescent in the swirling darkness surrounding her—the light of her love, stark against the demon's dark power.

The creature's face twisted and changed. Instead of a toad, she was staring into the eyes of a rabid cat. Anger laced its next words like poison. *"I will destroy you, insolent mortal. By the time I am through with you, you will curse the day you were born."*

Phaidra took a steadying breath and jerked backward as hard as she could. The cloud shifted with her, following her, partially freeing Eris' body.

The sound of skittering insect legs assaulted her ears. She clenched her teeth, trying to stop her body from shaking and jerking. It felt as though fire ants were crawling up her legs, eating her flesh from the outside in.

Her cries were lost in the rushing noise that surrounded her, but despite the intolerable sensation of insects creeping over her skin, one small part of her mind held onto sanity and awareness of her surroundings. Immortals were dangerous and capricious, but they could be bargained with, if one knew what drove them.

"A wager, then!" she cried, trying to make her voice heard over the rush of noise. "You call me his whore, but I know the truth of our bond! I will wager that our love is stronger than your evil! If I'm wrong... if I lose... you will have everything you want. You will get to watch as my heart shatters with grief, and afterward he will be your creature."

There was a pregnant beat of silence. Encouraged, she continued. "But if I'm right, you will spare his life. He will be forever protected by the sacrifice of true and unconditional love."

As Phaidra spoke, she struggled to unsteady feet and took one stumbling step backward, pretending that her trembling legs could not hold her weight. The creature paced her, and the movement completely freed Eris from the dark cloud surrounding the demonic being.

The silence stretched longer, and she held her breath.

"If he is so important to you, human, it will be as you say it is. You are but a mindless beast, in the end. Your fear will overcome your sickening nobility the moment you see the truth of what I have done to him."

The air escaped her lungs in a whoosh. "You're wrong. He is worth everything to me," she said. "And that is what I am offering you as my part of the wager. Everything."

There were no more words. The demon did not speak again. Its power coalesced above her like a heavy stone, crushing her. She fell beneath its weight.

As her body dropped to the ground, her gaze flickered and came to rest on Eris, covered in blood, twitching weakly on the sand a few paces away. As she watched, he curled onto his side, facing her. His eyes glowed red, and his handsome face twisted into a mask of animal hunger. There was no recognition in his ravenous gaze.

With a sinking feeling, she wondered if her beloved was already gone forever, his soul sacrificed to a demon's lust for power. But… no. The creature had agreed to her wager. Her love could still redeem him. She had to believe that. She *had* to.

What the demon didn't understand, was that she couldn't bear the thought of living in a world without Eris. She had no fear of what might happen to her, because it couldn't possibly be worse than losing him.

Eris was struggling onto all fours, now, stalking toward her like a predator. She felt the demon retreat, leaving her prostrate and helpless in the sand as it fell back to watch. She could feel its bloodthirsty glee.

Her beloved was close enough now that she could read the anguish behind that blood-red gaze. The *need*. He hungered, and her eyes fell to the full-lipped mouth that had brought her so much pleasure over the years.

He had *fangs*.

The demon's words returned to her. *He will serve me loyally, feasting on blood and skin and sinew. Your fear will overcome your sickening nobility the moment you see the truth of him.*

That fear tried to rise now. She didn't let it.

Eris crawled up the length of her body, caging her with his arms and legs. Looking down at her. A drip of saliva fell from one of his fangs, to land warm and wet on her throat.

She swallowed. "Eris, my love," she said hoarsely, "I know you can't see anything but the Darkness right now. And that's all right. I will be the Light for both of us. I offer you everything I have to give, and ask only this in return. *Don't let this creature win*." Her voice fell to a whisper as Eris wrenched her head back by the hair, and lowered his mouth to her neck in a sick parody of a lovers' embrace. "I love you. Through death and life—"

Eris snarled, and sharp pain pierced the sensitive flesh of her throat. She cried out, blood gurgling. As her soul was dragged forcibly from her body, a single thought flickered before her awareness slipped away into nothingness.

But now, I'll never know if I won the wager...

-o-o-o-

Trynn shivered violently. The air against her back felt icy, but there was warmth beneath her. Was she still in the dream? She *hungered*, as Eris had hungered on that beach in the distant past. A feast lay a mere hairsbreadth from her lips. She could feel it. She could *smell* it. All she had to do was—

Her teeth buried themselves in salty flesh, and warm nectar flowed over her lips. She lapped weakly at it, and some slipped down her parched throat. It should have been horrific, but she knew it couldn't actually be real. She was still sleeping, no doubt, her brain concocting some kind of fantasy dream-revenge on dream-Eris for biting her earlier. That was all.

A hand cradled the back of her head, holding her steady. "That's it, beloved." The hoarse voice sounded relieved beyond measure. "Drink from me. Everything will be all right, now."

She suckled like a hungry newborn, completely on instinct. The warmth inside her grew, driving back the icy chill. Exhausted, she slipped into sleep.

-o-o-o-

Trynn still couldn't open her eyes. They were too heavy. Her aching body weighed a ton; her fingers might as well have been made of wood for all the feeling in them.

What — ? Where — ?

Indistinct voices murmured above her, the words unintelligible as she drifted in and out of sleep. Trynn tried again to open her eyes. The lids parted reluctantly, only to slide closed again as the world around her spun.

She moaned, and wrenched a numb, heavy hand up to her head, pressing the heel clumsily against her temple.

"Easy," a voice whispered. Strong arms held her against a warm, naked chest. "Rest now, Trynn."

She nodded, past the point of caring what she was agreeing to or with whom she was agreeing. She knew that voice. She trusted that voice. That was all that mattered.

Trynn drifted vaguely for what seemed like a long time, resting with the warm body on the soft pile of pillows. Someone pulled a dusty blanket up over her shoulders and she relaxed further, concentrating only on the feeling of blood pumping through her veins and arteries. It was strange, hearing the soft, rhythmic *shush-shush* so clearly, though she couldn't have said *why* it was strange.

Some time later, she became aware of an odd chasm inside her chest that had not been there before. She didn't like it. Something about it made her feel lopsided. Off-balance.

Don't be stupid, she thought. *You're lying down. How can you be off-balance when you're lying down?*

Realization struck.

Oh. Right. Snag had ripped her soul in two earlier. She probably should have remembered that part sooner. It was kind of important. Did that mean she was going to hell now? Which… yeah. Apparently hell was a real place, so…

I certainly hope not, a voice murmured inside her head. *For one thing, that would require dying first. But if you do, gods forbid, I will be by your side the whole way down – my word on it.*

She was so startled by the mental intrusion that she physically jerked in surprise. A warm hand settled on her arm, rubbing soothingly.

"It's all right," the voice said aloud. "Sorry about that. Don't worry, that's normal."

Trynn's tension bled out when she recognized the person lying next to her as Eris. Warmth enveloped her, knowing that he was with her and standing guard over her while she recovered.

Still too exhausted to speak, Trynn wondered if she could communicate with Eris mentally. It was worth a try, she supposed.

Am I a vampire now? she thought as hard as she could, hoping that Eris would be able to hear her.

"Yes, and there's no need to shout at me," Eris responded wryly.

"Shout?" The word emerged a bare rasp of sound.

"You were projecting very loudly. I don't doubt that every vampire in the vicinity could hear you."

Oh. Whoops. Trynn tried again to open her eyes and found that the world was still swirling. The longer she held them open, however, the more the view righted itself. She was curled up in a familiar, run-down room with bare stone walls and floors.

A cheerful fire burned in a dilapidated, crumbling fireplace, warming the air around them. The other vampires were lounging comfortably in chairs and on the floor, all dressed for survival and combat.

Trynn's eyes fell on Della, who was studying her with a worried expression.

"How do you feel, Trynn?" Della asked, coming closer to the bed where Trynn and Eris were lying and crouching next to them.

Trynn cleared her throat, though the terrible dryness persisted.

"Tired," she finally managed to croak.

Della nodded. "I bet. You've been through a lot this week."

Eris squeezed her shoulder in comfort as she nodded, still fighting sleep.

"She'll bounce back," Eris assured the room. "Her life force has already grown stronger since the turning, and it's only been a few hours."

"Hours?" Trynn murmured, allowing her eyes to fall closed again. "God. It feels like days."

Eris brushed her short hair away from her forehead. "I don't doubt it. You'll feel much better after you've fed again."

At his words, Trynn felt bone-deep thirst flare inside her, followed closely by repulsion at the idea of drinking blood.

"Can we take that part slowly?" Trynn asked, a note of apprehension in her voice.

"Of course," he replied. "It won't be as bad as you think. You've done it once already, though you may not remember it. Honestly, though, it's perfectly natural for us."

And I'll help you, he whispered in her mind.

Relieved, Trynn nodded again. Her head fell back against Eris' strong shoulder, and she slipped into a light sleep.

What seemed like mere moments later, a hand on her shoulder shook her gently awake.

"Huh?" she slurred, cracking her eyes open. "Wha's wrong?"

"Trynn, you've slept too long. It's time to feed now." Eris' voice was quiet, but insistent. She could feel him spooning her back—his body wrapped around hers protectively.

"I can't," Trynn whispered, unable to gather enough breath to raise her voice any more.

"You have to," Eris said. "Trust me, it will help."

Trynn ran her swollen, dry tongue over her teeth and discovered that her canines had lengthened into fangs. She shivered. Clearly, her body knew what she needed, even if her stomach clenched at the idea of preying on a human.

Eris seemed to know what was troubling her. "Not yet, beloved. Not until you gain enough control not to hurt them accidentally. There's no need. Feed from me, for now."

With her eyes still closed, Trynn felt his wrist touch her lips. Before she could stop herself, instinct took over and she bit down hard on his exposed flesh. Blood gushed into her mouth, tasting like the sweetest gift from the heavens.

Eris groaned as her teeth sank deeper into his skin—not from pain, but from longing. She could feel it, through the tenuous mental link joining them. His breathing grew rough and uneven in her ear as she sucked hard, drawing his lifeblood into her body. She felt energized, even as the evidence of his growing desire pressed against her from behind. As she continued to feed, he lowered his mouth to her exposed neck and nibbled playfully along the sensitive skin. He pressed the entire front of his body against her, as if trying to meld them into a single being. His breath hissed out sharply against the side of her throat, and goose bumps erupted along her arms.

"You are the most perfect thing I have ever seen," he said in a husky voice. "Absolutely flawless."

She did not answer, too focused on the feel of his body against hers and his blood flowing across her tongue. The heat of it filled her up, sending ecstasy coursing through her. As his life force passed to her, she felt their souls connecting and intertwining. What had been the pain of a broken soul became completion, the likes of which she had never known before.

This was what it meant to be truly alive. And to think, she'd only had to die to achieve it.

Eris chuckled, still breathless behind her. "Well stated. I can tell you still have the same sense of humor. Twisted... just the way I like it." He kissed the back of her neck. "You are mine, Trynn, and I am yours forever."

Finally sated, Trynn lowered his arm from her mouth and let him wrap it around her waist. She rolled over to face him, feeling whole and complete for perhaps the first time in her life as she buried her face in his neck.

Exhausted from their recent trials, Trynn and Eris slipped into a deep, easy sleep, resting peacefully in each other's arms.

SIXTEEN

Wakefulness crept up on her slowly, many hours later. She stretched, feeling completely refreshed and healthy—somewhat to her surprise, it must be said.

Opening her eyes, Trynn saw they were still in the same room as before. The fire next to them had burned low, only a few embers still glowing red. Eris was obviously already awake, and he stroked gentle fingers through her close-cropped hair.

"Hello," he said, his voice raspy.

Trynn turned towards him, studying him as the events of the past couple of days finally started to sort themselves out in her memory. Surprise and relief swelled as she took in his handsome features. "Hey! You look great."

Eris laughed, a deep rumble. "Uh… thanks? As opposed to before, you mean? Yes, I'm feeling much stronger, mostly because of Snag's generosity. There's something to be said for getting a top-off from the most powerful vampire in existence. His blood has me pretty much healed, I think."

To demonstrate, Eris lifted his arm. Where there had been cuts, deep bruises, and broken bones from hours of torture at Kovac's hands, there were now only faint pink lines. The wounds were almost completely knitted back together. Many had already faded, revealing new, tender skin underneath.

"Will I heal like that now?" Trynn asked in awe, glancing at Eris' face.

"Yes, I expect so. You've got Snag's blood running through your veins now, too—even if it was filtered through me first." His gaze narrowed. "However, that is *not* an invitation for you to go out and do something dangerous."

"Of course not... *Dad*," Trynn answered with an eye roll. She strongly suspected that even though she was functionally immortal now, Eris would still worry about her safety.

Remembering the others, Trynn looked around and realized that the room was empty except for the two of them. "Where is everyone?" she asked.

Eris jerked his chin toward the door, and the corridor beyond. "They're in another room down the hall. They got tired of waiting for you to wake up, and went out to explore the building. It's daylight, so there's not much else to do at the moment. I gather Tré and Xander are unearthing a partially destroyed piano right now, trying to figure out if it still works."

Trynn stared at him. "Okay. Why?"

One dark eyebrow quirked. "Now that you have an immensely long life, you'll find that there's time to dedicate to those types of pursuits."

She continued to stare. "Pursuits like abandoned and destroyed pianos?"

He snorted. "That... or old vehicles, like Xander. It just depends, honestly. Oksana is obsessed with human junk food and wine, of all things. She considers herself a *connoisseur*. I love to read, and Duchess spends more than an hour a day putting on her make-up. She claims that it's for the purposes of disguise, but I suspect it's actually a vanity project." One muscled shoulder lifted in a shrug. "You just... find things to occupy your time."

"Like Snag and his chess, I suppose. What about Della and Tré?" Trynn asked, genuinely curious.

Eris wagged his eyebrows suggestively. "Oh, I'm pretty certain they're still in their honeymoon phase."

"Ah," Trynn replied as understanding dawned—followed by amusement. "Since when?"

"It hasn't been long since we found Della, and she was turned. Only a few months. I don't think the novelty of near-constant sex has worn off yet. We haven't seen much of them during that time, to be honest."

And that brought to mind another question. The seven of them were obviously close, but—

"So, how does this work? Are you neighbors with the other vampires or... ?"

Eris shook his head. "We all live together, usually. It's safer that way, with Bael's power growing stronger, day-by-day. Every now and then, one or more of us will go off on our own, as Snag and I did when we traveled to Cyprus. But we are a family. We always return to the nest eventually."

"And where is this *nest*? Someplace in America, right?" Trynn asked, fascinated. No doubt she should have thought more about things like that before she was turned, but she still couldn't bring herself to regret it.

Eris scrubbed a hand through his tangled mop of dark hair, mussing it further. "Most recently we lived in New Orleans. An old plantation house that we've been working on fixing up. It's on the market right now, and I think we've just about got a buyer lined up. While the others were closing the deal, I came here to sell a Greek artifact that I've kept over the centuries."

Trynn gave him a sidelong look. "Part of our ill-gotten gains?"

Eris paused, his eyes crinkling at the corners, as if he were reveling in her use of the word *our*. "Yes. Just so. I still have a store of artifacts and exotic pieces. I sell them off one by one, as needed. I didn't see much point in keeping them—too many memories attached."

Trynn nodded thoughtfully and said, "I'm surprised you held onto them for this long. Why not sell all of them immediately and get the cash?"

"Too dangerous. I don't want to flood the market. It might raise suspicion. Besides, in the normal course of things, we're hardly short of money," Eris answered with an indifferent shrug. "Xander's the businessman. He's got his fingers in everything. My little contributions are a mere drop in the bucket."

Trynn settled back against him, thinking.

"Also," Eris continued, as an afterthought, "I'll admit to feeling a pang whenever I sell one. It feels too much like losing another little part of you."

Her chest tightened. "I can understand that," she said quietly. "It was something we did together."

Eris nodded, his dark eyes tracing her features like a caress. "I still keep half-expecting to wake up, and find that these last few days have a been a dream. We've studied ancient texts about the so-called Council of Thirteen for centuries, but we'd assumed it referred to existing vampires we simply hadn't found yet."

"And now you think it's us?" Trynn asked, fascinated. "People like Della and me, I mean?"

He gave her a small, helpless shrug. "I think it must be. Until Tré found Della, none of us had ever come across the reincarnations of our soulmates. We were beginning to assume the whole thing about the Council was nonsense—a myth. I certainly did. And I'd long ago given up hope of ever finding love again."

Saddened and touched, Trynn wrapped her arms around his neck and clung. "I'm sorry I made you wait."

Eris huffed. "Don't be daft. You had no control over that." He nuzzled into the crook of Trynn's neck and took a deep breath, as if inhaling her scent before pulling back and continuing, "I'll never hold that against you, Trynn; I'm just glad you're here now. I can barely remember my life before you walked back into it, even though it was only a few days ago."

"That's how I feel," Trynn said, wonder coloring the words. "It's like... I can remember things that happened, but they feel foggy and disconnected, almost like a story someone else told me."

"Maybe you are a different person now, in a way," Eris suggested. "Tré thinks that we are completely reborn as vampires, just as you were reborn from Phaidra into Trynn—and who knows how many lives in between."

Trynn considered this possibility, readjusting her body against Eris'. "I don't think so. I still feel like *me*, but it's like… I've woken up now. Like, my life before you was all a dream, and everything after has become so much more real to me."

"The fog has been lifted," Eris concluded.

She snorted. "Yeah, I guess." Silence reigned for a moment before she continued. "So, if you're selling this plantation house, where will we go next?" she asked, still curious about their living arrangements. "I guess I'll have to call my boss and give her my notice. Pity. I liked that job. But this way, I'll have more time for MASQUE... and that's more important, by far."

He nodded. "I don't know yet what we'll do now," he replied thoughtfully. "I suppose we'll have to see where the next vortex of chaos forms. We think that's the best way to try to locate the others like you and Della."

"Seems impossible that one place could even stand out, when pretty much the entire world is mired in violence," Trynn murmured.

Eris shrugged agreement. "I know what you mean. Though I'm starting to wonder if it's more a case of the chaos finding us, rather than the other way around."

They lay quietly for a few more moments before Trynn got up and stretched out her arms and legs. Eris rolled into a sitting position to watch. She could feel the new strength in her muscles, unlike anything she'd felt before. It was intoxicating.

Eris followed the path of her thoughts effortlessly. "You have many new powers now," he said. "We'll teach you how to use them over the coming days and weeks."

"*Powers*?" Trynn echoed. She narrowed her eyes playfully, suddenly intrigued. "*Do tell*. Powers like what?"

Catching onto her mood, Eris grinned, slow and dangerous. Something in her belly tightened.

"Well," he began airily, "Let's see. You have an owl form, now. That's always an interesting experience — being able to fly."

Trynn took a step closer, reaching down to touch Eris' cheek. "What else?"

He swallowed and looked up, his pupils blown wide as he continued to play the game with her. "Hmm. Oh, yes — you can also transform into mist. I believe you've seen that trick already, haven't you?"

She nodded. "So I have. What else?"

"You can press impressions into another person's mind," he murmured, his voice going husky. "You've seen that one, too. I still have the imprint of your knuckles on my jaw to prove it."

"Show me again," Trynn breathed. "I probably won't hit you this time."

Eris nodded and shut his eyes. As he took several slow breaths, Trynn felt something heavy and sweet creeping over her. Heat radiated outward from her core, but it was not the same kind of consuming fire that she had experienced while being turned. This fire warmed, rather than burning her. It settled in her belly, turning liquid.

"Oh. Is that all?" she asked, reaching for affected nonchalance as the sensation lifted.

Eris raised an eyebrow at her. "I believe you called it a *mind-whammy*, back in Nicosia. You seemed... rather affected, at the time."

Trynn laughed. "All right... *guilty*. And you're obviously never letting me live it down. So, as a vampire, I can make horniness into a mind-whammy. That's, uh, useful, I guess?"

"Do *try* to get your mind out of the gutter, Trynn." His voice was smug as he sent another wave of desire rolling through her body. "You can transmit any emotion. Anything."

Trynn gasped and ran her hand down her stomach, trying in vain to hold herself together. "And... how would I go about doing that? Exactly?"

Eris sprawled back on the bed of cushions they'd recently vacated, and let his legs fall open. He was wearing only the pair of well-worn, low slung pajama pants she'd first seen him in at the hotel, and Trynn thought he had absolutely no business making them look as good as he did. For fuck's sake, he looked good enough to *eat*.

Her mouth watered.

"Take the feeling you want to pass on," he said, "and force it into a ball inside you, like crumpling up a wad of paper. Turn it into something you can grasp. Then, pick it up."

Trynn nodded and concentrated on bundling up the hot, liquid feeling in her gut.

"Now," Eris whispered, "pass it along to me, just like when we were speaking telepathically."

In her eagerness, Trynn shoved her arousal towards him hard, unsure if she would be able to separate it from herself… or if she even needed to.

To her surprise, it passed easily along the mental connection they shared, but at the unwonted force of her attempt, Eris cried out in surprise and arched, his hips flexing. "Too much, *too much*!" he protested, the words caught between laughter and sexual agony.

With an evil smile, Trynn shook her head, remembering the second time she'd come to his hotel room for answers. "*Oh, no.* That's just a taste of what I'm going to give you. It's payback time!"

"Immortal or not, you're going to be the death of me, woman," Eris said around a chuckle, flopping back with his legs akimbo. His grin turned as devilish as hers. A golden light glowed behind his eyes. "But don't mind little old me. Do *please* continue."

She tried, but now the connection on his end was shielded, somehow.

"You're cheating!" she accused.

"I'm sure I have no idea what you mean," he said, right before he hooked an ankle around hers, taking her feet out from under her and sending her sprawling on top of him. He caught her in his arms, breaking her fall, and suddenly she was nose to nose with him, her mouth open in a round *oh* of surprise.

She met his golden eyes and tried again to regain the upper hand, scowling when her mental attempt slid away from the edges of his mind like droplets of water on an orange peel. "You're blocking me somehow."

Eris' look of faux-innocence wouldn't have fooled the most credulous of onlookers. One moment, she was lying on top of him, taking a mental measure of the *very* promising bulge nestled against the crease of her hip. A heartbeat later, she was pinned beneath him on the pile of cushions, held effortlessly in place by a careful strength that far outstripped hers, even now that she'd been turned.

Trynn didn't really need a mind-whammy of horniness at this point; her body had that angle taken care of, all on its own. She wriggled in his grip, not yet ready to throw in the towel in whatever game they were playing.

Right. *Shit*. So, maybe she didn't *need* the mind-whammy… but it looked like she was getting it again, ready or not. A wave of hot lust swept over her and ebbed, dragging an undignified noise from her throat. Somehow, Eris was still able to press desire into *her* mind, even though he was blocking her from doing the same to him.

"*Definitely* not fair," she groaned, her head falling back against the cushions as the next wave came.

"Nonsense," he said, though the hint of gravel under his voice betrayed his own dwindling control. "There ought to be *some* advantage to being as old and experienced as I am. It's *perfectly* fair."

She writhed, wanting to feel that strength holding her in place… loving the way it ratcheted her raging desire even higher than before. Trynn redoubled her efforts to shove the molten ball of lust back across the link, and was rewarded by a sharp intake of breath as he thrust against her hip. The one-way shield strengthened a moment later, and he made a tisking noise.

Trynn felt like a volcano about to erupt, all pent up, with nowhere to go.

"*Touch me,* damn it," she demanded. "God! You're driving me mad, Eris!"

He smirked. "I *am* touching you," he said, squeezing her wrists and thrusting against her hip again to demonstrate.

She groaned aloud. "*Argh*! Not like that. *Touch. Me.*"

He still looked inordinately smug. "Hmm… not yet, I don't think. For one thing, I'm quite enjoying you like this." He rolled his hips, and she bit off a frustrated curse — which he ignored. "And for another, I don't think we've really explored the *mind-whammy* in sufficient depth, yet. I did promise to educate you in the use of our powers, after all."

Trynn made a desperate noise as the tide of *want* rose even *higher*, building impossibly within her with no outlet for release. Sex had always been a casual game for her in the past — a harmless amusement. It was a game she was used to winning. She had always been a *champion* at getting what she wanted in the bedroom.

Right now, she was definitely *not* getting what she wanted. She had a suspicion, though, that by the end of the night, she was going to get exactly what she *needed*. A new wash of lust washed over her, stealing her breath. Her body shuddered as she tried to hang onto control, but it lasted for only a moment before the thread snapped.

She went limp and heavy, surrendering to the overwhelming feelings coursing through her. Satisfaction rumbled through Eris' chest, her mild-mannered lover transforming into a growling, possessive panther before her eyes.

"So beautiful," he said, releasing her wrists to run his thumb over the seam of her lips. "And *mine*."

The touch ignited every nerve as she lay beneath him, pliant and waiting. "Please," she whispered against his callused fingertip. "Eris, *please*."

His thumb slid past her lips, the skin tasting of salt and musk as he pressed in deep. Her body balanced on the knife-edge of orgasm, aching and untouched.

"Yes," he said. "You're so close, aren't you? I want to feel you come merely from the touch of my mind against yours."

She whimpered around him. He stroked over her tongue and pressed an image into her thoughts of his cock sliding inside her with a single smooth thrust. Trynn cried out around the flesh in her mouth and came hard—still fully dressed, and without him having come within six inches of her clit, or even her breasts.

"Jesus *fuck*," she whispered after he slid his thumb free, and the aftershocks had died down to tremors. "I can see already that I'm going to have to up my game in the bedroom."

He stroked the backs of his knuckles over her cheek tenderly. "Your game is magnificent," he said, his tone sounding nearly reverent. "But, right now, I think it would be even more magnificent if you were naked."

Coming untouched might sound like serious fantasy material, but the reality was that it only left her wanting more, with a deep, empty ache that longed — no, *demanded* — to be filled.

"Naked is absolutely a plan I can get behind," she agreed. "As long as it's mutual, anyway."

"Very, very mutual," he said, sliding the soft cotton pajama bottoms he was wearing down and off without ceremony.

And... *yup*. The bulge had not lied, earlier. He was hung. And she was staring, to his evident amusement.

"No wonder you and Phaidra fucked constantly," she said. The words emerged sounding a bit faint.

That startled a bark of unrestrained laughter from him. "Should I even ask?"

She shook her head, trying to clear it. "Uh... I may or may not have had a whole series of extremely raunchy sex dreams about us in the past, those first few nights after we met."

His expression grew far away, and she ached for him in a new way as he looked down, breaking eye contact for a moment before peering through the tangle of his messy hair at her.

"I have tried for a long time... not to think about that part of the past," he said, all hints of teasing gone.

She smiled up at him sadly, and lifted a hand to stroke his jaw. Mirroring his earlier action, she brushed her thumb over his full lower lip. He grasped her wrist, holding her in place as he pressed a kiss to the pad.

"The time for sadness is past," she said. "I'm here. You're here. There's no reason to be sad any more, is there?"

His eyes closed, and she felt a fine tremor run through his body. When he opened them again, they were wet, but gold glowed behind his gaze.

"Trynn," he whispered hoarsely.

She smiled, and reached down to grasp the hem of her shirt so she could pull it off. She watched him watching her as she removed the rest of her clothing, piece by piece. She knew her body was fit, but not classically beautiful—she was a bit angular, a bit boyish.

But one glance was enough to tell her that in Eris' eyes, she was perfect. Part of her wondered if she resembled Phaidra physically. She guessed not, since he hadn't seemed to recognize her when they first met. Apparently, it didn't matter to him in the least. He was watching her avidly, hunger in his golden gaze.

"No more games," she breathed.

"No more games," he agreed. And then, he was stalking up the length of her body, pressing closed-mouth kisses along her inner thigh.

Oh, thank god, she thought, as he nuzzled between her legs and breathed in, rubbing his stubbled cheek against her, openly wallowing in her scent. Watching him like this... it was... *fuck...* it was the sexiest damn thing she'd ever seen in her life.

She could feel arousal not her own resonating along their bond again as his tongue darted out to taste her folds. This time, though, it wasn't a tease or a contest of wills, she knew. He just couldn't stop himself. Somehow, that realization made it even sweeter. Trynn felt the echo of desire flow freely back and forth, growing as they fed off each other's lust.

There was no reason to hold back.

It took almost no time at all for the touch of his mind and his delving tongue to bring her to the edge and push her over. She came, gasping, feeling him struggle not to follow her down into release.

A torrent of deliciously filthy images flashed in front of her mind's eye, a movie reel of her dreams and fantasies from the past few days. She very clearly saw herself masturbating in the Merit Lefkosa's decadent bathtub, to thoughts of Eris sinking his fangs into her neck.

Just as clearly, she felt Eris go still between her thighs, shock and uncertainty echoing through the connection. It took a minute for her to gather her wits after her orgasm. When she did, Eris was looking up the length of her body, his brow furrowed.

"What?" she asked.

He blinked. "You… want such a thing? After what I *did* to you, all those centuries ago?"

Understanding dawned, and the breath left her lungs in a slow exhale. "Oh, *Eris*." She swallowed. "Not everything has to be about the past, does it?"

He was still watching her intently. "The past defines us."

She shook her head. "Only if we let it," she argued. "Is it so difficult to accept that maybe, just maybe, I have an untapped vampire fetish that doesn't have deep, dark implications from millennia in the past? Especially given the fact that *I'm a vampire now*."

The crease between his brows deepened. "But —"

"But nothing," she insisted. "It was just a passing thought. I'm not asking you to do anything you don't want to do. I trust you, though. I trust you with that completely. And I *want* that kind of bond with you. It's the same bond you share with the others, isn't it? The bond of blood?"

His expression softened into desperate longing, but she was relieved to see a hint of humor underneath. "Well," he said, pressing a kiss to her mons, "perhaps not *quite* the same."

She laughed, breathless. He kissed his way further up her body until he was poised above her. When his mouth closed over hers, she tasted herself, and moaned into the kiss. Her legs circled his hips, urging him forward. His hard length slid into her, stretching her passage deliciously. Filling her to perfection.

She gathered him close to her body and held him tight as they rocked together. She might have expected urgency from him during this, their first coupling. Instead, it was sweet beyond measure… slow and tender. Exquisite.

The world fell away, and for the first time she understood what he had said about having *time*. There was no hurry. They had forever.

She could feel what he felt; he could feel what she felt. It was the same. It was love.

When the sharp slide of his fangs pierced her neck, it was painless — the most natural thing in the world. When the deep pulling sensation as he drank from her joined the feel of him moving inside of her, a profound, all-consuming release washed through her body. He followed, filling her up even as he drew from her, the connection between them whiting out with ecstasy.

When he was finished, he kissed the fast-healing twin wounds left by his fangs, and buried his face against her neck. She felt the warm wetness of his silent tears, and held him close, cradling him to her.

"So long," he whispered against her skin, his arms clutching her. "It's been so long, beloved."

"I know, my heart," she soothed, stroking his messy hair. Feeling wise and strong. Cherished and protected. "I know. It's all right, now."

-o-o-o-

Some considerable time later, Trynn pushed open the door and the two of them emerged, turning left down the darkening hallway. Eris led the way, moving expertly through the maze-like corridors, and Trynn understood that he must be receiving directions from another vampire.

His large hand clasped her slender one. She could feel the power pulsing between them as their life force intermingled, tangled together after the hours of lovemaking. Adoration swelled in Trynn's chest, filling up the unpleasant empty place in her soul that had plagued her after her turning, until it overflowed. It seemed that being reunited with her mate bridged the gap between the Light and the Dark within her. She wondered if it had done the same for Eris, but she wasn't sure how to ask.

Apparently, they had reached their destination. He gestured towards a door and ushered her inside.

Trynn had a sneaky suspicion that she'd spent the last couple of hours projecting ecstasy to every vampire within mental listening distance. In the dwindling light of the room, she felt a hot blush creep over her cheeks as the others looked up. Della smiled, having pity on her.

"Yeah, I'm afraid you did, a bit," the other woman said, her eyes crinkling. "Don't worry, though. Anyone who didn't want to hear it shielded their minds against you. You'll get used to it, and it'll be easier to control next time."

Della's gaze flickered involuntarily to Tré, and Trynn spared a brief moment of embarrassed curiosity over the idea that certain people might *not* have shielded. She cleared her throat to cover it. *Yup… none of her business.*

"Yes," Xander said. "You, uh, really might want to work on that. Before *some of us* have to leave the country for some peace and quiet."

Trynn blushed harder, and Eris gave Xander a look that was *thoroughly* unimpressed.

"Hey!" Xander raised his hands defensively. "Don't give me that glare. You don't understand how it is, being celibate while having to listen to the *happy couples* sneaking around."

"Goodness. Celibate *and* sober at the same time?" Eris asked. "The horror."

"Well… sober-*ish*," Xander clarified, making a waggling, half-and-half motion with one hand.

"My heart bleeds for you," Eris said, dry as dust. "Oh! Wait. No, I was wrong. I think it was just a moment of indigestion."

Xander slapped a palm over his chest, playing at being wounded. "*Ouch.* I feel like you're not fully appreciating my suffering, here."

"From the hangover, you mean?" Eris mused. "Or the existential angst?"

"As entertaining as this is," Duchess interrupted, "I think everyone is looking forward to leaving this run-down shithole as soon as it can be arranged."

"Yes, the whole *bombed out war zone* thing is getting kind of old," Oksana agreed. Her gaze settled on Eris. "Also, the whole *people I care about nearly getting themselves killed* thing."

Eris had the grace to at least look regretful. "I'm sorry, Oksana. Not least because my misjudgment put the rest of you in jeopardy. But there were nuclear bombs involved, and an unknown timeline regarding when they might detonate. You weren't here, and I had to leave Snag behind to guard Trynn. I regret the way it turned out, but I'm very much afraid that under the same circumstances, I'd do it again."

The others were quiet. A lump rose in Trynn's throat, but she swallowed it down. "And would you lie to me again, about what you were doing?" she asked, remembering the way he'd looked when she'd first arrived here with Tré and Della. Broken. Half dead.

Eris' face softened. "No. No, I wouldn't lie. Tré told me what you did, with the email to the Russians. If I'd talked to you first, the whole thing might have been avoided."

Honesty compelled her to say, "I don't know. Maybe not. I only came up with the plan because I was so desperate to save you after Snag showed me what that fucking bastard Kovac had done to you."

Tré had been silent, but he spoke up at that. "At least now we know the truth about Bastian Kovac. We know what kind of power we're facing. A power almost equal to Snag's, even though Kovac was turned only a short time ago."

Trynn looked towards Snag, who was standing still and silent in the corner of the room. As she gazed at him, she felt a surge of affection stir in her heart. Perhaps it was because they were connected now — bound by blood. Maybe it was due to that newly fledged bond, or maybe becoming a vampire had adjusted her eyesight, but he appeared less like a spectral monster to her now. His burns were healed, and his face seemed less gaunt than before.

She could detect a hint of warmth in his pale skin, and light in his eyes, which moved to rest on her.

As their gazes connected, Trynn felt the corner of her mouth lift up in a smile.

Thank you, she sent. She felt fairly sure that she'd managed to keep that message for him alone.

Snag tipped his head towards her in a tiny gesture of acknowledgement, before turning his gaze back towards the window.

"So. Where should we go next?" Oksana asked, brushing dust off her dark trousers.

"I need a vacation after this," Xander answered, looking aggrieved. "This has been one gigantic clusterfuck from start to finish."

"Yeah, it has, at that," Eris agreed, abandoning their earlier sniping. "Let's just be happy that it's over and—"

Without warning, the entire building rocked on its foundation. Trynn and Della staggered and fell to their knees. A wall of sound crashed against their ears, and dust rained down on their heads as beams and chunks of plaster fell from the ceiling.

Trynn felt herself being dragged sideways just as something heavy smashed where she had been crouching. Eris flung his body across hers and shielded their heads with his arms.

As more debris rained down, Trynn heard a scream from somewhere to her right. It sounded like Della.

With a final quake, the building grew still. The only sound was the clatter of falling masonry. Trynn coughed and pushed Eris off of her.

"I'm all right," she croaked. "Is everyone else okay? What the *hell* just happened?"

The others stirred, pushing debris aside, seemingly unhurt.

"I've no idea," Eris said, wiping dust from his face. "Anyone?"

Listen. The silent order echoed across the mental connection between the vampires, and after a moment's confusion, Trynn realized it came from Snag.

"Listen to *what*?" Tré demanded. Through the gloom, Trynn could see him helping Della to her feet. They both looked shaken.

Snag was the only one of them who had remained standing through the shock wave. He stood before the window, clutching the windowsill with tension radiating through his slender body.

"*Mon dieu.*" It was Duchess. She had gone pale, her china blue eyes wide and unseeing. "*Merde.* The screaming. Can't you hear it? It's coming from the city…"

Trynn couldn't, and looking at Duchess' expression, she was immeasurably glad of that fact.

All of them rushed to join Snag at the window. They crowded around, in time to see a mushroom-shaped fireball of brilliant orange, yellow, and red slowly lifting into the sky a few miles away.

"Oh my *god*," Della exclaimed, horrified. "No, it can't be. It *can't* be! Not after all that!"

Trynn's heart sank, even as nausea rose. Dear god. She hadn't stopped it. *She hadn't stopped it.*

"This is a nightmare," Xander whispered, running a shaking hand through his hair.

Tré broke free of his paralysis. "Satellite phone," he said. "We can try to get a signal on the cell phones, but the system is likely to be down. Xander, who can we call to find out what's happening elsewhere? We need to know if this was the only detonation, and how the world's governments are responding."

Xander took a deep breath, visibly gathering himself. "I'll try some of my business contacts in the UK. They have dealings with the government there, and should have some idea of what's going on."

-o-o-o-

It took well over an hour for Xander to reach someone and get news. Trynn *itched* for a data connection — Twitter... IRC... *anything* that would let her put a finger on the pulse of the outside world. Tré had been right, though. Those parts of the cellular network that hadn't been destroyed by the blast were overloaded with everyone trying to use their phones at once.

Finally, Xander put the satellite phone aside and scrubbed a hand over his face. "This was the only explosion. It's touch and go, but it looks like the western governments and Russia are tentatively willing to view it as an isolated act of terrorism, not the beginning of all-out nuclear war. There will be boots on the ground and drones in the sky within hours. Every country with a suspected terrorist presence is about to become a hot zone — including this one. But the world's nuclear warheads are still in their silos. That tiny thread of sanity appears—somewhat shockingly—to have prevailed."

Trynn thought she should probably feel more relieved than this, at the knowledge that the world was not about to end in a rain of fiery ICBM-fueled terror from the skies. But she wasn't relieved. She was numb.

"What do we do now?" she asked, turning towards Eris.

He seemed to be at a loss for words as he stared out the window at the aftermath of destruction.

"I'm... not sure there's anything we *can* do," he replied slowly.

"But we're immortal, right?" Trynn demanded, turning towards the other vampires. "*Right?*"

"Yes," Oksana said hesitantly.

"*Then let's go help*," Trynn said, tugging on Eris' hand.

She felt a sudden urgency to rush to the aid of the people of Damascus. Her heart broke, knowing that she was witnessing the slow, painful death of thousands—perhaps tens of thousands—of men, women, and children.

"You're suggesting that we rush into a fire-riddled, radioactive pile of rubble to help a bunch of humans who will probably die anyway?" Duchess challenged, her voice brittle.

"Yes!" Trynn said, staring the other woman in the eye. Not backing down.

Their gaze locked for a long moment before Duchess shrugged, feigning indifference. "All right, then," she said. "That's what we'll do. Just clarifying."

"Can the radiation hurt us?" Della asked, looking at Tré.

"No," Xander answered, his tone clipped.

They all looked at him.

"And you know that… how, exactly?" Tré asked, brow furrowed.

Xander shifted on his feet. He took a deep breath "There was an incident in the nineteen-fifties… and… I, uh, just happened to be at the scene during a leak at an experimental nuclear reactor…"

He trailed off, looking pained. "You know what—never mind. Suffice to say, there shouldn't be any lasting effects on us. Probably."

Tré's eyes lingered on Xander for a long moment before he blinked and dragged his gaze away.

"Are we all in agreement, then?" he asked, his piercing silver eyes meeting each of his fellow vampires' in turn. They nodded in response.

"Do we have any supplies that would be useful?" Eris asked, looking around at the destruction surrounding them.

Tré shook his head. "I don't think there's anything we can really get on short notice that will help much. This… is going to be terrible."

Trynn saw Eris' chest rise and fall. He took her hand, lacing their fingers together and lifting her knuckles to his lips. "Not the honeymoon I'd envisioned, beloved," he murmured.

She felt tears threaten. "It doesn't matter," she managed. "We're together. Not just you and I, but all of us." Her gaze took in the others—battered… shell-shocked… and poised to fly straight into the heart of hell, in hopes that they could make some small difference in the face of horror. "We're to-gether, and we're going to do what's right. Demons and madmen be damned."

"Hear, hear," Xander said quietly.

Eris squeezed her hand. "Yes. We're together. I will never leave you again, Trynn. Never. We'll face whatever the future throws at us, shoulder to shoulder—my beloved."

She looked up at him, a single tear slipping free to slide down her cheek. "*Beloved*," she whis-pered, echoing the endearment. "Come on, then. Let's do this."

Surrounded by her strange, unexpected new family, Trynn turned toward the fiery night sky in the distance, and the others turned with her. She felt Snag gather her under the cloak of his power, guiding her first transformation into cool mist.

The others transformed, swirling around her, and the eight of them plunged forward into the unknown.

EPILOGUE

Bastian Kovac limped awkwardly through the rubble that covered every street and sidewalk in what used to be central Damascus. As he listened, he could still hear parts of buildings crumbling, sounding like heavy rain on a crashing ocean.

He breathed, smelling the heavy sent of burned flesh and decay.

It had been two days since the bomb had detonated in the heart of the city, and while the single point of destruction had not been exactly on the scale he had originally planned, it was effective as far as it went. With so much death to feast on, Bastian had recovered quickly enough from the Russian bullets that had ripped through his body.

However, the punishment from Bael for his failure was not so easy to shake off.

As he drew the radioactive air into his lungs, Bastian sucked in the dark power of his master, thrumming through the scene of devastation like a current.

This was their time. Their victory. Their chance at dominion over this twisted, pathetic world. Evil swirled through the air around him, palpable as a cold wind.

As Bastian's dark hair whipped around his face, the reek of death penetrated straight to his still, cold heart, calling like to like. His dead eyes surveyed the darkness around him, easily able to discern the lifeless bodies hidden under the rubble, away from the sight of men and vampires.

Oh yes — the abominations had been here, picking at the edges of the kill zone like vultures in search of the living. He'd watched from the shadows as they plucked injured men, women, and children from half-collapsed buildings under cover of darkness. Bastian had shielded his presence carefully, knowing that he was too weak to risk another confrontation with them so soon.

Around him, Bael's power swelled.

"Bring forth my army, to rule over all." The deep voice resonated through the earth, making it tremble.

Bastian climbed to the top of a mound of debris near a demolished building. Even though his left leg was mangled and bloody, he pulled himself upright and stood, spine straight, looking out over their kingdom.

"My master, your wisdom is as endless as the seas. I will build your empire with the help of your new servants, who now await your command," he proclaimed.

As he lifted his voice to the demon, Bastian held out his hands in front of him, palms facing downwards. He could feel power vibrating between his body and the earth as Bael's force grew and solidified.

"I will build your sovereign nation," he whispered, closing his eyes and allowing the darkness to flow through him.

A black bubble formed in the center of the zone of destruction, and expanded outward. Evil spread like an oil slick, coating everything it touched. The power balance between the Light and the Dark strained, and burst its bonds.

With a sudden, deafening *crack*, the bubble of power exploded, forcing animation into every frail, broken body in the city.

"Let your will be done!" Bastian cried, cold sweat pouring down his face as he concentrated on maintaining his connection with the earth. He would not fail his master now.

All around, he could hear the sound of feeble limbs scraping at the dirt, cracked fingernails scrabbling over broken concrete and twisted metal as the undead pulled themselves free of their unmarked tombs.

Bastian opened his eyes and looked around, surveying his new creations in wonder and ecstasy. Unbridled joy flooded him. He closed his hands into fists and threw his head back, uttering a roar of victory.

An army of the dead was rising from the ashes of Damascus, patiently awaiting their creator's command.

finis

The *Circle of Blood* series continues in *Book Three: Lover's Sacrifice*.

To get the free prequel to the *Circle of Blood* series sent directly to your inbox, visit
www.rasteffan.com/circle

27520278R00178

Printed in Great Britain
by Amazon